PRAISE FO

RIVERLA

2019 Andre Norton Neb

"Heartbreaking and heart-mending in turns, *Riverland* is
truest, deepest portrait of sisterhood and survival that I've read in a long time." —Rachel Hartman, *New York Times* bestselling author of *Tess of the Road* and *Seraphina*

"Bright, beautiful, and incandescent magic runs right through the heart of the this book. *Riverland* will mend so many fractured things, as only the best fantasy can." —William Alexander, National Book Award–winning author of *Goblin Secrets*

"I love everything about Fran Wilde's writing, from her gorgeous prose to the extraordinary worlds she creates. The right book can change a life, and *Riverland* is one of those books." —Kate Milford, *New York Times* bestselling author of *Greenglass House*

"Like childhood, the space between dreams and reality is both magical and perilous. Fran Wilde brings that to life with fierce tenderness." —Ellen Klages, Scott O'Dell Award–winning author of *The Green Glass Sea*

★ "Painful and heartwarming all at once . . . A must-read." —*Booklist*, starred review

★ "About courage and truth overcoming denial and fear, *Riverland* is an important book." —Shelf Awareness, starred review

"Skillfully blurs the lines between fantasy and reality in a haunting middle grade story of sisters connected through trauma and a shared mythology." —*Publishers Weekly*

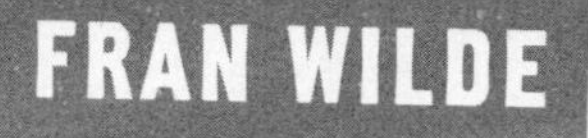

RIVERLAND

AMULET BOOKS • NEW YORK

PUBLISHER'S NOTE: This is a work of fiction. Names, characters, places, and incidents are either the product of the author's imagination or used fictitiously, and any resemblance to actual persons, living or dead, business establishments, events, or locales is entirely coincidental.

The Library of Congress has cataloged the hardcover edition as follows:
Names: Wilde, Fran, 1979- author.
Title: Riverland / by Fran Wilde.
Description: New York, NY: Amulet Books, an imprint of Abrams, 2019. | Summary: When their parents fight, sisters Eleanor and Mike hide, whispering stories and hoping house magic will protect them, until the night a river carries them to a place of dreams and nightmares.
Identifiers: LCCN 2018030956 | ISBN 9781419733727 (hardcover with jacket)
Subjects: | CYAC: Family problems—Fiction. | Sisters—Fiction. | Magic—Fiction. | Fantasy.
Classification: LCC PZ.1.W5328 Riv 2019 | DDC [Fic]—dc23

Paperback ISBN 978-1-4197-4338-2

Book design by Hana Anouk Nakamura

Printed and bound in U.S.A.

ABRAMS The Art of Books
195 Broadway, New York, NY 10007
abramsbooks.com

For my sister.

"Once upon a time . . ."

"Why do you always start like that? Why not someday, or tomorrow?"

"Because that's how stories start, Mike. They're already over when you tell them. They're safer that way."

"Fine. But make this one scary."

"Okay. Once upon a time, two sisters weren't very good. One sister was sent far away until they could both learn not to back talk or bring trouble, not to get mad or break things, not to cry."

"Didn't anyone notice the sister was gone?"

"No, because their parents replaced her with a better version. One who didn't do bad things."

"That's too scary, Eleanor. Does your head hurt?"

"It doesn't hurt."

"You always say that."

"If I say it, it's real. Like a magic spell."

"The sister who was sent away—what happened?"

"She made a magic spell that let her visit home whenever she wanted. But their father discovered that she kept coming back, because he'd been replaced too, by a troll, long ago, and trolls can smell kids really well. He made the girls' mother, who was a witch—a mostly good one—magic the house to keep the disappeared sister out and the other sister safe. And to keep anyone else from noticing that a troll and a witch lived in a nice house and not under a bridge somewhere."

"You sure it doesn't hurt?"

"Nothing hurts. Are you going to listen or not?"

"I'm listening."

"But the remaining sister knew that, when she followed the rules, sometimes her mother's magic would ease and the other sister could come home. She would hide under the bed and wait until her sister appeared. And they'd stay in that safe place, where the troll and the witch couldn't find them. They'd stay until morning whispering their own magic spells. Trying to get them to work."

"Eleanor, I don't want anyone to go away."

"Poppa was just joking, Mike. I'm not going away."

"Can I say our spell now?"

"Not yet. Shhhh."

. . .

"They're loud tonight."

"It's the stress. He'll be better soon. Momma said."

"Keep telling the story."

"The sisters stayed together for a long time in this way. But there was a price for these visits. If the one sister stayed past sunrise, she had to disappear for good, or they'd both disappear."

"I don't like that story. Tell a better one. A better spell."

"You can try yours now, if you want."

"Now?"

"Yup."

"Someday . . . our real parents will come for us."

CHAPTER

HOUSE MAGIC RULES

ONE

Some days, my sister and I could sense trouble coming.

Other days, like the weather, it caught us by surprise.

Today, from up the hill where the school bus dropped us off, our house looked trouble-free. Safe.

Momma had been busy.

The blue clapboard box with its wooden shutters anchored our cul-de-sac like it had been on Riverland Road forever, which it pretty much had. Mike's small purple bicycle leaned on my larger blue one in the shade of the garage. Our lawn, smooth all the way to the shoreline and carefully cleared of leaves, wrapped the house like arms with hands clasped at the pale concrete driveway.

Everything seemed perfect.

Better than perfect: The house didn't look magicked at all.

But today still felt like trouble. That's why I wasn't in a rush to go home.

If I was lucky, Pendra would invite me over. Her house was closer to our bus stop.

I formed the beginning of a wish—to be honest, it was more of a spell—in my mind. A spell that would turn Pendra toward her house, not mine. Two words: *Please, Pen.*

But Pendra Sarti had other ideas. She was looking down the hill too.

"We always go to my house," she said like she'd read my mind. "We haven't been to yours since summer. You always have some excuse. And you still have my book. We'll get it and then we can sit on the dock and work on our science posters until the rain comes."

As the bus, empty now, rolled away from our development, Pendra adjusted her backpack and ignored my frown. She started down the hill.

Spells never worked that well for me. Not even in the stories I told Mike, even if she did believe them.

And it *had* been months since Pendra had come over. Poppa was trying to buy more of the land around us in order to grow the development he'd named Riverland, after the road we lived on. He was stressed out a lot. That shouldn't have mattered, but it did. We had so many new rules.

The dock, Pendra's favorite place to sit, was just visible behind the house. The old wooden frame was mostly barnacles and cracking planks. Once, a dinghy had bobbed beside it. I'd seen pictures. But now, as river and wind whipped together into meringue-peaked waves, the dock swayed. The leaves on the trees near the house flipped over to their silver sides.

"Storm's going to be here too fast," I said hopefully, catching up to her as we neared her house. If it rained, Pendra and I couldn't sit outside. "We'd better wait. Your house instead."

But Pendra shook her head. "Yours." Her elbow poked me in the side, nudging me down the hill. "Mine's always a mess. Yours? Your mom waves a hand and cookies appear. My brothers are home and loud. Mike's not there to bother us."

I bristled about Mike. "Bothering is what little kids do. I don't mind it."

"You minded it this morning on the bus. You got so angry."

That was low. Mike's big mouth was why Pendra was insisting on going down the hill now.

"She was just kidding about the house." From where I stood, the beginnings of the late fall sunset hit a second-floor window and reflected off the blue fishing float—what the locals called a witch ball—hanging on the landing.

Everything in its place.

"Besides, no one's home." Momma had taken Mike to buy shoes after school. And a house rule was no surprise guests, especially if Momma wasn't home. I reached for excuses. "Poppa's working hard on the permits for the Lawton Farm."

Definitely no cookies to be had at the wave of a hand today.

"El, no one's at my house either. What's the difference?" Pendra was impossible to refuse when she wanted something. And what she wanted right now was to brainstorm science projects at my house. Preferably with cookies. Where she could look for magic. "Mike said . . ."

I knew what Mike had said.

She'd blurted to her friend Kalliope on the bus that morning: *Momma's doing house magic and I get to help her.*

I'd kicked the back of the seat and she'd gone quiet. Kalliope had shrugged it away with an *I bet you don't* and Mike hadn't replied.

All better.

But Pendra had heard. And she was as interested in magic as anyone.

The difference, magic or no, I wanted to say now, *is that your house is easy. Mine is hard.*

There were rules for my house Pendra didn't understand. Only my sister, Mary (everyone called her Mike, except Poppa), and I knew them all. Bringing Pendra home would break a rule, and rules helped the magic go.

At least, that's how I explained it to Mike when she was upset. No rules, no magic. No magic, everything would break and stay broken. And in our house, broken things disappeared.

I crossed my arms over my fleece jacket and cupped my elbows in my hands so the fuzz warmed my palms. I rocked a little on my heels, and the road grit ground beneath the thin rubber soles of my sneakers.

"We can't have surprise guests," I said. It was a big rule, based on how many times Momma had said it to both Mike and me. "And the difference is your house is noisy and happy even when no one's home. Mine's all creaks and groans," I finally argued. I wasn't lying. Our house was especially loud when the magic wasn't working.

I wished Mike were here. Pendra and I would go to her house then, at least until dinner. Problem solved.

Or else Pendra would try to drag more magic stories out of Mike. Problem not solved.

But Mike wasn't here and the temperature was falling fast. Gray clouds gained a greenish tint over the rough water. The smell of a dead fish carried almost all the way up the hill.

Two gulls cut tight circles over the beach but kept getting blown off course.

And Pendra kept walking away from her house and the bus stop. Her feet aimed past the three houses on the hill, down to the end of the street, to my house.

I wasn't one bit surprised my spell didn't work. They rarely did for me. And rain wasn't enough to put Pendra off.

I tried stubborn next. Stopped where I was and raised an eyebrow. Tilted my chin, leaning back toward Pendra's house. I tried to pull my friend that way, like the fishermen we sometimes watched work the river. I cranked a bright smile. "Come on, Pen, your house is closer. We can work on algorithms once we figure out the science project."

I didn't want to fight. Not with Pendra. Not with anyone.

The Sartis had moved three houses up from us that summer, into my friend Aja's old house. It hadn't taken long for Pendra's dad and mine to get in an argument and for Pendra and me to become friends.

Pendra said what she wanted. She did things and didn't worry about the consequences. Like now.

Her mouth curved, a half-smile. Her brown eyes crinkled at the corners. She turned again and continued walking down the hill, past the next house, toward mine. Her sneakers flashed silver in the afternoon light.

My feet wouldn't move.

"El, come on. I want *The Hobbit* back for the weekend. You've had it too long, and if you can't take care of my books, we simply can't be friends." She was kidding. The laugh at the end said she was.

Still, I grumbled. "If you like paper better than people, maybe we can't be friends either."

She slowed but didn't stop. Overhead, heavy clouds pressed the sun into stormlight and made her cheeks glow.

"We have the sleepover at my house this weekend and the science fair. Let's not fight. Come on," Pendra said, without turning around to see if I was following. Her dark hair swung side to side as she picked up speed. "We'll sit on the dock and decide our topic once and for all. What's stopping us?"

I pressed my lips together. Nothing was stopping us. Everything was.

Four months ago, when I'd hesitated over a pile of books at the library, Pendra had stepped up beside me at the desk. The librarian had squinted at her. Said to me, "You still have two out. Can't have these yet." And I'd felt my face heat up.

"I forgot," I finally said. I hadn't, but it was a good spell. One that worked, usually.

Pendra had elbowed me. "You're our neighbor, right? Eleanor Prine?"

I'd nodded, and she'd added my books to her own pile. "All of these, please." She'd deployed an enormous smile. One I learned later almost no adult could resist.

The librarian shrugged. "They're *your* fines if she doesn't bring them back."

Pendra nodded solemnly but cut a glance at me and winked. Saved.

I was so jealous someone could just *do* that. I kept myself from staring by grabbing my books and wrapping them in my jacket.

"My dad can give you a ride home too. It's raining," Pendra said.

A second save. I couldn't let her do it. Too embarrassing. "Thanks, but I like to walk."

If I drove with them, we stood a good chance of passing my dad on the road. I'd made him mad. He'd left me to walk back from the library on my own. In the rain. A lesson. If I didn't take the lesson, there might be other consequences.

I squeezed out the heavy library door and down the road, starting the long walk back on the overpass sidewalk. By then it was pouring. Halfway there, as cars roared along the highway below, the Sartis' car squeaked to a halt and the door opened.

"No discussion, Eleanor!" Mr. Sarti had called.

"Can't let *my* books get wet," Pendra added.

I wiped the rain off my face with the back of my hand.

She'd passed me a towel, whispering, "Sorry it smells like the dogs." And then she started telling a story about riding the metro from their old apartment into the city as I tried to sit as close to the edge of the seat as possible so I wouldn't get everything wet. I'd nearly laughed myself dry when she'd said everyone should take boats around Baltimore. She'd never seen Poppa try to handle a boat.

By the time we got back to the growing development that surrounded my house, we were friends.

Pendra and I, and sometimes Mike, spent a lot of time together that summer. Our dads still growled at each other, but they let us alone. There wasn't anyone else my age in the development, not since Aja's family had moved to the other side of the highway.

We'd taken advanced swim lessons together—Pendra's mom had insisted. We'd gone to the library. Sweated out the slow summer days on my dock, Mrs. Sarti insisting that Pendra put on sunscreen every time Mike and I did, which Pendra thought was ridiculous. "I don't need it nearly as much as you do," she'd laughed.

That had lasted until school began. Until the house started needing a lot more magicking again. Then I'd found more excuses to spend time at Pendra's. Sometimes with Mike along. And now Mike had let our secret slip and wasn't here to help me fix it.

What's stopping you?

I couldn't answer that. My heart started spider-crawling up my throat, tickling at the sides until I had to cough. Pendra didn't slow. Didn't turn around.

She was almost halfway down the hill.

There was one thing that might at least stall her. Pendra loved magic stories as much as I did. If I told her Mike had been right and there was house magic, she might listen, at least long enough for Momma to get home.

But I couldn't.

That was the most important rule. No talking to anyone about house magic.

If we talked too much, then house magic would absolutely stop working.

And if the magic stopped working, Mike or I might disappear.

I ran down the hill after my friend.

+++

Just before the hill started to level out, I caught up to Pendra. Our sneakers mashed the gravel side by side. A splot of rain hit my nose. "Not for long, okay? And I have to go in first. We can't bother my dad if he's there."

"You just said no one was home." Pendra switched her orange-and-pink backpack to the other shoulder. She kept walking.

"I forgot. It will probably be okay." My own backpack felt heavier the closer I got to the bottom of the hill. *Say okay, Pendra. Please.*

More terrible spells. Why couldn't I just say *no*?

Because Pendra might just leave and maybe find other friends.

And then . . .

Well, everyone left. Right? Aja had moved across the highway, and I didn't care—much. But I didn't want Pendra to go, too.

When I fished my key from the inner jacket pocket, the cold metal and the blue plastic ring around the rim against my finger felt solid. Nearly unbreakable. "Just give me a minute." I passed her quickly so she didn't have a second to reconsider or press me about going into the house with me.

Because no matter how safe it looked from the outside, I didn't know if the inside had been magicked yet.

That morning, when Mike and I left to catch the bus, a pile of torn-up photographs littered the living room, trailing all the way to the fireplace. Three broken frames lay in the foyer, plus the mirror, next to what was left of the white vase. As the front door closed, we'd overheard Momma phoning the cleaning lady, asking her to come another day.

The house had been full of trouble then, but Momma was going to work until it was better.

"Big house magic can't be done by the usual people, right Eleanor?" Mike had whispered knowingly on our way out the door.

"Right. And we have to help too. Don't notice anything's different when we get back. Don't say anything to Momma." Mike and I had our own house magic. Lesser spells but still important. "Don't break any more rules." That's what I'd told her on the way up the hill.

Mike had chewed on her finger and nodded. I took her hand and squeezed so she wouldn't tear at her cuticles. "We can do it."

But then she'd repeated what I'd said on the bus.

If Mike had come home instead of going shopping with Momma, none of this would have happened. Or if Pendra had listened. Or if my spells actually worked.

Say it's okay, Pendra. Say you understand.

I shifted the straps on my backpack, tightening them.

Pendra slowed as we neared the walkway. "Okay," she finally said. "Don't be such a worrier."

Easy for her to say.

By the time she joined me on the stoop, I'd undone the lock and cracked the door just wide enough for me. "Back as fast as I can," I said as I slipped through.

Behind me, Pendra sighed. "Fine, fine." She dropped her backpack with a thud and a rustle as the weight of her notebooks tilted the bag over. She sat down on the stoop just as noisily. "Your mom's a much better hostess than you, El."

I couldn't care. Not until I made sure the house was safe on the inside too.

The door clicked shut behind me and I set my purple backpack down soundlessly on the foyer floor. Laid my jacket over it inside out, ready to throw on if I needed to leave.

At Pendra's house, the entry hall was always a swirl of mail, backpacks, boots, dogs, a cat, and sports equipment. Since that first day they'd given me a ride from the library and Poppa had come to find me there, the jumble had kind of swooped me up too. Did I want a snack? Watch out for the dogs! Did I want to stay for dinner? (Yes, very much.) Someone laughing upstairs. So much fun that I'd forgotten the time.

"You're welcome always," Mrs. Sarti had pretty much sung from the kitchen then as I rushed out the door, and every time she saw me outside of school after that too. Being there felt like spring sun on bare skin—warm and comforting.

In my house this afternoon, the foyer sparkled. A new vase with heirloom roses in it lined up against the mirror over the entry table. I didn't waste time looking in the mirror as I passed—I knew I was a windblown mess.

My sigh of relief bubbled up on its own as I looked into the living room.

Momma's house magic had fixed everything while we'd been at school.

The broken glass and china were gone, like always. A new game console sat in the same place as the one that had crashed to the floor last night. The television screen had actually grown larger.

I almost loved this kind of magic. The kind where nothing was really lost, only bettered.

Nothing that mattered to the house was lost, that is.

Mike and I? We both worked really hard to matter, but sometimes we made mistakes.

In the living room, one new silver frame had the word *happiness* engraved on it. There wasn't any photo inside yet. The black mat looked like a hole.

House magic wasn't perfect, which was okay. I'd read enough books to know that no magic was. Still, Momma needed us to believe in it so that others would too.

And this was good enough magicking that Pendra wouldn't notice anything wrong. I swung the front door wide. "Come on, but don't shout. Your book's up in my room."

Mike would be sad *The Hobbit* was gone. I'd been reading it to her under the bed, some nights. I loved watching her expressions at each surprise, her excitement about the ponies and wizards. "But not the trolls." She only liked *my* stories with trolls, she'd said.

Now, Pendra jumped up from the stoop and swept through the door. Her hair hung straight, unbothered by the wind, all the way to her jeans pockets. When she shook her head, it made a beautiful curve, then settled back down. My own hair would barely stay in its braids.

Maybe it wouldn't rain. Maybe we could take our books outside soon. Then no one would know I'd broken a rule.

After Pendra dropped her coat and backpack in a jumble beside mine, we both took the stairs two at a time to the landing. That's what got my heart beating so loud, laughing quietly and climbing stairs at the same time.

For luck, I brushed a fingertip over the old glass witch ball that hung on the landing. Cool and reassuring, the smooth surface an illusion: small, stilled ripples and bubbles met my touch. Then the deep blue sphere swung gently on its cord, the glass strands inside picking up the last afternoon light and throwing it on the walls. Hand-size and weighty, the ball had been Momma's great-grandmother's, brought over from Norway.

It was the last of a net full of floats from when the Favre family—Gran's last name—used to fish the neck of the river until everyone started using foam buoys.

Pendra reached out too, but her hand hovered just above the sphere. "It always looks like a water bubble hanging in the air," she whispered. "That's probably part of the magic, right?"

My fingers stuttered on the glass, then stilled the ball in its sudden, broader swing.

She meant the float, not the house. I'd told her once how the colorful balls had supported fishing nets here in the nineteenth century, that the threads fascinated fish, luring them to the trap. That they were all very scientific, the fishing floats. Even one that hung alone on our landing, capturing light.

But Pendra had heard Momma call the float a witch ball once, and the idea that it was magic had caught, just like Mike's words had stuck today.

The bauble fascinated Pendra as much as anything in the house.

"Not everything can be magic," I laughed. "Most things are just superstition."

Pendra stuck her tongue out at me, then flipped her retainer in her mouth the way she did sometimes when she was thinking. I envied the trick, even if it was a little gross.

I let go of the ball. "They're supposed to catch evil spirits before they can harm a house, I looked it up." Pendra's face lit hopefully, and she leaned closer, like she was looking to see what the ball had caught. "I love them, but the ones in the shops are all fakes. This one's real."

"Real, like magic real," Pendra mused. She didn't listen.

"They catch fish, that's all." I tried to move her down the hallway. If I was truthful, I loved the float too, but not because it might be magic. I loved it because no matter what else broke during the night here, the witch ball stayed untouched. Unbroken.

Even though it was made of glass, it was the longest-lived object in the house. I wanted to be that strong. That beautiful.

Pendra's retainer clicked another circuit. "Know what isn't magic? Two brothers and all their gym clothes, everywhere. And being the youngest. Even the dogs are older than me. In dog years." She inhaled deeply. "Your house smells nice, like the river. My house smells like sports gear."

I sniffed. I didn't smell anything much. Maybe a little freshener to conceal the fireplace-burnt-photograph smell. "Come on, Pen." *Let's just get the book and get out before anyone comes home.*

My turquoise Converse All Stars kicked up the pile in the tan carpet. So did Pendra's silver Keds. We left a trail of scuff-marks in the neat vacuum swaths all down the hall, but it would have looked the same if Mike and I did it, so I didn't worry too much.

A closed door on my parents' side of the house blocked light from the brightest windows. The hallway, lined with relatives' photographs going all the way back to when Favres lived here and not Prines—and even further than that—was dark except for the light thrown by the witch ball. Some photos glittered in the shadows, silvered with age. Grandparents and great-grands. A few older still.

"Did you know any of them?" Pendra's voice was quiet. Her grandfather had died over the summer, right after they moved. I wished we'd been better friends then. It felt strange to say sorry now.

"Only Momma's mom is still alive and she travels a lot. The last time she came here was when Mike was a baby." I couldn't remember Gran's voice. Just her face. But my memory was grainy and black-and-white, just like the photographs.

Momma said they'd fought once but wouldn't say why.

At the far end of the hallway, as far as you could get from my parents' room, Momma had her own photo with Gran by the dock. The dinghy bobbed, its dock line wrapped in a half-hitch around a piling. Momma wore a white dress. Neither she nor Gran looked very happy. The photograph inside the frame had been taped back together, twice.

The light from Mike's room made the new frame on the photograph shine.

Like the witch ball, few of the heirloom frames besides that photo required house magic to fix. Mostly just Gran's. The rest seemed impervious and smelled slightly stale, like old books.

I liked old things. They lasted.

Sometimes, especially when no one was home, I wondered what it would feel like to break one. Sometimes I almost got mad enough to try. But I never did.

Pendra lingered, looking at the other photographs. "Imagine what this place was like when there were no other houses but yours." She reached out to touch a frame.

"Lots of fishing and crabbing and farming." I echoed Poppa's sales pitch for the development. "A lot of hard work." One last farm remained near our property. Poppa was trying to buy it so he could add more houses by the river. "Before the farms, there was a fishing camp. Before that? The Susquehannock and the Algonquin." Mike and I had looked it up at the library last summer. "Come on, Pen. Do you want your book or not?"

"It's just so quiet here," Pendra said, closing her eyes.

It wouldn't be quiet for long. We were going too slowly. Someone would be home soon, and if it was Momma, that was mostly fine.

We hurried past the guest bedroom, kept ready though no one ever stayed there. Down to the two rooms at the end of the hall. Mike's, then mine. Connected by a shared bath.

Mike's door was open. Mint-green walls, all the lights on. The space clean and neat.

Pendra lingered, looking back at the witch ball again.

At the end of the hall, the door to my bright turquoise room stood open. "Oh." I could barely breathe.

My sneakers crackled static across the carpet, I moved so fast.

Everything in my room had been straightened.

"Oh no."

My notebooks and sketchpads were stacked magazine-perfect. But that didn't matter. Those were decoys.

The dolls too. They'd been arranged against the wall, by period. The room felt smaller, then larger, too hot, then too cold by turns. *Calm down, Eleanor, they're just dolls.* The pioneer doll, then the Victorian. The one from New Orleans, the World War I doll. The dolls from India and China. I rarely played with them, but Grandma Favre had sent them, so I kept them nearby, in their boxes. Now they were on display.

Words I'd heard often but couldn't say pricked my tongue. Curses that would maybe not shock Pendra because of her brothers, but ones that would absolutely crack house magic. Much worse than *dammit* and other words.

"What's wrong?" Pendra, suddenly right behind me. I startled and she held up a hand. "El, you're so jumpy. What is it?"

I couldn't answer. Breath held, I dropped to the floor and lifted the thick bed skirt. A row of tiny bells jangled a merry warning.

"What are you doing?"

Nothing. Everything. "Just checking something. Shhhh." I tried to sound cool, but there I was, crawling on my carpet in broad daylight in front of my friend.

In the shadows, the space beneath the bed looked undisturbed. The old pillows were there. A blanket. The Halloween lights. Just like Mike and I had left them.

Pendra crawled under the bed with me. "You still make forts!" Her voice was right in my ear. The bed frame was close above our heads, and Pendra's shoulder pressed mine. "A bit low though."

"It's for Mike, when she can't sleep," I said, scanning the shadows, looking for *The Hobbit.* Not there. I startled and hit my head on the wooden slats of the old frame. Ow. On an old bruise too.

But, Pendra's book. My eyes itched, and not from the carpet. There were only two books under the bed now, not three. A book on birds. An old book about a tollbooth.

The Tolkien was missing.

I scootched back out, carpet fibers grating my elbows. Knelt by the bedside table, counting books: *one two three four five six seven eight*—not there either. Had it been magicked?

House magic didn't come into bedrooms unless a rule was broken. Mike and I had been so careful lately.

I winced at a memory from the night before: I'd slammed a door. I'd lost my temper. I'd yelled. I'd been so tired of the shouting from downstairs and Mike snuggled tight against me asking if I could make it all stop.

I'd made it worse instead.

Momma and Poppa slammed doors too, but their rules were different. I should have stayed under the bed.

That was our safest place. No one knew about it except Mike and me. House magic had never gotten under the bed before.

"Pendra, don't tell anyone, okay?"

She didn't hear me. She was looking in every corner, as if she might find something magical there. But she wouldn't even find the missing book.

In the entire house, not one place was safe anymore. For a moment, I wished I were small enough to crawl inside the glass float. Maybe that was safe. Because now I had to tell Pendra I'd lost her book, and then I had to get her out of the house before she decided to search everywhere.

I felt panic build. We were going to get caught.

Once, Mike had gotten chocolate on one of Pendra's books, and now I had to promise to never eat over a book when I borrowed one. It had been months. But a lost book? "It was right there."

This wasn't magic. This was just mean.

I crawled backward until the bed skirt ruffled my hair. Then I sat back on my knees and looked all around the room. Pendra's feet and legs stuck out from under the bed. Striped leggings, the hem of a pink skirt. "Maybe it's under a pillow?" The bed skirt rang merrily as she moved around. Jarring music for my growing doom.

While she searched, I checked one more thing. Not a book, not at all, but still a good gauge of the doom. "Please be there," I whispered to the house. I flipped back the blue comforter and picked up the pillow. I'd tucked the edge of the pillowcase in, so it didn't flap or look sloppy.

Pendra's sneakers wriggled under the bed. "I don't know how you and Mike both fit under here," she said.

Practice. I bit my lip. If Pendra knew how much time we spent under there, telling stories, I know she'd look at me funny.

I unfolded the edge of the pillowcase and reached inside. The pillow's rough seam was still safety-pinned together, a good sign. Careful not to prick my fingers, I unclipped the pin, then reached into the foam insert. I pried off the piece I'd cut away then pasted back together with washi tape. My fingers touched the hard weight of the small paring knife I'd stolen last spring from the kitchen.

It was a tiny theft. So far our parents hadn't noticed. So many things came and went in the house.

But on days when I worried about disappearing too much, it helped me feel better. Even if I didn't know what I'd use it for. I had it, and that was what mattered.

It was the most daring thing I'd ever done.

But I couldn't ever brag to Pendra or Mike, or anyone that I'd done it.

If slamming a door got books magicked away, a stolen knife would be far, far worse trouble. I smoothed the foam down and stuck the tape back in place, repinned the pillow, and refolded the outer case. The pillow went back on the bed and the comforter over it in one well-practiced move.

A shadow darkened the window and I jumped again. Just a heron landing on the tree outside. Spying on fish in the river maybe. The afternoon sun had cast its shadow far into my room. I relaxed my fingers, which had curled up tight into fists.

“Bad bird,” I murmured. “Go lurk in someone else’s tree.” We still needed to leave the house. “Come on, Pen.” The words came out sharper than I meant them to.

Pendra slid out from beneath the bed. She’d gotten pale carpet fuzz on her leggings and yellow T-shirt. She began to brush it off slowly, not looking at me. “Hey, Eleanor, don’t worry. Take three deep breaths and let them out slow. That always helps me relax.”

Three deep breaths weren’t going to cut it with a missing book and family bound to come home soon.

“Did you find the book?” she asked.

“No, nothing.” I braced for a proper scolding. I hoped that was all I’d get.

Downstairs, the front door opened and shut. “Eleanor?” Momma. “Who’s here with you?”

Worse and worse.

CHAPTER

CONSEQUENCES

TWO

Mike passed us on the landing, her new shoes still in their box. Her eyes widened when she saw Pendra. "Ooooh. Trouble." She mouthed the words. I fought back my own annoyance, but I let Pendra shush Mike.

Still, Momma didn't seem mad once we got downstairs. She waved her hands merrily. "You can't do homework without a snack! But it's late enough to call it dinner."

She wouldn't let us in the kitchen. Plates with heart-shaped grilled cheese sandwiches and mugs of hot cocoa appeared in the dining room and she sat with us to watch us eat. "Eleanor, really, you should know better than to not feed your guests."

She'd put pesto in my sandwich. My favorite. Avocado in Pendra's. Pendra practically glowed with happiness while she texted her mom to let her know she was eating here. "Your mom is so great."

Momma *was* being great. Better than great. She was being magic.

I tried to chew my sandwich while Pendra's phone buzzed with reply texts.

I longed for a phone like hers, but it was easy to make myself not want one right now. That would be the first thing to disappear in house magic. And there was absolutely going to be some house magic after this.

We ate, but Mike wouldn't quit goggling at Pendra and me, so wide-eyed she looked like a fish. I couldn't meet her gaze, so I kicked her under the table. I knew what she was thinking and hoped it didn't come right out of her mouth. Poppa would be home any minute. I had a surprise guest. And this was not a proper dinner.

Trouble.

When the doorbell rang, we all jumped, Momma included. All except Pendra, who kept chewing the last bit of my sandwich, which I hadn't been able to finish. But it was only Mrs. Sarti.

"Thought I'd swing by when I got Pen's text," we heard her say as Momma stood on the threshold.

Momma smiled and stepped back, and Mrs. Sarti followed her in. "So many surprises!" Momma laughed. Mike choked on the crust of her grilled cheese. "Would you like some cocoa?"

"We can't stay long, the boys have a late game," Mrs. Sarti said.

Pendra slouched in her chair. "Can't I stay while you go? It's so much better here than at a game."

But Mrs. Sarti cleared her throat and looked at Momma. "A quick question, Moira? I've left messages. I thought since I was coming by anyway, we could talk for a moment. Maybe in the kitchen?"

Mike kicked me back under the table. *So much trouble.*

Momma's face shifted so that it was hard to tell what she was thinking. She still smiled. "There's nothing my girls can't hear. No secrets in this house. All's well, I hope?" She put her hand on the back of my chair.

"Of course. Maybe a later time." Mrs. Sarti smiled at me. "I'll try and reach you on the phone again."

The door squeaked open in the silence that followed. Poppa nearly tripped on Pendra's backpack as he came inside, took in all of us sitting around the table, and raised his eyebrows. "Quite a crowd!"

Mike didn't kick me again. She froze in her chair. I couldn't move either. Only Pendra and her mom seemed to be impervious to Poppa's sharp cheer.

Momma's smile didn't change. "Mrs. Sarti was just about to take Pendra home."

As if she'd willed it, Pendra jumped up from her chair and dodged around Poppa to get her bag. Poppa frowned as if he was chewing on unasked questions and they all tasted terrible.

I had a horrible, acidy taste in my mouth too.

"Good to see you both." He held the door open for them.

"And you too," Mrs. Sarti said. "Perhaps when I speak with Moira, you can join us."

Poppa's frown deepened. Mike and I, trapped at the table, couldn't break for the upstairs if we wanted to, which we did. Momma looked caught in the middle. Finally, under the increasing weight of Poppa's gaze, Momma broke.

"Vandana wanted to have a quick conversation, that's all. It can wait."

"About? Something at school? Let's have it." Poppa's voice had a rumble of thunder behind it.

"I think it would be better without—" Mrs. Sarti said. She looked terribly trapped too.

"We're all here. Let's get things out in the open," Poppa said, laughing a little. He winked at Momma. He didn't look at Mike or me. He sounded reasonable.

We watched Mrs. Sarti nod. "Pendra, why don't you head up the hill?"

Pendra looked at me as she shouldered her backpack. "My book," she mouthed. "Tomorrow."

I whispered back, "I'll find it." *Please don't be mad*. And then she was out the door, Mike and I were trapped in our seats, and Poppa was staring at Momma. Who wasn't looking at any of us.

So much trouble.

"It was an idea I had. That's really all," Mrs. Sarti began. "I noticed since we've been at school that Mike sometimes gets pushed around at the elementary." Mrs. Sarti was the district's traveling guidance counselor, and our neighbor. Right now she looked as uncomfortable as Mike and I felt, but she pressed on. "And there's the fight from last spring in her record, which I know she said she didn't start."

Mike groaned and sunk lower in her seat.

"I'm sure you're well aware we took care of that." Momma's voice turned icy cold, but her smile remained. How she did that always made me squirm, but I wasn't sure why. Wood squeaked as her fingers tightened on my chair.

Mrs. Sarti spoke as if she thought the chill in the room was just a draft from an old house. "I thought, perhaps you'd like to look into an assertiveness class, or a mentor for Mike and maybe Eleanor too. To get out ahead of things a little." She smiled at Mike. "You're very bright. I want to see you get the most out of third grade." Then to Momma and Poppa: "We could talk about it more officially at school, the next day I'm there."

Momma released the back of my chair. I scooted back as soon as she was clear, looking for my exit. Mike did the same. The sound of our chair legs squeaking on the dining room floor was the only noise in the house besides Poppa's long sigh.

"Thank you," Momma said, making each word distinct. She glanced at Mike. "But we would appreciate you not pressuring her. Mike is fine. Aren't you?"

Mike nodded, her face bright red.

"I understand sometimes these things come off as a failing," Mrs. Sarti hurried to say, "but they're really not. I thought—"

"I think the question's been answered," Poppa said. His voice was calm, but he held the door open with fingers tight around the knob.

Mrs. Sarti nodded. "Of course. Anything I can do. I hope you understand."

"I understand that you were right earlier. This should be kept on school time, if there is any problem," Momma said. "And there won't be." She walked Mrs. Sarti to the door and then through it. Poppa barely moved. I saw Pendra standing just beyond the driveway. Had she heard too?

When the door swung shut, our house seemed to turn in on itself. Poppa glared at all of us, one at a time.

Momma smoothed the air with her hands like she would a wrinkled bedspread. "I'll take care of it," she said.

Poppa let go of the doorknob, walked up the stairs, to the landing. He pulled the remaining air through the house with him. "What just happened?" His voice was overly calm.

Momma bit her words tight. "Eleanor knows what happened."

I shook my head, the terrible taste in my mouth getting worse.

"Mike, what did Eleanor do?" Momma said without moving from where she stood. She cast her words so that Poppa could hear them.

Mike stared at the table. She kicked her feet but didn't say anything.

"Mike, you were asked a question," Momma said. She said it like she needed an ingredient for a recipe. Or a spell.

Mike looked at me and I nodded, barely. *Say it.* I hoped it would be enough.

"Eleanor brought trouble," Mike whispered, her eyes locked on mine.

The dining room was silent for a moment. Momma let out a small hiss of breath. "She did. She brought it right into the house. Eleanor, we don't need anyone from the school coming around. Your father has enough to worry about. Even if you're friends with their daughter. All right?" She was asking all of us.

Was it enough? I didn't look at Momma. Just at Mike. Mike looked at Momma, eyes wide, lip trapped beneath her wide-gapped front teeth. Neither of us looked out to the landing.

"They need to remember," Poppa said from upstairs. From the upstairs light, he cast a shadow on the foyer floor.

"I agree," Momma said. "Everyone will."

Poppa said, "Yes. They will." His shadow danced silently on the wall. A twang broke the quiet, a string snapping. There was no more warning. But consequences rarely came with warnings.

We didn't see him drop the witch ball.

We saw his shadow arm move, the bright glitter of glass rippling blue on the pale wall.

We heard silence so loud it sounded like horses' hooves galloping. Then an enormous *pop* and shatter. Thick glass connected with hard floor.

Then the ancient blue glass was everywhere. The thick string dangled empty above the landing.

Shadows swirled and rippled blue on the ceiling, then disappeared. A single shard skidded into the dining room.

I thought I could still hear hoofbeats. Probably my heart trying to run away. Was there more to come? Was this enough?

Poppa walked down the stairs without a word, back through broken glass, his shoes grinding pieces to dust. He didn't stop. Didn't look at us. His feet crunched on the wood floor all the way back to his office. The door slammed.

"You promised," Momma whispered to me. "But that's never enough."

Not enough. Oh, that hurt.

We looked at the air for a long time, as if the space between us could harden. "I didn't break the—"

My voice was louder than it should have been. Momma winced.

"Mind your temper, Eleanor. From now on," Momma said to us, her words as bright and sharp as shards, "no friends here unless I'm home. Absolutely no Pendra."

I bit my lip so the sour taste wouldn't get out. No more broken rules: no back talk. No crying either.

Crying wasn't for someone who'd turned twelve two weeks ago, anyway. Even though, since I'd agreed to wait to celebrate at Pendra's sleepover, it really didn't feel like my birthday had passed yet. Still, no crying. That would make it worse.

And what about the sleepover? The science fair project?

"For how long?" Mike saw my concern and asked for me. Her words vibrated in the air. But she could ask. She wasn't in trouble. Not today, at least.

"Pendra and her mother do not get to make free around this house or our business. You see what happens when they do," Momma said. She saw my face and her voice shook. "Eleanor, you can visit up there sometimes, as long as you're discreet. But that's the rule now. Clean up, then stay in your rooms."

She walked into the kitchen fast, leaving Mike and me alone at the dining room table.

Mike slid from her chair and came to stand next to me. "I'm sorry."

"Nothing to be sorry for," I lied. "You helped." It hurt to hear her tell on me, but it would have been harder if she hadn't. If she hadn't gone shoe shopping. If she hadn't talked about house magic. We were actually lucky, I told myself. Maybe Poppa had taken it all out on the witch ball. And Mike, still embarrassed by Mrs. Sarti's visit, had done her best.

Now, what I could do was fix things.

I added another rule to our list. "I won't break any more

rules," I promised Mike. So often, broken rules led to broken things. The photographs. The television. The witch ball.

Mike brought the dustpan and I began to sweep up the blue glass. I wrapped the big pieces in paper towel and put them in my jacket pocket.

"House magic will fix it," she said, as if this was nothing new. "We'll get a better witch ball, that's all."

I wanted to tell her house magic wasn't real, right there. But I bit my tongue. She needed to believe. "We'll get a better witch ball," I said instead. Even though I knew that sometimes broken things didn't come back. We'd had more glass floats, once. They'd broken over the years and couldn't be fixed or replaced—so they, like Pendra's book, just disappeared.

+++

Sometimes, one broken thing was enough.

I was lying on my bed, halfway through my math homework, when voices drifted up from the kitchen.

". . . School drama. Ridiculous new regulations. Waiting periods," Poppa said. "This seller's agent is a monster."

Momma responded with bright words. "It will be all right. Things work out. You know they do."

Then there was a crash, like a dropped plate, or a mug. "Oh, damn. Clumsy of me."

The quiet was tense like the green clouds curled up on the horizon this afternoon.

"Things are tight, Moira. Especially now. Especially with two goddamned girls to take care of. How much did that cost?"

"I dropped a mug," Momma said. "A few dollars. It happens."

From the echoes through the air vent by my bed, I knew Momma was standing at the kitchen sink. Her voice was muffled like her head was bowed. Poppa's voice grew louder and softer. He was pacing as if trapped in there. I'd stood at the same sink, in the same pose, during an angry prowl.

"A few dollars." I knew his hands were probably shaking with the effort of holding his anger together.

That was hard to do when people brought trouble into the house.

The witch ball hadn't been enough.

I knew another thing with creeping certainty. I knew I wasn't going to go downstairs and get in the way again.

I hated that I knew this.

My homework slipped off the bedspread and rustled onto the floor. I eased off the bed, one sock foot on the carpet, then the other, bare. I'd kicked off a sock while wrestling with algebra, trying to memorize algorithms for Monday's test.

The sock was probably sandwiched in between layers of covers and sheets. I left it there. I tiptoed through the bathroom I shared with Mike. Where my bare toes met the cold tile, I hissed.

Then the hard music of more stoneware mugs hitting the kitchen floor punctured the fight. One cup. Two.

"Do another one," I murmured as I went through to Mike's room. "Then they're even at least."

Crash.

Good.

Crash. Crash. Crash.

Bad.

Mike was awake, bunched up in her blankets, looking out at the doorway like an owl. Waiting.

"Come on," I said. "You don't need an invitation anymore."

Mike slid down from the bed, but she did it very slowly. "Maybe they'll stop."

Crash. I shifted from my sock foot to my other, bare foot. Felt the rough carpet between my toes. "Not likely. Let's go. Story time."

The stairs creaked. First step. Second step. "It's been a stressful day for everyone, Simon. You'll upset them."

"And whose fault is that? Moira, don't be stupid. They're asleep. They don't care about you." A hard hand met a soft cheek. "No more than the neighbors do."

There were different kinds of quiet. Just like different kinds of magic. There was shame quiet, and angry quiet. Worry quiet.

There was the quiet of someone deciding what to say, which way to turn.

"Eleanor." Mike tugged at my arm, finally free of her bed. I stuffed her pillow beneath her comforter and punched it a few times. Made it look like she was sleeping. Pulled Mike by the elbow until she followed me from her bedroom, through the cold bathroom, and back into my room.

She stepped carefully around my math pages and crawled under the bed.

I paused, listening. A moment, just one while I rethought which way to go. Mike would be safe under the bed. I could crawl under too. Or I could go try to help, like I'd done last night.

Got a good bump for that on the back of my head, from the wall. Mike and I had whispered, "It doesn't hurt," under the bed until I didn't know what hurt felt like, which was the same thing as not hurting.

Which was why Pendra's book had disappeared. Consequences.

I didn't want to get in the way again. I had nothing much left to disappear.

Momma broke the enormous quiet. "Eleanor's friend was by, and that's why Vandana came. As the girl's mother. She's been trying to track me down about Mary."

"That girl. We could send her to military school, like I said. Or Eleanor, if her grades slip. They're nothing but trouble together." His voice was the low, looming storm quiet again. "How did she—"

"Eleanor gave her the opportunity. Had her daughter over when no one was home. She knows she broke the rules."

No. I was most certainly not going downstairs to help. I wished I was a bird and could fly from the house.

I got down on my belly and crawled under the bed. I could see Mike curled against the far wall, pushing aside pillows to make room. Maybe she hadn't heard.

"The guidance counselor. What next, Moira? Blaming me for everything?"

Mike had wrapped a blanket around herself. She bit her lip and snuffled.

No such luck. She'd heard every word.

Momma's reply was too soft and I couldn't make it out over Poppa's footsteps on the landing. Sometimes we could make him so mad that he'd get in his car and drive away. That was better. Sometimes.

The quiet built again.

"Tell me a scary story," Mike said. "With magic in it."

A crash of glass against a wall. "Do you think I'm stupid? Do you think I don't know what the girls are telling people behind my back?" His voice broke the silence like a wave.

"Simon, no." Pleading from the landing.

Another crash. A breaking frame. Another. The old photographs. And something heavier. I closed my eyes and hugged my sister tight.

+++

"Once upon a time," I whispered, hunched beneath the bed frame, "two girls lived in a lighthouse where the old lighthouse keeper was sick. They kept the light going so no one would know."

"Scarier," Mike murmured into the heaviest of quiets. He hadn't left. Mike curled on her side and pulled her knees up to her chest. Wrapped her arms around them.

"Okay. Give me a minute." I peeked out from beneath the bed skirt carefully, holding the bells to keep them from chiming. No one was in my room.

I rolled over, careful not to catch my hair on the frame, and lay on my stomach on the carpet.

Pendra was right, I was getting too big to fit under here. Mike snuggled hard against my side. "Tell a story, El."

"Once upon a time, there were two girls who weren't very good at rules," I began.

"I'm sorry about the magic." Mike pulled her sleeves over her hands and began to twist the fabric. "I didn't think it would matter."

I closed my eyes. I'd been trying for funny, but what I'd said was so mean. "We both broke rules." I would be nicer. I would.

A door slammed. A car started.

"We're not good at family either," Mike added solemnly.

"Or that." I thought of Momma and Gran. How they rarely spoke and Gran didn't visit. "I'm not going anywhere, though."

Mike nodded. "Okay."

I tried again. "Once upon a time, two sisters set out to rescue their real parents, who'd been kidnapped by a troll."

Mike shivered at that and I reached for the toggle that turned on a string of Halloween lights beneath the bed. The bed skirt was thick enough they couldn't be seen from the outside. I'd made sure.

At once, the space beneath the bed sparkled. Small bits of purple edged the shadows. I'd done what I could to make it nice under here, once I'd started getting Mike in the middle of the night. I'd tied back the thin box-spring cover where it was torn. I'd put unmatched socks over the exposed springs so they couldn't grab Mike's hair or mine.

But now the lights glittered purple on the carpet. No. They gleamed across a skim of water where the carpet had been.

"Did you spill something?" I looked at Mike suspiciously.

Mike shook her head and stared at the water, which had formed a stream. A slice of light swung over the water and then moved away.

After a long time—and we didn't take our eyes off of it—the light swung back across the darkness again. Yellow, like fireflies.

"Ooooh," Mike whispered.

A blue-gray feather rested on the water's surface and turned, like a low gray boat, adrift in the breeze.

I rubbed my eyes and reached out to touch the water. Lifting the feather, the small breaks and whorls coming off the quill caught the light. So delicate, like it was made of glass. But the feather dripped cold water, real enough. The stream reflected stars and a pale lighthouse, tall against the night sky.

I lifted the bed skirt again and looked out. My room looked just the same.

The pool of water didn't extend past the bed.

Downstairs, the waiting kind of silence held. The kind that could still get us in trouble.

I let the bed skirt drop again. Mike put her fingertip in the stream. I could smell the bay now, like salt and fresh water, mixed.

"Impossible," I whispered. "Mike, pinch me." She pinched hard. That didn't wake me. The stream was getting bigger and I shivered at the breeze coming off the water.

The stream expanded just as the door slammed and the shouting began again. Poppa's feet banged on the landing, crunching broken glass. Mike switched the lights off.

"Mike, wait," I said. But in the dark of the underbed, I heard an enormous splash. "Mike!"

The lighthouse beam slid across the water's surface again. I saw Mike's footie pajamas kicking up a splash. Spray struck my face. Then Mike disappeared.

I didn't stop to think. I dove after my sister.

CHAPTER

THE RIVER

THREE

Cold water pushed my breath from my chest in one quick rush. Bubbles rose around me and my hair wreathed my head, loosed from my braid by the tide. Which way was up? I flailed and kicked, disoriented, until my head broke the surface of a wide, night-dark river laced with moonlight.

Gasping, I struggled onto my back and floated for a moment beneath stars pricked bright into a pitch-black sky. The bed frame was gone. The carpet, too.

Where was Mike?

I nearly sank again looking left and right. Water, cold and fast, sweeping around me. Wind strong enough to drive clouds across the sky. Sky.

We'd been hiding beneath my bed. Now a river pushed and pulled at me, carrying me where it would, dragging at my hair, my clothes.

There was an explanation. There had to be. I sputtered and coughed, fighting what my body knew already as it kicked and scissored my legs, circled my arms in the water.

Survival came first. Understanding would have to wait.

My one sock grew heavy and my pajamas twisted around my legs as water swelled the fabric. I tried to kick them straight. Long tendrils of bay grass tickled my ankles.

I recoiled, pulling into a knot. If I could have jumped straight out of the water like a fish, I would have.

What had happened? We'd been telling stories, the water had come in over the floor and—

Had we fallen asleep? Both of us? We were no longer in my room. Or the house. I couldn't even see the house.

I kicked and splashed. My pajamas clung too cold and wet for this to be a dream.

House magic was just a story, I knew. Unless I was wrong about that too? What if we'd been magicked right out of my bedroom?

Where was Mike?

I stopped kicking and sank below the surface of the river. Fought my way back up, my arms aching with the effort. The taste of brackish river water real as anything in my mouth. Sour and salt.

I'd told house magic stories for Mike's sake, to explain why so many things disappeared when we broke rules. But I'd broken so many rules lately. I'd brought trouble. What if this was a real consequence? There were always consequences.

"Mike!" I yelled. No answer.

Had we really been magicked?

I deserved this, whatever it was. The river pushed me along, spun me around, and I didn't fight it.

As I floated, I saw lights from a distant bridge far downstream, strung low across the water. The large lighthouse on the other shore loomed closer, its sides pale in the moonlight, the great glass enclosure for its lantern glittering with reflected stars. There was no bridge or lighthouse like this near our house.

My heart pounded fast, but I wouldn't cry. Not now.

The beam arced above me, passing across me almost painfully, a bright path in the river's darkness. Then it was gone.

Pockets of air began to fill my pajama top and pants as I fought to stay afloat. The water might try to drag me to the bottom, but I realized I could use my clothes to float me to shore, house magic or not.

Except I couldn't see much of the shore.

An eddy in the river tried to yank me under again.

Stay calm, Eleanor. I started to swim across the current, against the rush of water. Mike had fallen in first and I'd followed her. Where was she? Which way took me to her?

Moonlight over the dark pulse of the river revealed little that could help—patches of lily pads, a piece of tree branch, floating. I grabbed that branch and held on. The solid wood against my arms and chest calmed me as it bore me up. I kicked again, searching the river for my sister.

What if Mike drowned? What if I drowned?

If this was a dream, we'd wake up screaming for sure. And that would call Poppa's attention to our hiding spot under the bed.

But if we weren't dreaming? If this was a real river, and we'd been magicked away? How could we escape it and find our way home?

I held on to the branch and let the current spin me while I tried to think. Tried to calm my heartbeats. My fears.

I didn't want to be magicked. I didn't want to disappear.

A whimper and a splash broke the river's rush. Another splash, closer. I rolled to my stomach and swam toward the noise, using the branch as a float.

The lighthouse beam returned. It swept across the river, highlighted my pale arms, and revealed Mike struggling in the river's rush, wavelets building against her shoulders and breaking over her face.

She coughed and sputtered. Yanked at something below the water between strokes. Tried to keep her head up.

She was caught on something.

"I'm coming!" I called. She couldn't hear me above the river.

A bird flew overhead, its long shadow and broad wings blocking the moonlight.

Calm down, calm down. Each stroke, each kick, I made myself think only of how to get out of here. How to survive. When I thought past that, the fear of having been disappeared threatened to push me under.

Calm down.

When I reached Mike's side, my head cleared. Taking care of my sister was something I knew how to do.

"I've got you," I said, as calmly as I could. I helped her grab the branch. Watched as she caught her breath.

I treaded water, working to stay beside her. Carefully, I felt below the surface for whatever had caught my sister's feet.

Last summer, Pendra's mother insisted on junior lifesaving at the local pool since they lived near the water now. Momma had agreed I could go too, as long as Mike took lessons also. We'd all piled into the Sartis' car and sometimes into Momma's. Practiced drills until we knew how to help without thinking.

"You're okay. Tell me what's happening."

"Foot's stuck," Mike said. She shivered and struggled more. Nearly slipped off the branch.

"Stop kicking." I tried to keep my voice level. She was making it worse, whatever it was. "Can you float?"

I treaded the dark water, keeping my own feet away from the tickling grass, while Mike leaned back against my arm. Her eyes reflected the stars, then focused on me. Trusting, hoping I knew things she didn't.

How could I? I didn't even know where we were.

"You're okay. It's going to be okay."

"I can't float. There's grass wrapped around my ankle." Panic in her voice.

"Shhh. It will loosen if you relax." I hoped that was true. Small solutions could build into bigger ones. I used the same tone I'd used to get Mike back to sleep after a bad night. But I was tiring too.

Kicking against the current to stay even with Mike was hard. *Don't think about the other hard things—the strange river, the strange sky.*

Mike calmed. Eventually, the grass around her ankle loosened. I threaded my fingers through the tangled grass and began to pull it away.

"Bicycle your legs higher instead," I said as Mike began to swim in earnest.

As another tendril grazed the bare skin between my sock and my pajama bottom, I did the same. We were both tiring now. Rescuing someone was hard work, magicked or no.

I turned to let Mike lean on my shoulder so we could both hold on to the branch and rest. The wood was growing waterlogged, sinking low in the water and starting to come to pieces. How long could we float on our own?

As long as we had to.

A pale ribbon of sandbar loomed ahead. "Do you think you can make it?" I asked Mike.

"Okay," Mike said. She said okay when she wasn't sure but was willing to try. She rolled to her stomach and kicked, pushing the branch in front of her.

I was close enough that I got a face full of water from the splash. Choking and coughing, I struggled forward, one arm, then the next. Kicking. Finally, Mike did what I did. Slowly we swam diagonally across the current.

When my knees ground against the rocky shore, my pajama leg tore. I hissed as skin scraped off my exposed knee, my bare foot. The sand was sharp.

Too tired to walk, I crawled up the beach, pulling Mike with me.

"So cold!" Mike complained through chattering teeth.

I lay on the wet, pebbled shore, grateful we were no longer moving downstream.

Mike shivered next to me. "Where are we, El? Where's your bed?"

"We're somewhere on the bay." I tried to sound certain. The grasses, the smell of the water, the gritty shore. All of it felt so familiar but still not the same. The sky was a deep purple, the stars unfamiliar from the sky at home.

Home.

I'd wished myself away, hadn't I. Was that how we'd come here? I'd made a spell of it. Swept Mike up in it. Maybe the house had heard me and sent us both for good measure. Or one of the stories I'd told. Maybe the house had heard that. The lighthouse. I'd told a story about a lighthouse. But then there would be an ocean. And an ill lighthouse keeper. I shivered.

The river licked at the shoreline. From the reeds and cattails edging the sand, something croaked.

"How do we get back?" Mike's words rolled like a river. She didn't think we were dreaming any more than I did. Dreaming meant you could wake up.

The moon slid behind a silver-dark cloud. The stars dimmed as a fog rose from the water.

As my sister and I recovered on the beach, everything around us turned to shadow and shade.

+++

A repeated beat—which, to me, sounded like garbage bags being dropped into cans half filled with rainwater—sloshed closer: one, two. One, two. Mike grabbed my arm and almost climbed into my lap.

Another beat caught up and passed it. Hooves moving over sand and through water.

A bird screeched in the darkness.

When the cloud shredded and the moon shone through, the lighthouse sparkled on the distant shore across a wide span of river. Out in the deeper water, the current moved very fast. Moonlight highlighted a log careening downstream and, closer, two figures moving through the shallows, near where we'd landed.

One, an enormous, smoke-colored horse, galloped through the water. Steam curled up with each splash. Its breath shook the river reeds on the sandbar.

"Careful," said the shadowed figure keeping pace with the horse. "We can't be seen up here. The birds are too strong, too many." Her voice was like a long velvet gown. Wet, muddy velvet. The kind that hissed softly when you fidgeted. She wore plastic bags knitted into a dress and her thin hair was held back with twist-ties, pulling her scalp tight and making the scales above her eyelids and snout glitter with tension. She stood as tall as the smoke horse. Her tongue darted, tasting the air.

"Troll," Mike whispered.

"I don't think so." Trolls in books didn't look much different from big, angry people. This one looked like pieces of things, all stuck together. And coming our way.

We shrank into the reeds, trying to hide, trying to be quiet. Still not anywhere close to safe.

The smoke horse and the snake-headed monster turned in our direction. Walked up the beach to where we'd rested. Where my sock had stuck to the sand.

"What is this?" She bent to lift my sock—dingy in the shadow of her hand—between two greenish fingers. She looked around, squinting in the dark, tongue flashing in and out.

We crouched lower in the reeds.

The horse snorted and pawed at the sand.

"We'll take the upriver tunnels faster this time. The crabs must be working overtime to fix them, if they're cracking as badly as your 'mares say. If we can beat them to it this time, maybe we won't need the bridge. One way or another, I'm telling you, we'll find a way out." She stopped and licked the air. "But there's something else here. Something new. I can almost taste it."

She kept searching as more birds flew overhead. I pressed my sister and myself as low to the ground as I could.

Soon a flock of birds had assembled, with more rising from the reeds around us. The snake's head shot up. She muttered under her breath, "Can't be caught here."

She stepped away from the sandbar and mounted the smoke horse. She held my sock to her nose and inhaled. Looked at the sandbar again.

"Grossss," Mike whispered so quietly it sounded like the wind.

"Shhhh," I breathed back. "Maybe she can't see in the dark, but she can hear."

The snake's scales shimmered as what passed for her ears pricked and her head turned. She nudged the big horse forward. Mike and I tried to make ourselves as small as possible in the reeds. The horse left the water once more and its hooves crunched the shoreline.

"I can hear better than you think," she said. "Your thoughts. Your innermost fears. Your guilt. Your anger. All of it ripples out from you and gives you away, whoever you are."

I tried to make my mind as blank as possible. But now I was so afraid. My thoughts were the worst part of me.

The lighthouse's beam began its slow swing across the beach. In a few moments it would cross our hiding place. The snake's eyes would see us clear as day. The smell of smoke and ash worked its way into the reeds as the horse's snorts came close. My eyes watered.

One of the reeds near us moved. It walked toward us on the sandbar, and I saw the sharp beak and long neck of a heron, and also the gleam of metal, the glimmer of glass. Garden shears for a beak. Beach glass feathers draping driftwood wings.

It was the strangest heron I'd ever seen. I couldn't stifle a small gasp.

The snake-woman laughed and turned toward us. "There you are, little one." But then she gasped too. "And *you*."

The lighthouse beam caught her in its glow and she squinted as if it hurt. The horse beside her screamed and bolted for the shadows.

The heron screeched alarmingly, metal on metal, and several dark shapes whirled up from the reeds to join the birds already aloft. A flurry of wings gathered as the heron spread its own and flew to meet them. Then they all turned and dove as one.

Sharp beaks pierced the horse's flanks and more wings circled in a swirl around its head.

The enormous horse collapsed into an eddy of black smoke. The snake-monster fell to the ground, then rolled to her knees and began to run through the shallows. "Terrible birds!" she yelled. "Terrible light!" Her bag dress crackled as she fled, still carrying my sock.

The heron rose and circled high, moonlight and lighthouse beam making its glass wings sparkle blue and purple. The rest of the birds—I could see bitterns and osprey, a few dark ravens—swept over the reeds in a cloud of wings and chased the monster down the river.

But the heron returned to the beach.

"You can come out now," it said in a clipped voice. "You who fell through the leak in the river."

+++

We held a long silence. The heron waited, unmoving.

Mike clutched my arm hard enough to leave a mark. Finally, the weight of quiet became too much for her.

"Who are you?" Mike tried to move backward, but there were too many reeds. More seemed to have sprung up during the battle.

"You're on *my* beach. I grew up right there," the bird said, pointing at a reed. "I'm the Heron and you fell into my river."

I stood, bristling like I, too, had a beak made of shears. "We fell through a leak? Your river got under my bed." I put a protective arm around Mike's shoulders.

"Well, obviously," the Heron clacked. "We've been fighting more leaks in the past day than ever before. It's been bad since we lost the tunnels below the bridge to Anassa—the snake-headed monster you saw. The pressure builds across all the other tunnels and the crabs can't keep up. Still, the big leaks in your area were held back by a boundary guardian's agreement. What happened?"

The wood-and-glass bird turned a red eye toward me and waited as if what it had just said made complete sense. It waited more as I groped for words in the dark by the strange river. I didn't understand at all.

I tried to be as polite as I could to a flotsam-and-jetsam bird. "I don't know of any agreement."

"Of course you do. You wouldn't be here if it hadn't broken."

The bird shifted so that both its glass eyes reflected Mike and me and trapped us in its gaze. "The Favres protect this portion of the river. The agreement's held since your great-great-grandmother nearly drowned and got lost here." The Heron closed its garden-shear beak as if this was the most obvious thing in the world.

I shivered in the night breeze. "Favre is our grandmother's name. But we're Prines. And we haven't agreed to anything." *Besides,* I thought, *lots of things got broken all the time.*

The reeds behind the Heron knocked together in the breeze. Crushed seagrass's tart smell and salt air combined. My stomach growled. I hadn't eaten much of the grilled cheese earlier.

This wasn't a dream. Whose stomach growls in a dream?

Another dark horse galloped by, the riverbed knocking hard at its hooves, the splash carrying up the sandbar and shaking the reeds. It kept well away from the lighthouse beam.

The Heron opened its beak and hissed.

"Why are those horses so scary?" Mike whispered.

"The 'mares?" the Heron asked. "They have to be."

The horse's midnight-colored ears pricked, and it started to slow. My fingers tightened on Mike's shoulder, ready to pull her back down onto the sand. A flock of ravens erupted from the reeds and chased the horse off the beach and out of sight.

"An unkindness," I whispered.

"A what?" the Heron said.

"A flock of ravens. It's called an unkindness. I read it." I was glad to know one fact, any fact, in this strange place.

The Heron lifted a driftwood leg and scratched its belly, unimpressed. "Ravens *can* be somewhat stern."

"But where did they come from?" Mike asked.

"The ravens," the Heron said, "grow in the reeds. As dreams always do. When they're young and small, they fly up, into your bedrooms and back. The wrens, gulls, and other birds too. When they're old enough, they fight for the river."

I just stared at the Heron. "Dreams do a lot of things, but they *don't* fight."

"Not when they're young, no. But once they have more experience? Sure they do." The Heron brushed a reed with a wingtip. The reed made a *tac* sound against the worn sea glass feathers. "But we're running out of places to grow them, especially along this river."

All of the Heron's words were familiar ones, but their meaning was still as strange as the sandy bank we were stranded on.

Dreams lingered. They wrapped you tight and left you stranded. They didn't grow. They didn't fight.

But even as I watched, an eggshell egret stretched from the reeds. It crackled as it shook its tiny wings dry. The Heron touched the tip of his beak to its crest, and the small wisp of bird climbed into the air, a white star in the dark night.

Just before growing too small to see, it shone bright for a moment, then disappeared.

"Just like that," the Heron said, satisfied. "One very good dream on its way to someone."

My mouth hung open as, speechless, I searched the sky for more dreams.

But Mike twisted, pulling away from my arm. She marched down to the edge of the sandbar and peered out across the river. "Where did the other birds go?"

"They're chasing the 'mares back below the bridge. Every day a few more try to come up this way." The Heron's stillness and its even tone made its words seem all the more concerning. "The 'mares didn't use to cause as many problems. But my birds have so much trouble with Anassa that the 'mares are taking advantage too."

A snake-headed monster. Horses made of smoke. I tried to find my words. "There are only mares?" The horses that grazed the farm next door to our house had been mares and colts, sometimes a stallion.

The Heron picked at its wings, smoothing a crooked bit of glass back down. "Not mares. 'mares. Nightmares."

I took a deep breath of river air. Mike stared at the Heron. *"Nightmares."*

The Heron nodded. "They don't start off that way, of course. They have to accumulate. They're made of failed dreams, smoke, and the river mist at the base of the falls beyond the bridge. Used to be, the same magic that kept dreams and reality apart also held back the nightmares. But they've been moving a lot faster upriver lately. And now? Anassa's helping them. She's an invasive monster. We don't have many ways to defend against her. And she's doing everything she can to get to the other shore."

The bird spread its wings with a clatter and nodded at the lighthouse across the river. "All of us are fighting to keep them below the bridge and away from reality. If we don't, she and the nightmares will try to gallop through in force."

"Like we fell through the other way?" My voice wavered. Nightmares loose in the world sounded scary, but something else worried me. Did the Heron think Mike and I were monsters and nightmares too?

The Heron stalked in front of us on stick legs, tilting its head this way and that. "Nothing like how you fell through. Your family comes here to help strengthen the boundary when the agreement breaks. Or when we have a problem we can't solve for ourselves, like the snake." A single bright eye fixed on me and the Heron's beak gleamed in the moonlight. "If you can help us, then we can stop the 'mares. Nightmares pouring into the world instead of seeping in when they're faded and weak would be very bad."

"Why can't *you* stop her and the 'mares and fix the leaks without us?" Mike asked. "Why are there nightmares here at all?"

"Nightmares are a natural part of the river," the Heron answered. "We have to keep them in balance. That's part of the fight. Too much of them, like too much of anything, is bad news. But Anassa changes the balance. Worse, the lighthouse beam can't defeat her, only scare her back. So, let's get to work. You'll need some dry clothes and something to eat first."

"Wait," I stalled, buying myself time to think. The Heron had said Anassa was invasive, that we were needed here.

But this wasn't our fight. We had too much to worry about at home. "We're not good at things like this. We're not fighters. We hide under beds and when we do try to fix things, we make them worse."

The bird looked down its sharp beak at me. "That's not true. You're very much fighters. All of your family is. Since before the agreement was made. And you should know that telling untruths is very dangerous on the river."

"I am telling the truth. We can't help you. We have to go home." I had a math quiz on Monday and the science fair soon. My friends to make peace with. A book to find and return. A birthday sleepover.

"How do we leave?" Mike asked the question, sounding much younger than seven. "I want to go." She looked at me. "Away from the 'mares."

I put my arm around my sister's shoulder again and stared the Heron down. "We fell through by accident. Help us get back out."

"You can't," the Heron squawked. "You'd risk making any crack wider if you tried to squeeze through. That would let more nightmares and leaks into the world behind you. The 'mares search for any such weakness now that Anassa has them convinced crossing over before they get too old means they'll never fade. So you would do great damage trying."

"Cracks." I pictured all the broken things in our house.

The Heron bobbed its head slowly. "Mostly the cracks are in the underground caverns and tunnels where I can't go." The bird scratched its belly again. "The small ones are part of the filtration system and the natural river balance. The crabs do most of the maintenance on those when they're not helping the old 'mares fade through. But that's dangerous work. You'll want to work here, close to the flock." The Heron turned in the direction I'd seen the snake, Anassa, go—toward the bridge. It bent its neck into an S and looked at the sand. "Anassa collects anything she can get from your side. She'll want to collect you. Anyone who minds a river boundary can help her as easily as they can help us, but especially someone with a broken agreement. She's so obsessed with getting back across to your side, she'll be eager to have you. We've kept you from falling into her grasp for now."

Mike shook in the cold breeze and I pulled my arm tight around her. "Why?"

The Heron pulled a tiny worm from the sand and ate it. When it had swallowed, which took a long time with its beak pointed up to the moon, it spoke again. "Anassa was once like you, but she's too changed—more than half nightmare herself. The river does that sometimes. She hates it. She wants to be real again. But she's not small like the baby dreams. Or mist like faded nightmares. For Anassa to pass back through, she'll need a very wide break in thc boundary. And the nightmares are all for that. Right now, the only way they can cross over is when they grow weak and faded enough to sift through the filters under the river, but they're looking for more opportunities to cross over in strength." The Heron snapped its beak shut like that was the end of the discussion.

As far as I was concerned, it was just the start of one. *She was once like you*, the Heron had said. "Was Anassa magicked here too?"

"She helped a friend mind a boundary, once. The nightmares pulled her over and she got stuck here. Some people do. Anyone who stays here past sunrise risks getting stuck."

The way the Heron said it gave me chills.

"I'm glad you chased them away," Mike whispered. Her clothes were nearly dry, but she still shivered in the breeze.

"It's my job to chase away what doesn't belong and to tend what does. To keep the place where dreams grow safe." The Heron bent for another worm. "It's your job too. Your family are Favres. That's the agreement." The Heron stepped back from the shore, but Mike and I didn't follow.

The sand prickled cold beneath my bare feet. The wind tugged at my hair. The reeds knocked together at the top of the sandbar, making dreams, maybe. The moon and stars above illuminated the deep purple river, outlining the edges of the landscape in silver. If it weren't so scary, I could love this place. But I didn't want to stay here. I wanted to sleep in my own bed. To see Momma. I wanted to work on my science project. I wanted to get Mike out of here more than anything. Before we got stuck, like the snake-woman.

"We don't have an agreement," I repeated. This was all a mistake. "We've been swept away here. Disappeared."

"Almost like house magic," Mike whispered.

I winced. If house magic really did disappear things like I'd told my sister, we were in a lot more trouble than I could handle.

The bird nodded. "You do have an agreement. Round, pretty thing. Shiny." We stared at the Heron some more while the last of the birds that had chased the monster downriver returned to roost in the reeds and the cattails. We watched them fold up into dreams and shadows and disappear. "First agreement with your family was the lighthouse, there." The sharp beak pointed across the river. "It helps us spot nightmares and holds them back. And your great-great-grandmother added some of the glass balls she had with her to trap whatever slipped through. Favres have protected your side of the river for generations. Sometimes one of you forgets, but the rest of you always kept the agreement safe. If it's broken, then cracks begin to get worse in the tunnels that feed the river. Those will grow, unless you make a new agreement, or help us stop Anassa and the nightmares from crossing over. And keep them from tearing the river apart."

Running water blended with the Heron's words, tumbling them nonsensical. What did the bird mean? An agreement? Nightmares? A lighthouse? My great-great-grandmother? I wanted my own bed, my friends. Something familiar.

What would Pendra do if she got caught in a river beneath her bed? I tried to think. *Pendra*. She was never, ever going to believe me, was she? If I ever saw her again. "If this agreement got broken—and I'm not saying it did—were we magicked here?" I finally asked. "Is that why the leak happened?"

Mike let out a gasp. "Magicked. Lost. Unless . . . will we be like your story, Eleanor? Or the television? Replaced with something better?"

I squeezed her shoulder. "Nothing is replacing us. We're leaving before the sun rises."

"Let me explain," said the Heron. "May I tell you a different story? You might have heard this one. I hope you have."

Mike nodded, and then I did too. "Go ahead."

We sat and the bird squatted on the cold beach at eye level with us. The wooden parts creaked and the glass parts squeaked and the shears trembled a little as the bird drew itself in. Once it was settled, things quieted down and the Heron began to speak. "Once upon a time," it whispered.

I braced for Mike to interrupt, but she didn't.

"Once, there was a fisherman and his wife and their children. One day, the fisherman didn't return from the river. His boat and three of his fishing floats washed up on shore.

"The fisherman's wife waited as long as she could, but then she eventually had to take the family's glass fishing floats and the nets and go out in the boat to catch food for the family. She left bread and broth for a couple of days. A storm caught her. She didn't come back, either. She could have drowned, but instead, she came through to this river. This happened more before we had people guarding the boundaries."

Mike pressed closer to me. I crossed my arms around her. Shut my eyes, angry that this bird was frightening my sister, and me too. "Why are you telling us this?"

The Heron ignored my question.

"As the bread ran out and the children realized what had happened, they began to cry, even in their dreams. Their cries shook the wind. Birds of all sizes heard the children. Ravens. Herons. The river heard them too. Their cries shook the cracks deep between the worlds, and the nightmares began to run, looking for a way out and finding many. No one got any rest.

"The birds came to see what was the matter along the shore; first one bird, then three more, until there were birds resting on the riverside cottage's roof and the windowsills.

"The oldest daughter brought out what was left of the bread and shared a few crumbs with the birds. She didn't have to do it, but she did anyway."

The Heron looked down its beak at us. At me.

"Then the oldest daughter quick as lightning grabbed one of the birds and killed it with her bare hands so that she and her sisters would have something to eat. They were very hungry."

"That's a terrible story!" I was on my feet before I knew it, pulling Mike up too. Mike's eyes filled with tears. She gripped my hand hard. "You're supposed to be happy with her generosity and give her three wishes. That's what you're *supposed* to do."

Snick—the Heron's beak opened and closed. Opened again. "That's a fairy tale. This is a real story. In a real story, you see anything that will keep you alive, you grab it," the Heron said. "But the bird that the girl grabbed was a guardian of the boundary between the river and your world. Like me. Many birds are, whether they know it or not."

The Heron paused until Mike sat back down.

"Did the birds get mad?" Mike asked.

"There are different kinds of mad," the Heron said, not unkindly. "There's the kind that breaks and hurts. The kind that salvages and defends. Birds salvage. We defend."

I eased myself back down to the sand beside Mike.

"Sometimes birds don't remember being dreams, before they flew. Things work differently here. There's much forgetting, if you spend too long on one side or the other. But this was a bird of some importance. A heron of the river. We may seem calm and still, but we do not forget and we are not good to kill."

Mike shivered and pulled my arm around her shoulders. I crouched next to her, glaring at the Heron. The bird was not allowed to scare my sister like this.

"When they knew they could, the nightmares began to test the boundary again, flooding the waking world with terror through the leaks. The river the girls lived next to started to rise. And the big smoke horses began to come through, looking like enormous storms, turning the world darker, and bringing great fears and worries with them.

"The children were very scared. They apologized for harming the heron. They begged for the rest of the birds to bring their mother home, to keep the horses at bay. Some of the birds took pity on them, for they'd enjoyed the crumbs."

"And you found her? The mother?" Mike's voice filled with hope.

The Heron nodded solemnly. "She'd nearly drowned. Like I said, it was easy to fall through then. But she'd held on to the nets containing six fishing floats and washed up on our shore. The birds helped the oldest daughter through to find her. And the daughter worked here until she'd made the river stronger, building the lighthouse that helps us see and slow the nightmares before they travel upriver. But she missed her sisters. So then the daughter spoke with the birds. She made an agreement in exchange for their mother. The birds returned the floats that had saved their mother's life as symbols of the agreement. They'd survived both the real river and the dream river; they were strong enough to help maintain the boundary.

"But sometimes adults forget. When they got home, the mother didn't remember anything but that the floats attracted fish and provided a lot of food. The daughter knew they were more. That they captured wandering nightmares. She passed that knowledge to the next generation, and her children's children did so too. They helped keep the river from crossing into the real for many generations. Until now."

In my mind, I could see the witch ball hanging on the landing. I heard again the sound it had made when it broke.

When Poppa broke it as a lesson to us.

"What did the children give up in exchange for their mother?" I asked. There was always a trade. I hoped it wasn't one of the children. The Heron had said the monster had once been like us.

"She promised the family would help guard part of the boundary between dream and real forever. More people help in other places, in their own ways. Some stay here, some stay on the other side. Favres guard this boundary and the agreement—the fishing floats. They're the promise. These fishing floats have been on both sides of the river; they're magic that way, maintaining boundaries, catching nightmares. Or they were."

Mike looked at me, eyes wide. "Our witch ball?" she said. "I knew it was magic. I *knew*!"

"It *was*," I whispered. I pressed my fingers to the shards of glass in my pocket. It was realer than my magic, anyway. And I'd never seen any others like it. Ours must have been the last one.

I'd never thought about magic as an agreement before. It made an uncomfortable kind of sense. Even a small magic that anyone could do needed someone on each side: someone to cast the spell and someone to believe in it.

The Heron stretched one wing, then the other. The settling moon shone through its glass feathers, casting a pattern of blues and greens upon the sand. "The boundary always leaks a little. Usually only small things pass through: dreams and little nightmares from our side, lost socks from yours. But if there's nothing on one side or another to ward off the larger leaks and trap the nightmares, things get bad fast. They run wild. Cause people to fight, to fear. Weaken boundaries even more. When your fishing float—the last of them—broke, I'm not surprised you two fell through."

The Heron said this matter-of-factly, like it happened all the time. Mike and I looked at each other. It didn't feel matter-of-fact to us.

The Heron continued, "The question is, how you will help fix the river now."

CHAPTER

THE LIGHTHOUSE

FOUR

Where the sandbar met the waterline, I put my bare toes into the cold water and threw pebbles at the river.

Plunk. Yesterday, I'd woken early, settled Mike back in bed, and slept until my alarm buzzed six.

Plunk. I'd herded both of us onto the bus on time, where Mike had said too much. *Plunk*. I'd sat through math review for Monday's quiz. Pendra and I had eaten third-period lunch together, which was way too early, and we'd talked about the science fair.

I held on to that memory of normal schedules, homework—a buoy of sorts in this strange place.

Plunk. I'd turned in a five-paragraph essay on the War of 1812. Then the bus home and Pendra. *Plunk*. *Plunk*. Then I broke rules. And now here we were. Trapped like a great-great-grandmother I hadn't known except for silvering photographs in the hallway.

Except no one was coming to find Mike and me and bring us home.

Reeds rustled as the Heron stepped through the shadows, nudging more baby dreams with its beak to see if they were ready to fly. I turned to watch, one last pebble in my hand. One dream chortled as if the rusting shears tickled, shaking the reed.

The Heron plucked the dream from the reed and lifted it to the sky. The dream—a soft blue puff this time—shook out wings made of tissue paper and flew.

Mike stared, her mouth an O. She whispered, "This is beautiful."

Mike was right. The river was beautiful. But we couldn't stay here. The dreams were wondrous, but this wasn't home. "Can a dream get lost?" I asked the Heron, trying to distract Mike. "You said they find their way through to our bedrooms. What if they don't?"

"Of course they get lost," the Heron replied. "But they still find people to dream with for a little while. And when they make their way back, they have more interesting stories to tell."

The lighthouse beam swung across the beach, broad and thick. "Our great-great-grandmother built that in order to help you," I said, trying to understand.

If the birds wouldn't help Mike and me in return? I flexed my fingers. I toed the light as the beam brightened the sand. We would have to help ourselves.

"Have you made your decision?" the Heron asked. "Where will you help protect the river?"

Staying and helping meant fighting nightmares on the river and finding a way to make a new agreement. No more school. No more future.

Those things mattered to me. School was what I did well. If I missed it, or messed up . . . or if we started turning monstrous like Anassa . . .

No. We couldn't do it.

I looked down at my feet, still lighthouse-beam-bathed. My toes felt warmer than the rest of me. When I wiggled them, the light caught between them and pulled. It tickled.

The lighthouse's beam had come to a complete stop, because I was standing on top of it.

The Heron hadn't noticed. Its eyes were focused on the reeds, like it was giving us time to pick a correct answer. Meanwhile, I was more confused than ever.

The beam, caught by my foot, tugged and wavered but couldn't budge unless I lifted my toes. Confused, I dug them into the sand instead.

The rope of light drew taut. *How?* I looked behind me. Light that caught like a rope and held was as strange as reed-born dreams or talking to a flotsam heron. Or having a troll for a father.

Things work differently here. The nightmare and the snake-woman had both reacted as if the beam was more than just light.

I dragged my foot in the sand. The light pulled with it. Like a rescue line.

Quietly, I made my choice. "Mike." Maybe I could get my sister home safe. Our parents liked her better. She'd go first. "Time to go."

Mike was watching the ravens tend the baby dreams. If she went home without me, who would protect her? Who would come get her at night?

The lighthouse's glow rode atop the river like a man-made moonbeam. No. A girl-made one. One of my family members had made the tower and the light and then she'd brought her mother out of dream and home.

How had she done that, I wondered.

"Mike," I said more firmly. "Come here now."

Another baby dream distracted the Heron. This one struggled and steamed, clouds of gray all around it.

"Sometimes a dream's really a nightmare," the bird whistled. "This one has to go to the falls before it spoils the others. Won't be a minute. Will you stay?"

"Yes," I said.

And as the Heron flew away, long legs dragging the sky, I grabbed Mike's collar and pulled her onto the wet sand, then into the water with me.

"Get *off*, Eleanor! I'm watching the dreams. And you told the Heron we would stay—"

"Just do it, Mike. Take a step." Annoyance flared again. What if we ran out of time, or the Heron came back?

For once, she listened, though she went too slow. She stepped, then steadied herself. Mike stood on the beam of light that I'd trapped. She looked at her own feet the way she'd looked at the baby dream flying away.

"Run for the lighthouse. I'll hold this as long as I can." I made another decision. "I'll be right behind you."

This was my answer. We weren't going to stay and help. Either of us.

The light tugged harder beneath my toes. The lighthouse's lantern in the distance didn't spin, though I heard an echo across the water of gears grinding, as if it was trying to turn. I scrunched my toes tighter. Bent down and grabbed the edges of the beam too. The edges of the light felt soft in my fingers.

Mike wobbled and caught her balance out over the river. She began to climb the beam, all the way up to the glass windows at the top of the lighthouse.

Because I couldn't catch my sister, I caught my breath and held it.

When she reached the other side, she climbed into the lighthouse dome and I could see her, a tiny dark figure against the light, waving.

I bent down and crawled onto the beam, and it held me too. But, freed from the beach, the light began to move again, slowly sweeping across the river. I scrambled to keep up with the sideways motion while moving forward but wobbled and nearly fell. This was hard.

Helped by the beam's swing, I was halfway across the river much faster than Mike had gone. But when the light swung so far that I couldn't see my sister or the dream reeds and the Heron, I wavered, dizzy.

The bridge was visible in the distance, and the span of the river sweeping far in each direction. Then the beam swung me across the land and out over the water, and I fell and hung on, my arms clutching at the light.

The beam started to shred beneath my fingernails and I clawed at it again. "Mike, find a way out!" I wasn't going to make it.

I was going to fall onto the rocks, or into the waves below.

I could see Mike's face inside the lighthouse guardrail. She was shouting. Her cheeks were wet with tears.

Taking a deep breath, I gave one last push and scrambled up the steep beam and over the lighthouse railing. Then I let go of the light and fell against the grating. Mike piled on me. "You made it! You made it!" The birds wheeled overhead, screeching.

In the tower, a large, oval lens made of layers of yellowing glass was held together with fishbones. Inside, stacked jars of fireflies, old bulbs, and bright witch balls filled with moonlight generated light, and the lens magnified it. Fishbone clockworks dangling far below on eel-skin tethers swung the beam around. Above, in a ceiling made of whale vertebrae, a hatch hung open and a rope ladder hung from the hatch.

"Can't we take a witch ball from there?" Mike asked, pressing her nose against the lens.

I remembered what the Heron said. "They need the light to hold back the nightmares. We don't want to make things worse."

She frowned. "Okay."

Spiderwebs were everywhere. There was no sign anyone had been here in a long time. But the light still worked. Except for the small holes where my fingers had dug through the beam.

Like the ceiling, the lighthouse walls were made of fishbones, large and small, woven together. It must have taken my great-great-grandmother so long to build. She must have wanted to go home very badly.

Like us.

The birds had swirled up into a flock and were trying to fly across the river, but the wind slowed their passage.

"What's up there?" Mike pointed to the hatch.

"Maybe a way out?" Panting hard, I pulled Mike toward the opening. She balked at the ladder.

Always, my sister with the questions. I counted to ten instead of losing my temper and shouting at her to hurry. "The ladder's the only way I can see someone might have climbed out. We fell down, remember? We need to go up to get out. And someone did get out—remember the story the Heron told us?"

Mike nodded. She pulled her pajama sleeve over her hand and chewed on the cuff as she looked up. The hatch opened onto darkness. "Will you go first?"

"If you stay right behind me," I said. I didn't want to lose sight of her.

"I promise."

I grabbed the ladder, which was made of old fishing nets, and pulled myself up. Climbed carefully and slowly, my fingers crusting with salt, my dried pajama bottoms sticking to my legs. My hair got in my eyes, but I couldn't brush it away.

By the time I reached the top, I was sweating. But I pulled myself through, over the edge of the hatch on my belly, the wood scraping at my ribs. My fingers dug into damp carpet. I spun myself around and helped Mike up and through the hatch too. I pulled her out of dream, into my room.

We lay on the carpet, beside the slowly drying pool of water, beneath my bed.

+++

The river slowly disappeared as the first hint of sunrise lightened the space between the bed skirt and the floor.

We'd escaped. I'd gotten us out of there, barely. I shivered and Mike huddled against me.

"I don't like it there," Mike whispered. "Except for the baby dreams."

I put an arm around her. I didn't like it there either. "Soon, we'll wake up," I murmured. My sister's eyes drifted closed, though she fought it.

A heron feather made of blue glass lay on the carpet where the river had been. I was too tired to reach for it. I fell asleep staring at it instead.

And when I woke, the feather was still there. I put it in my pocket.

If I said it was a dream enough times, maybe it would feel like one. But I knew better now.

Mike murmured in her sleep. I peeked out below the bed skirt.

Outside my window, the sunrise outlined the form of a large bird in the tree. It slept with its beak tucked beneath its wing. A heron.

The Heron? Watching us? This one had always hunted the river and slept in the tree by my window. Now it was strange and tinged with magic.

Magic. Monsters.

Those had just been stories to tell Mike. Except now? Now magic was real, and dangerous.

At least we were home.

My stomach felt achy and heavy, like I'd eaten too much popcorn. I watched the day come to life. Listened to the birds chirp in the trees and wondered which belonged to the river and which to the real.

I knew one new thing. Our house had another rule: The space beneath the bed wasn't safe for Mike and me to hide under anymore.

CHAPTER

BROKEN THINGS

FIVE

Especially on weekends, in the very early morning, house magic was slow.

Before today, I'd loved being awake, alone in the moments when things hadn't yet disappeared.

I moved through the darkened house like a shadow over water. My sock feet—dry ones—slid across the carpet. I wiggled my toes against the thick, warm cotton and looked over the damage.

The hallway looked fine at first, long and clean. I already knew the witch ball wouldn't be at the other end. I didn't look at where it wasn't hanging.

But then I realized that the hallway was bare. No photographs hung on the walls, only slight shadows where they'd been. Except the one of Momma and Gran. That was still there, next to a dent in the wall. A bit of broken frame on the floor. Where were the rest? Those photos were Momma's. They'd always lasted.

I went downstairs, my throat tight with loss. In the kitchen, the computer screen lay propped against a wall, cords dragging, case broken, panel shattered. All the mugs and most of the glasses were gone from the cabinet and hadn't yet been replaced.

I shook the garbage bin. It clanked: full of broken things.

Outside the window, Poppa's navy-blue truck was already gone from the driveway. Fresh tire tracks dug half circles on the perfect lawn.

Don't think about the grass. It'll be fixed soon. That's how house magic works.

Don't think about what happened last night either. Not a single minute of it.

I whistled slowly as I poured two bowls of dry cereal and tiptoed back up the stairs. My parents' door was closed. Momma sometimes slept late after a loud night, especially when Poppa was already gone. At the landing, where I would usually stop to touch the witch ball, I paused. The bare hallway, bright with sunrise, hurt my eyes. Glass sparkled on the carpet and I put the cereal down to try to pick shards loose before Mike had to walk here. Mostly picture glass, but a piece of the float—what was left of the family agreement—had made its way up here. I wrapped that up and put it next to the rest.

What were Mike and I going to do? Where would we go now when things got loud?

Mike's bed was too low for me. The rest of the house, too visible.

The hallway seemed longer without all the photos silvering in their frames. I peered at the one remaining picture. Momma and Gran.

"Did you know about the agreement? About the river?" I whispered. "Why didn't you tell us?"

The photograph didn't answer. I hadn't really expected it would.

Back in my room, Mike was still under the bed. "Come on out of there," I whispered. Who knew when the river would come back?

She crawled out and climbed up on top of my bed. A damp spot darkened the navy comforter while her hair dripped. I handed her a cereal bowl.

She pushed the bowl back at me. "I like it with milk now. Is he gone?"

I fought back a wave of frustration as the edge of the bowl pressed my foot. Mike could get her own milk if she wanted it. I wasn't ready to walk down that bare hallway again.

"What's wrong?" Mike asked, pulling the bowl back when she saw my expression.

"House magic for the lawn again." I felt bad about being cross with her. "We can go get milk if you want."

Mike's fingers reached into the bowl, then brought a fistful of Cheerios up to her mouth. Crunching noises were her answer. "Do you think house magic will bring the witch ball back?"

Oh! Slow relief hit me. If house magic was real, then of course the witch ball would be fixed. And then we wouldn't have to go back to the river. Our safe place would be all right again. At least I hoped it would be. I smiled at my sister, hoping to comfort her. But I couldn't stop thinking about the witch ball. "Maybe? There aren't any more like that one—the stores sell fakes, and the real ones are in Japan and China. So it would really have to be magic if it came back." And if it didn't come back, we would have to find one ourselves.

But if it did reappear, then we wouldn't have to worry about the Heron, or getting trapped on the river, or Anassa anymore. Just the regular stuff. I felt lighter at the idea.

"House magic will fix it. I know it," Mike said. She put so many Cheerios in her mouth that she looked like a fish. "Eleanor, we could stay under the bed while we wait for it to be fixed. You could finish the lighthouse story."

I didn't want to tell her that I was still worried. That the witch ball might not get fixed. That we couldn't go under the bed until it was. The river would come back for us, I was sure of it.

"I forget where I was in that story." My lighthouse in the story had been so different from the one on the river. "Besides, I can't tell any more stories today. I need Momma to take me to the bookstore. And then maybe we can go somewhere else, until things are fixed around here."

I'd been saving money to replace a pair of broken binoculars, but with the cost of a book, replacing the binoculars would have to wait.

"The bookstore?" Mike still chewed. It sounded like *ookstore*. "What book?" she crunched a single Cheerio.

"The one with the dragon. The one we were reading. It got magicked." I hated admitting this out loud. Even to Mike.

Crunch. Swallow. "It's not magicked! It's in my backpack. In my room." Mike grinned. Her teeth were gritty with cereal.

My face grew so warm it must have been bright red. Relief, mixed with building frustration. "You didn't ask! Pendra was so angry I lost it!" I forgot to count to ten. "You're so unbelievable sometimes, Mike. You don't even like *The Hobbit*." Mike flipped her letters and couldn't read long things on her own yet. We read together for fun. "Why'd you take the book?" I heard my voice rise.

One-two-three-four-five. Momma kept telling me it was possible to keep my cool by counting to ten, but sometimes even she couldn't get that far. I knew I had to keep trying, that I couldn't yell at Mike, especially about books, but I was so mad. And when I got mad, I'd be as bad as—

"I just wanted to show Kalliope." Mike reached out to touch my hand. "I'm sorry. I wanted to tell her how you were reading it with me."

Six-seven-eight. I started to cool down, setting aside Pendra's anger with me. Thinking about my sister wanting to read with me.

But Mike's eyelids were red and puffy already. The edges filled with tears even as I watched. *Nine-ten. Oh no.* My face must have been pretty scary, my voice too loud. My temper had gotten away from me.

"Mike, shhhh. Don't cry. I'm sorry I shouted. Hey. I'm glad I know where the book is now. And we can try a story." Anything, if it would help her forget how mad I'd gotten. "I'll think up a new story. Something without monsters."

But if the carpet grew even slightly damp, we'd get out of the bedroom, maybe even out of the house, fast.

"Okay." Mike snuffled. "But I want more ponies."

"No ponies in this story." I thought of the nightmares and fought back a chill.

"Why not?"

If she didn't remember, I wasn't going to tell her. "Too predictable. Every little kid wants a pony. And they never get one."

Mike nodded but pulled the edge of the navy comforter closer around her, pulling it off of me. She smelled like the bay. "You have seaweed in your hair," she said.

I reached up and pulled a long piece of seagrass from my braids. Crushed it in my hand until the place smelled like salt and fish. "Now I don't anymore. Ready?"

I thought of anything but the lighthouse. Kept myself from imagining it cracking and falling apart. I wondered if anyone in our family had ever heard stories about it. Had Momma, long ago? Is that where I got the ideas for my stories? Did Poppa know?

Mike bobbed her head. "Ready."

But a knock on my bedroom door made us both jump. I sucked my breath in fast so I wouldn't cry out.

"Girls?"

Momma couldn't see us like this.

Another knock. "Girls. How about we get in the car? Let's take a drive." Her voice was bright, but it had a sad undertone I'd heard before.

I slid off the bed and stood by the door. Cracked it open and peered out. "Where to?" Maybe the library. Maybe we could live at the library until the house went back to normal.

Momma's eyes were puffy, with a dark purple pillow beneath one. But she was dressed and she had car keys in her hand. "Just a drive. Maybe to a museum? We can go visit your grandmother? Would you like that?" She was reaching for ideas. Momma didn't have a lot of friends or family. Just Gran and us.

We'd never done anything like this before.

"You don't talk to Gran. Why are we going now?"

"Gran travels a lot, painting, doing work with museums. She's in DC for a while doing an extended residency."

I remembered a kind smile and loved when she sent us things, but most of what I knew of her was from photographs. "Okay."

Momma sighed. "We had a silly fight. I'd like to talk to her if she'd talk to me. You'll understand someday."

"Was it about the witch ball?" I said it all in a rush, and then bit my lip to keep from saying too much more. Still, hope bubbled up. Maybe this was it.

Momma looked confused, then mad. "The fishing float? I don't know why you'd think that. It was just a decoration, and we will not talk about that today."

I could usually tell when Momma was fibbing, and this wasn't one of those times. She stared at me, her forehead furrowed, her arms folded. *Sometimes one of you forgets.* She didn't remember.

Momma forgot a lot of things, but they were usually things Poppa did. Not house things.

Maybe Gran would know about the agreement if Momma didn't.

"Stop dawdling. If we're going, we need to go now. Gran's taken a townhouse near DC during her research fellowship at some gallery. The National, I think. We can bring her a housewarming present. That will be fun." She tugged at the door. "Is Mike in there too?"

"Yes, Momma." Mike sat on my bed, getting crumbs everywhere, like normal, but I still didn't let the door swing wide. River grass stuck to Mike's foot.

"Get ready. You can dress up if you want. Let her know we're not heathens? Yes, definitely dress up. And maybe bring your toothbrushes? Some pajamas."

I could tell when she was nervous, but Momma always had a plan. Now she sounded like she was making things up out of thin air and worry. Unease churned my stomach. This was new.

"Can't Momma magic it so we can stay here?" Mike whispered so quietly only I heard.

I opened my mouth to ask why when Momma said, "Let's hurry!" as brightly as I'd ever heard her say anything.

"Okay, we can get ready fast," I said, to ease her. But everything felt wrong. Something had definitely changed. As if a big 'mare had gotten through and darkened things, like the Heron had said.

We had to figure out a way to fix it, without getting trapped on the river.

Gran. Maybe she'd know about the agreement. Maybe she had another one of the original witch balls to replace ours, in case house magic didn't fix it. Maybe we wouldn't be stuck helping the Heron after all. I nudged Mike. "We have to help her this time."

"We'll get ready," Mike agreed.

A quiet sigh. Momma's shoulders relaxed. "Good. Twenty minutes. Be ready to go, all right?" Then she let go of the door. A moment later, I heard her bedroom door open and shut.

Mike put another Cheerio in her mouth. *Crunch.*

"Come on. You can eat in the car. Go get dressed." I reached out for the bowl.

She didn't move. "What will Gran be like?" she said. "Will she like us?"

Maybe. She might. But maybe not if she and Momma fought. "I don't know. Let's find out?"

Crunch.

"Mike. Let's go!" I twisted my sister's fingers. The kind of casual thing Poppa did to get our attention sometimes.

"Ow!"

We could have started fighting then, but Momma called "Girls!" with a tone that made us both snap to attention. We hurried. In the bathroom, we towel-dried our hair. Got the worst of the river off, stuffed our toothbrushes into my backpack, and went to get dressed.

+++

Mike wore her usual green sneakers and a pair of socks decorated with monkeys, but she'd heard Momma's suggestion. The dress she'd chosen to visit Gran in was the velvet kind that demanded she sit perfectly still or it would crease.

Sitting still wasn't one of Mike's specialties.

Even before we left the development, she was squirming. So much that Momma didn't want to stop the car so I could drop off Pendra's book. "Later, please, Eleanor. It has to wait."

Fine. I fumed a little. They could take my books, tell me to go here and there. No one cared what Pendra thought of me.

Or Mike. As long as we made a good impression on Gran. On everyone, really.

During the long car ride, Mike scratched at the starched lining and picked at the satin bow. She kicked her feet in the air.

I'd brought my math book to study, but as we hit beltway traffic, the car slowed. Momma's sighs grew louder. She wore large sunglasses even though it was cloudy out, so I couldn't see how annoyed she was. But I could tell from her sighs that things were getting worse.

I tried to think of a story to help. "Once upon a—" I began.

But Momma cleared her throat. "Gran's nice, girls. She thinks about you all the time. Look at all the presents she's sent you on your birthdays." She sounded nervous. "She'll be fun to talk to. It will be like a sleepover. I bet Gran wouldn't mind putting you two on a train to come home. I can pick you up in Baltimore after we get the house settled again. It will be fun. Just don't mention your Poppa, all right? Or anything else?"

No bringing trouble. No surprises. No talking about house rules or Poppa or the broken witch ball. Even with family. I'd made sure Mike understood. House magic didn't work if you blabbed.

"We know, Momma," Mike said. She scratched a scab on her knee until I stopped her.

"Mike, I mean it," Momma said.

"We know!" The words tumbled out before I could stop them. A little too loud.

Momma winced. "Temper, Eleanor."

But I fumed some more. She was talking about leaving us with Gran. That's why she'd said to pack, not just to dress up. "We're staying there alone?"

"You won't be alone, you'll have each other. Just for one night," Momma said. "It will give Poppa some peace and quiet, a little trouble-free time at home. Everyone needs some time to think."

I didn't. But staying overnight did mean more time to search Gran's apartment for a witch ball.

"Do you think Gran's a monster or a witch?" Mike whispered.

"Mike! Shhhhh." Horrified. Gran was Momma's mom, not Poppa's. She wouldn't be a monster. Would she? "Let's meet her before we decide."

It was impossible to be angry with Mike most days. Just like Momma couldn't stay mad at Poppa. Besides, everything was such a jumble this morning. *What if?* A small worry tugged at me. *What if Momma was just making things up as she went along? Maybe there wasn't enough magic to fix things this time.*

I felt the same way as the night before by the river. I wanted to go home—as long as everything was fixed there. I wanted things to be normal. Go to school, see my friends.

We drove through the dark harbor tunnel and all the way down the highway in silence.

Momma stopped at a gas station to fix her makeup and leave a message for Gran. Traffic zoomed by on the street as she patted concealer on the dark circle and used purple liner on the other lid so they matched. "You'll be back before supper on Sunday. I just need some time for your father to calm down. And after the land deal closes next week, it will be better, you'll see. He's just so stressed." She smoothed pale gloss on her lips.

Momma said the words as if we jumped in the car and went visiting all the time. She was casting a new kind of spell, the kind that made this not new at all. Then she fell silent and drove the last of the way to Alexandria.

"Once upon a time, there were two girls on a quest," I whispered to Mike. She was staring out the window, and her chin was wobbling.

Mike dipped her head and replied softly, "Okay." But the word curled like a question mark at the end. She didn't add anything to the story.

By the time we were in the elevator of Gran's new building, going up to the twelfth floor, quiet echoed off the mirrored walls. Momma chewed the gloss off her lip and Mike played with her sash.

"What will we wear tomorrow?" she asked. I'd only brought pajamas and toothbrushes, like Momma had said.

"We'll figure it out," I said quickly so Momma wouldn't worry. Characters on a quest didn't think much about what clothes they'd wear. We wouldn't worry either.

I had on a black skirt, the same fabric as Mike's dress, and a white button-down shirt. I'd worn it for the spelling bee the previous year, when I'd placed second. I still wished I'd won. No point in celebrating if you didn't win, according to Poppa.

The skirt didn't fit anymore, because I'd grown a lot, but Momma said we'd go shopping once Poppa finished the deal for the farm.

When we knocked, Momma stood straight and smiled the way she'd done when Mrs. Sarti visited. Gran opened the door with a surprised "Well, hello!" after an uncomfortable minute or two, and then we followed her down the narrow entry hall. I couldn't see anything except Momma's back and shoulders and Gran's long, flower-print broom skirt, swishing over a pair of beautiful black cowboy boots.

Did Gran look like her pictures? I couldn't tell. Gran was smaller than Momma, I knew, with a nimbus of white hair that didn't seem to appreciate being corralled any more than Mike's. In my memories of her, like the pictures, she was smiling, her hair piled on top of her head in an old-fashioned way. Once, I remember, she'd stuck a paintbrush through the knot and had laughed when I'd tugged at it.

"Sit there," Momma said as she followed Gran into the kitchen. We sat for what felt like hours.

Mike started sliding back and forth on the sofa, her skirt making a *zzzzt* noise on the textured fabric. I tried to cast a binding spell on her with my eyes. *Please, Mike.*

We didn't look like a proper family.

Worse, something felt wrong.

Mike dragged a dark velvet sleeve across the underside of her nose. Snot left a damp, sticky trail. I twitched at the sight of it. Best behavior didn't mean snotty sleeves.

"Stay there," I said, and slid off the sofa, against Momma's order, and found the bathroom. Floral wallpaper matched the thick, rose-colored hand towels with embroidered *Ms* and *Fs* on them. No witch balls in here. None in the living room either.

I dampened one of the towels enough that it grew heavier and darker but wouldn't drip much. Back in the parlor, I grasped my sister's hand and cleaned off Mike's sleeve as best I could, all while keeping an eye on the door that separated us from the kitchen.

"Too cold!" Mike's voice toppled the room's quiet. The velvet looked weird too.

"Shhhh." She could never follow a rule. Mike pressed her lips together, then slowly stuck out her tongue and crossed her eyes. I couldn't help it. I snorted. Our laughter cracked the tension in the room and swept over us. We leaned against each other, unable to stop until Mike pinched me hard, using her nails, through my white cotton sleeve.

Ow! I yanked away fast but bit my lip so I wouldn't say a word. I looked hard at Gran's prize glass paperweights, arranged on the table in small patterns. Glittering and filled with bubbles and color, but nothing like a witch ball. Each held something trapped, dandelions, a shell, a jeweled beetle.

Each was a hard, clear moment that looked very heavy. I stared them down.

Don't cry. Don't let anyone see you cry. It only makes people meaner.

It wasn't working. I blinked once, twice. I imagined both of my eyes were paperweights, clear and colorful and hard as rocks.

In moments, the tears stopped pricking at my eyes. "Next time, clean up your own boogers, then."

"Sorry." Mike whimpered. "I don't even know why I—" Tears streaked her cheeks.

"It's all right. Shhhh." It wasn't okay. A tiny, dark dot bloodied my sleeve. It hurt, but I didn't know what else to say. We were both tired. And things had to be all right.

If I said it, it would be.

I didn't know why Mike got in fights, or why I got so frustrated. I didn't know why people did a lot of things. Like why Momma had brought us all the way here. It still felt wrong. We could have gone to the library like usual. Looked up witch balls on the computers.

Maybe Mrs. Sarti had been right. Maybe Mike did need a mentor. I looked at my sister from the corner of my eye. Neither one of us really fit in among my grandmother's nice things—the copper tea service, the table made of intricate tiles. But Mike really stuck out.

Her hair was a tangle of red curls, the kind that broke combs and ate brushes. Two barrettes held back most of it right now.

Momma had hastily applied them in the elevator, along with a battery of sighs and pleas to be careful. Be quiet. Be good.

A snarl behind Mike's ear stuck out sideways. Luckily, we'd gotten all the bay grass out. A scatter of equally red freckles crossed Mike's cheeks and the bridge of her nose. When she smiled, which wasn't all that often, her cheeks dimpled and her brown eyes nearly disappeared. But right now they were as big as an owl's.

I licked my hand and tried to get her hair to lie down. I could almost hear Momma sigh again. What would Gran think? We'd find out, and soon.

"I can't this weekend." Gran's voice rang clear as the door between the kitchen and the living room swung. "There's no room here for them to sleep, and I have a meeting at the museum on Monday—I wish you'd given me more notice."

Mike stopped fidgeting, transfixed. She squirmed closer to me. Her heart pounded through her dress, right up against my arm. I hugged her tight. "This will be okay," I said again. It had to be.

Mike kicked her feet. "It will be okay," she echoed. She squirmed until she was in the same position she'd sat in when Momma and Gran left the room. "Someday our real parents . . ."

Behave.

I squeezed her fingers so hard that her eyes glazed with tears again, but she hushed.

I tried to scootch back from the sofa's edge, too. My fingers brushed the damp softness of the hand towel. The leading edge of a water stain spread out from beneath the plush fabric, across the sofa's damask. *Oh no.* I froze. Mike was staring hard out the picture window, toward the tiny Jefferson memorial in the distance, blinking fast. She hadn't seen my mistake. I moved a fold of my skirt to cover the hand towel and the water stain. I'd hurt Mike; I'd messed up the couch. I couldn't breathe. I couldn't do anything *but* breathe. I did everything wrong.

The door finally swung wide. "We'll see what we can do for the afternoon, at least."

"I thought you'd be happy to see them," Momma said, holding out her hand to us. The air closed up in my throat and I wished Gran's couch were carnivorous. Two girls, unwanted, disappeared without a trace.

"They're happy to see you, aren't you, girls?" Momma smiled broadly and nodded at us, like she was reeling up a line with her teeth and Mike and I were on the other end.

Gran's smile bloomed quickly when she looked down at us, but faded a little, maybe, when she looked at Momma. Several different colors of paint rimmed her fingernails. More paint speckled the front of the chambray shirt she wore and the floral skirt.

"Will you please help me?" Momma whispered. "At least with the girls, if nothing else."

"Moira." Something ached in my gran's voice. "The last time I tried, I wasn't welcome."

“He wasn’t that bad,” Momma replied. “He was nervous and you were too sensitive.”

A silence pushed between them like a bubble. Mike and I looked back and forth at them as if we were trapped inside.

Finally, finally Gran spoke. “Not for the night. Not right now. Let me get to know them first?”

Momma gathered up her belongings fast. “I’ve been trying to do that for years. I’ll be back before eight. Hopefully I can get everything sorted out by then. If they give you any trouble, phone.” Each word was sharp, like it was about to crack.

The handcloth’s damp began to seep through my skirt, chilling my leg. How I wished for house magic now.

“We’ll be fine, I’m sure,” Gran said. She didn’t look certain. But Momma was already out the door. Nothing felt right or safe. When the elevator binged, I knew we were alone.

CHAPTER

BEST BEHAVIOR

SIX

I stared at my gran and she stared back. "Are you hungry? I think I have tea . . ." Her voice trailed off.

Mike leapt from the couch like she was on a spring. "Starving." She looked back at me and wiggled her eyebrows.

"Mike!" I tried to catch her sleeve. *Best behavior.* I might have whispered it. But Mike was already out of the room. The door to the kitchen swung wildly behind her.

Gran smiled a bit sadly. "I gave up best behavior decades ago, don't worry. I'm just not used to having kids around anymore."

I didn't move from the dampened sofa.

She waited me out, still smiling, ignoring the sounds of a seven-year-old searching through her kitchen cupboards. She winced now and then when a box crashed to the floor.

After a few moments, she pulled an embroidered handkerchief from her sleeve, the edge of the fabric tucked over her paint-stained finger, just so. She began polishing the dandelion paperweight as if she did that every day.

I couldn't stand the quiet, both hers and mine. "I made a mistake," I finally blurted, my voice rough. I hated mistakes. They started an avalanche of problems I could never fix fast enough.

In profile, Gran raised her eyebrows and turned from the paperweights. I held the towel up, dangling from my hand. "I got your sofa wet. I'll pay to fix it." I had no idea how, but I would figure it out.

Gran stepped toward the couch and looked at the water stain. Would she tell us to leave? Call Momma? How bad had the argument with Momma been to keep them from talking all this time? Would she stop talking to us too?

Gran laughed instead. "I've done that before. With paint! The old sofa can take it." The damask looked like it had been through a small storm, but only its first. "Go on, see if you can find something in the kitchen to eat. Help your sister. I'll take care of this." She took the washcloth from my hand. She smelled like baby powder and roses.

I slid off the sofa and into the kitchen. The door swung behind me, nearly catching me. On the other side, Mike stood at the counter, one hand holding a cookie, the other sunk deep in the box of Cheerios.

She beamed. "She likes the same food as me."

Out the kitchen window, wind tossed the Potomac River basin into a froth. Twelve floors up was higher than the lighthouse from the night before. I felt the dizzying spin again. No getting down from here until Momma came and got us.

But nothing in the kitchen looked like a witch ball. Papers covered the kitchen table. The window had a sheer curtain, and small canvases leaned against walls and countertops: bare ones, unframed and primed, some with sketches, some with notes and colors. Gran painted in here, or at least worked out ideas. I wanted to run my fingers along the canvases, to see how they went together, wanting to know more.

+++

"Tell me what's happened with your mother? Your parents?" Gran asked when she brought more food to the table.

"Nothing," I said too quickly. "Just a little argument, I think." Sometimes a small truth helped make a story more believable. Especially if both sides wanted to believe it.

I dipped the perfectly gooey grilled cheese sandwich Gran had made into a teacup of tomato soup. Lots of butter. Cheddar cheese. Perfect.

Gran swallowed a spoonful of soup thoughtfully. "Moira's not one to ask for help, usually."

Mike opened her mouth to say something and I kicked her ankle, hard. No more breaking rules. Not until we knew we could trust Gran. My sister looked angrily up and away, at the paintings. Stuffed more cereal in her mouth.

"She's not the kind to admit error either," Gran said. There was a leading edge to her statement. As if she was asking me to peel back layers of photographs, to one where Momma was much younger. "Not even when she made a mistake."

I took another bite of sandwich. Watching Gran carefully, I took my time chewing instead of answering.

The silence grew, until Gran coughed and looked at Mike's untouched sandwich. "Do you want something different, Mike?"

Mike wiped crumbs onto her dress after dutifully trying the sandwich. She stared at me mournfully, and I knew she didn't like the cheese. She couldn't bring herself to eat it, though Momma would have made her if she'd been here. "It's okay," I whispered. I moved her sandwich onto my plate.

Gran frowned but didn't fuss. She opened a breadbox high on a shelf and pulled out a quarter of a chocolate cake. "From an opening last night. It's still good. I had some for breakfast."

Mike's eyes were as wide as our teacups. "Momma never lets us eat dessert before a meal."

"If you break it down," Gran said, "it's pretty nutritious. Most things in there are in bread too. And dark chocolate's good for you." She winked and Mike stared at her, half baffled and half in love.

This was dangerous. Mike might say anything to show off, and we still didn't know why Gran had stopped talking to Momma or whether she knew anything about the witch balls.

I waited until Gran's back was turned and then pressed my lips together and made a fierce zipper out of my fingers. Mike nodded.

Gran had swept aside enough room on the kitchen table for our mismatched cups and plates, but papers teetered around us. Bills that read "canvas shipping" and "insurance." Letters, actual handwritten ones in colorful inks, with stamps from all over the world. Often more than one. I couldn't make out more than half the words on the letters.

"Can you read all those languages?" I asked before Mike could forget to be careful.

Gran's cheeks dimpled like Mike's did when she'd misbehaved. "Mostly. Some are from places I haven't been yet. But I like learning new things."

My fingers brushed an envelope. It felt like onion skins: light as a feather and as soft. "Do you answer them all?"

Gran laughed. "I do my best. But if I answered all of them, I wouldn't have time to paint, and that's why people write me. It's a tricky balance."

"That's why you travel so much?" Mike asked, cake crumbs dribbling from her mouth.

Gran nodded and handed her a napkin. "Plus," she said, the skin crinkling at the edges of her eyes, "I love it."

I smiled at the thought. But unasked questions hung in the air. Mike finally broke. "Why don't you visit us?"

All our smiles faltered at once, then flickered back. "What she meant was it's nice to be here," I said, fast.

"I think I know what she meant. It's a hard question to answer, because there's a lot to that story. Some of it is most certainly me." Gran sat down in a chair with a sigh. "Art is"—she spread her hands wide at the canvases on the kitchen walls—"a way of thinking that sometimes doesn't allow for much else."

Momma didn't have a single one of Gran's paintings in the house. I looked at the sketches and underpaintings. The lines and arcs of some future that hadn't happened to the canvas yet. "I draw," I said. "Sometimes."

"You don't draw like this," Mike said helpfully.

I elbowed her, wishing that I shared Gran's talent. "Not as good, no. A couple maps. Sometimes glass." I'd sketched the witch ball recently. Was that maybe a way into a conversation?

Gran's smile returned and spread wide. "I used to love maps. Anywhere special? Narnia? Middle Earth? England? Tibet?"

"Oh, Middle Earth, yes. And places with rivers," I said, though I'd never drawn a river map in my life. Even though Gran hadn't said anything when I'd mentioned the glass, I kept trying.

Mike's mouth hung open. "What do you know about rivers ..." I stopped her with a look, but Gran had pushed back from the kitchen table.

She opened another door that led to a small, box-filled spare room. "In here somewhere," she murmured.

We followed her, peering around the doorframe and toward the closet as she moved things around. No glass spheres here either. This was the only room not painted a bright color, not hung with pictures.

She pawed through a box, then opened another, clucking. At one point she laughed and then put a box to the side. "All of this was from my life with your grandfather. When I lived in your house. I can't bring myself to throw it away . . . There it is."

Mike and I both leaned all the way into the room as she lifted a box too small for a witch ball from the bottom of a larger packing carton. Metal and embossed with a boat, the lid squeaked when she opened it. Taped to the lid was a yellowing piece of watercolor paper. The kind that looked like pressed cotton. Done in brown ink, with triangles for the mountains and wavy lines for a river, it was a very simple map.

No, those weren't mountains. They were dunes and sandbars. A lighthouse.

I hid my excitement as best I could. No talking about magic of any kind. Not until we were sure. "What's that?" I pointed at the round wheel in the corner, the letters *N*, *S*, *E*, and *W* hand-lettered around it crookedly. It looked like map directions but much fancier.

"A compass rose. It means safe passage through rough waters." Her voice sounded wistful. "I drew this for your mother once. She liked to fish as much as my grandmother."

She did? I hadn't known.

The map wasn't a masterpiece any more than my drawings were now. This made me happy. "Did you draw it from memory? What happened to my grandfather?" There weren't any pictures of him in our house anymore—not after the other night.

Gran's smile faltered. "I drew it from a dream, I think. After your grandfather went out in a storm. The boat sank."

Her fingers played with the box. The map. She spoke quietly, just to me. "Your mom married your father soon after, and they nearly sank another boat. I couldn't live near the river anymore. Too painful. So I gave them the house and I was free to go where I pleased. I put away the memories and didn't look back." She looked at us sadly. "I forgot. A lot of things."

"What's that?" Mike asked wide-eyed, peering into the large box again. Something glittered there. She moved as if to reach inside. I stilled her hand with a touch.

But Gran tilted the box so Mike could see better. "This?"

Mike nodded eagerly. Reached for it. This time, I didn't stop her. I wanted to push forward too. Instead, I grasped the broken pieces of glass in my skirt pocket that I'd shifted over from my pajamas.

She pulled and the sound of packing plastic gave way to a curve of glass, light green.

"Careful," Gran whispered. My stomach churned.

The top half of a fishing float emerged from the packaging. A very old one. But it had taped edges. Broken. "We used to have a net full of those, if you can believe it," Gran said. "I lost track of the last few."

"We had one," Mike said fast before I could stop her. "Do you have any more?"

I looked at her hard and she bit her lip. We both waited for Gran to say something, but she didn't. *How could we ask about house magic or the witch balls when we couldn't talk about "anything else," like we'd promised Momma?*

Gran blinked and folded the half sphere back up in plastic and pushed it inside the box. "That was a long time ago. I'll keep an eye out for another one, all right?" She held her hand out for the map. "I'd like to keep that." Her voice was stiffer. More formal. We'd done something wrong.

I wished I knew what it was.

When I handed the map over, my fingers touched Gran's for a moment. Her paint-speckled hand held my bitten-down nails as she whispered, "Eleanor, what do you *think* is going on with your mother? Is she all right?"

She still smiled. Looked quietly into my eyes. Her irises were flecked with gray and blue and green.

We have rules. When we break them, things go bad. But I couldn't say that either.

I'd answered teachers at school this way before. Mr. Divner, the science teacher, had asked just a few weeks ago about the binoculars I'd borrowed, which had gotten broken, then cleaned up but not replaced. Yet. I kept hoping.

I knew how to answer questions like this.

The fight hadn't been that bad, not really. And if it hadn't been for me, it probably wouldn't have been anything. But I didn't want Gran to know that. I wanted her to think well of us. Besides, I'd seen worse fights on television at Pendra's house. I blinked once, slowly, and smiled a half-smile. "Money, I think?" I shrugged and blinked again. "Something she bought was too expensive. And Poppa's working on buying some land."

Gran's eyes rolled a little up and to the left. "Oh, mercy. Moira was always a bit needy. Never happy with just what she had."

And that was it. Just like magic.

It had actually worked on Gran. My mouth felt dry, then drier still.

This was what Momma had said to do, and I'd done it. And I knew that Gran had done it too, when she closed the box on the broken float. But I still thought my heart would turn to sand in my throat, I'd lied so hard.

I swallowed it down.

I thought for a moment that I saw Gran swallow too, but I always imagined things.

+++

Gran fed us peanut-butter sandwiches for dinner. The sun went down over the Potomac basin while Mike and I lay on the parlor carpet on the twelfth floor. When the moon came up, Gran's paperweights glowed in the light. So did the maps we'd drawn on scraps of paper, each with lighthouses, sandbars, and birds of all sorts, scattered across the rug. Gran stared at one, then shook her head and looked away. The doorbell rang, startling us all.

Momma stood on the other side. She looked tired.

"All right," she said. "Get your things."

We found our backpacks and jackets in the kitchen. Mike slipped one of her maps behind a frame. "In case someone needs to find us," she said.

I didn't stop her.

In the hall, Gran stood on one side of the door, Momma on the other. "If you were only more careful with money, Moira," Gran said. A purse unzipped.

"I don't want that," Momma replied fast. "We're managing. Better than managing. We have excellent jobs, both of us. The property sales alone will—"

"You're working for his company now?" A pause. Gran's shoulders shifted as she put her purse away. Momma's earrings jingled. "Okay. That's a good example to set for the girls. They're precious. I'd like to spend more time—"

But Momma interrupted. "You could have spent more time with them this weekend, like I asked you to. Come on, girls." She held her hand up when Gran tried to respond. I'd heard that note in her voice before, whenever she said, *We'll be fine.* I hustled Mike ahead of me.

We hugged Gran. Everyone smiled. Momma never took her sunglasses off. The three of us rode the mirrored elevator in silence and found the car in the lot.

Momma drove for fifteen minutes before pulling into a motel by the roadside. "It's not great," she said, "but we'll make do while everything works itself out. Things will be calmer tomorrow, I promise."

I imagined the house trying to calm itself. Imagined Momma trying to fix things from far away. As if that was safer, somehow.

Sleeping on Gran's sofa would have been tough, and the guest room had been filled with boxes. I looked at the long, low sweep of motel doors, the empty pool. "This is fine, Momma."

At least the river couldn't find us here.

Our room was right next to the parking lot, and the beds smelled like Windex. The wood-paneled walls felt greasy.

"Don't touch," Momma said. "Just one night."

She handed me my backpack. Familiar toothbrushes and a tiny tube of toothpaste nestled at the bottom.

We brushed our teeth. Washed our faces with the rough brown hotel washcloth. After Momma left the bathroom, I tried to see how messy my braids were in the mirror. The glass was so high that even standing on my tiptoes, I only saw my forehead. A row of small zits crossed above my brow, barely visible. Not even red yet. I scrubbed them again with the washcloth. Then I scrubbed Mike's face again too for good measure.

Mike hadn't spoken much since we left Gran's. She stood for the scrubbing in silence.

When I finished, she finally whispered, "Do you think Gran liked us?"

I replied with a question. "Do you think she knows about the river? Just doesn't remember it?"

Again, no answers.

When we came out of the bathroom, Momma was on the phone, sitting at the table by the window. She propped her head with her hand, and the light of the screen illuminated her cheekbone and ear. Her makeup had worn thin and the bruise had darkened.

"I understand. And I'm so sorry. Yes, I know. No, no one's fault. I understand. Land purchases are always very complicated, and frustrating. We won't lose everything. You'll pull this off and it will all be better soon. I'm so sorry for causing extra stress. We'll see you tomorrow." She closed the connection and shut her eyes. Rubbed the bridge of her nose.

She didn't see us crossing the brown carpet to the double bed we were supposed to share, which had a scratchy blue-and-orange spread. I coughed. Momma jumped. "Eleanor! Don't be so—"

Mike's hand tightened on mine. "Sorry, Momma."

Her broad smile flickered, then caught. "We'll be back home tomorrow, just like magic. There's so much up in the air right now, it's easy for misunderstandings to happen."

I nodded. Mike nodded. We avoided misunderstandings. It

was a good rule. If we wanted everything to be back as it should be when we got home, we had to follow the rules.

"I hope Gran was okay?" she said. "We just needed some time to sort things out."

"Gran was great," Mike said. "She's really nice."

"It seems that way, doesn't it?" Momma said. She didn't explain. "Everything is going to be better now." She smiled like she believed it, and I wanted to believe her.

I'd made the right decision by being careful. There was so much between Momma and Gran we didn't understand yet. Between Poppa and Momma. Especially if something had changed. Momma put her head in her hands again and we tried to be loud enough to not startle her while climbing into bed. Mike whispered magic words in my ear: "Once upon a time. Someday." We were tired and giggles came fast and easy.

"What's funny?" Momma sounded annoyed.

As if someone had put the stopper back in a bottle, both of us quieted. "Nothing, Momma. Good night, Momma. Love you." We curled up in a tight ball, my arms and legs tucked around Mike under the thin blankets.

We woke to the sound of an engine growling outside, loud enough that Mike startled and screamed before I could put a hand over her mouth. "Shhhhh."

Momma still slept.

I slid off the bed and peeked out from beneath the curtain. "Just a car. They're gone."

But Mike was down on her stomach on the gross brown carpet, looking beneath the bed skirt. "Eleanor, don't be mad. I'm scared."

I winced. "I'm not mad. What's wrong?"

"There's no underbed here," she whispered.

I looked. The bed ended in a solid-seeming block of wood. "They don't want people leaving things behind," I mused. "Besides, you don't want to be down there anyway." I patted the bed, glad there wasn't any space below for a river. Pulled Pendra's book from my backpack. "Come back up."

"I won't sleep knowing we can't hide if we need to." Her voice was a whisper.

"We just have to get by," I said. Like Momma did.

But I thought of Gran's kitchen and wanted to go back to the apartment in Alexandria. If she'd asked us to stay, I would have.

Why hadn't she wanted us?

I wasn't going to think about Gran. Mike couldn't either. Wanting something made it easier to lose.

I opened *The Hobbit*. I'd give it back to Pendra on Monday. Until then, I reassured myself, it was completely okay to use. "At least we know Gran's familiar with river histories. Someday, she might help us figure out our river too." Except that we couldn't talk to her about that yet.

Mike's face crumpled. "We already know rivers are dangerous."

No place was safe anymore, but I didn't want to tell Mike that. "Come on, I'll read until you fall asleep. Then I'll keep watch."

Very quietly, I read to her about Beorn's Hall until her eyes drifted shut. Then I watched the sun come up over the parking lot. The soft light glowed across the windshields of the cars, the motel windows.

I tried not to think about the river, or the Heron, or Anassa and the nightmares. Or about anything else. Eventually, I must have fallen asleep too.

Momma shook us awake when it was time to go.

By the time we arrived home the next afternoon, the house was better. The lawn, smoothed. The computer screen returned to its place on the counter. There were even fresh flowers on the kitchen table and in the entry hall.

Heirloom roses. Momma's favorite.

But the vase was off center and the roses were still bound by a rubber band. The garbage can was still full.

House magic had kind of worked, but not quite.

"Beautiful," Momma said, pulling the rubber band off the flowers. Her eyes softened. "It will be okay."

Poppa peeked out from his office. When he wiggled his eyebrows and made a funny face, Momma laughed. Then he tilted his head toward the bakery box on the table. "For Eleanor and Mary."

His voice was quiet. Calm.

Mike and I relaxed. "Maybe he's learning how to do house magic too," Mike whispered to me.

We opened the box to find chocolate cookies, still warm. Mike tore into them. I went to get some milk so we could all share.

But in the kitchen, there were only three mugs. And they didn't match. It wasn't quite the same.

And when I returned to the hall, I followed Mike's wide-eyed stare to a damp spot on the ceiling, just below my room.

I swallowed hard, feeling my mistakes pile up like I had at Gran's. It was just a leak. Nothing to do with the dream river. Nothing leaking into the real that we could fall through again.

The damp spot on the ceiling could be anything.

I pressed my lips together. Momma hadn't seen the leak yet. Maybe she wouldn't notice.

But maybe the Heron was right. We needed the witch ball. If that was fixed, then everything would be fine.

On the landing, a yellow suncatcher shaped like a starfish hung in the witch ball's place.

It wasn't the same at all.

Poppa caught us looking at it. "I thought you'd like it," he said.

"We do," Mike said.

"It's so pretty," I added brightly. But when Momma and Poppa went into the kitchen, we stood and looked at it.

The witch ball hadn't been magicked back. We'd only found pieces of old ones at Gran's.

This wasn't going to be fine.

House magic hadn't fixed everything, even though we'd followed all the rules.

Mike squeezed my hand and I shook her away.

We wouldn't be safe telling stories underneath the bed. Not for a while.

And now the nightmares and the monster were our responsibility.

"We'll fix it ourselves," I whispered.

CHAPTER

RETURNS

SEVEN

On Monday morning, I rushed to the top of the hill with Pendra's book under my arm.

Mike dragged her feet behind me, her puffy coat unzipped, hair a mess. "I'm so tired, Eleanor."

Neither of us had slept well, even though the house had been quiet. She'd ended up falling asleep reading comics in my bed while I studied for my math quiz and thought about how to fix the leak.

Mike was all elbows and sharp heels, and she thrashed in her sleep. I was tired too.

Both Poppa and Momma had an early meeting at the bank, so our lunches waited on the counter when Mike and I came down to get breakfast. I made Mike grab a snack bar instead of cereal. I wanted to get to Pendra before the bus came and other people were around. I made her hurry.

I hadn't returned *The Hobbit* on Saturday, like she'd wanted, but I hoped Pendra would understand. Even if I couldn't tell her why.

Everything was fixable. It had to be.

"Today, no telling anyone about house magic," I whispered as we passed Pendra's house. Mike nodded solemnly. But Pendra's mom's car wasn't in their driveway, and Pendra wasn't waiting at the bus stop. That meant she'd gotten a ride, and Mrs. Sarti was going to be at either Mike's or my school today. Great. I hoped it wouldn't be too awful. At least they'd been clear of the house before everyone got too upset on Friday.

A fog rolled in while Mike and I waited, and then it started to drizzle. Our fleece jackets grew damp. I squeezed *The Hobbit* into my backpack between math and science to protect it. "If Mrs. Sarti's at the elementary school, and she wants to talk to you, do you know what to do?"

Mike nodded. "I'll say I need to go to the nurse first."

"Good. Stay there as long as you can, okay? She has to split her time between both schools, so eventually she'll leave." The elementary and the middle school backed up on each other but opened to opposite sides of a long stretch of roads. It took some time to get between them. "We'll see Pendra on the way home. Please don't bring any trouble in the meantime?"

Mike scuffed at the wet blacktop with her sneaker. "I won't."

She looked tiny and upset. I pushed away my own worries from the weekend, from the strange river, from the leaks. Dropped my bag and grabbed her up, then swung her around until she laughed.

"Get off, Eleanor. You'll mess up my hair." She mock-pushed me.

I held on to her until she looked at me. "It's going to be okay. I promise."

"You sure?" Her eyes were the same colors as Gran's.

"I'll make sure."

"I wish we didn't have to go to school."

Mike didn't like school very much, but I did. Squeezing my sister's shoulder, I whispered, "I know it's hard. Wait, though. Middle school is better. Mr. Divner, the science teacher? You'll like his room. It's full of gadgets and things to look through and at, and you can do experiments. Sometimes when we've done all our work, he thinks of something really fun, like the time we went outside to measure distance with sextants. Remember when I told you about that?" Mike nodded. "Even the lunchroom isn't so bad. The cafeteria aide is really nice. She helped Pendra and me find her retainer last week when we had to go trash-diving for it. We'd cleared our table and she'd left it on her tray." Mike snorted.

"Pendra's so lucky."

"Yeah," I said. About a lot of things. Like not having to wait in the rain.

By the time the bus driver squealed to a stop on loud, wet brakes, we were all right again.

The driver squinted at us. "No one else today?" He said it as if we'd waited at the bus stop the wrong way.

I shook my head. Everyone was in a bad mood today.

"Hardly worth it coming all the way over here for two kids, but at least you're the quiet ones," he muttered. Slammed the door shut and was rolling almost before we found a seat together. The driver complained a lot that Pendra was too noisy. But she never was. Mike and Kalliope were much louder. I got ready to say something, to defend Pendra because she wasn't there to defend herself, until the bus hit a bump and jostled me to silence.

I grumpily tried to read on the half-empty bus, but the brakes squealed at every turn, and Mike's feet kept kicking the seat ahead of us. The driver frowned at me in the mirror. Trouble.

"Mike, knock it off." I put my hand on her ankle. She wore the same socks as on Friday. "Couldn't you find new socks?"

"Only ones left are singles, Eleanor. I lost my other good pair in the river. Like the Heron—"

"Mike!" She'd promised. How could we keep anything to ourselves if she leaked as badly as the river?

"Sorry," she grumbled. Once Kalliope got on, at the last stop before the highway, I switched to an empty seat across the aisle and let them sit together. They put their heads down and whispered. Then Kalliope laughed.

Don't talk about house magic, Mike, please. I thought really hard at my sister. I hoped the spell would work.

Mike quieted and I looked out the window at the pine trees still green and the bare oaks and maples. Then at the highway median as we took the on-ramp, then the next off-ramp to get to the elementary school.

I looked back at my math book open in my lap. I knew this as well as I was going to, even if my head was swimming with other things. But I had to keep my grades up, or else they'd send one of us away. Mike wasn't the only one who heard everything.

But I could do it. I liked school. It was the best thing I had besides books. Maybe not besides Gran, if she decided she liked us.

It didn't take long before we pulled up beneath the metal awning outside the elementary. Rain pattered against the metal, making a *tic-tic-tic* sound. Mike and Kalliope exited with muted, twin "bye Eleanor"s and the door squeaked shut. I was left alone with my worries. School and home. The river. What happened if it came back? But I felt myself relaxing too. Looking forward to the order of classes, the noise.

I loved those things. I was allowed to be good at school.

Then I froze. I'd promised to bring back Mr. Divner's binoculars this week. I'd been so focused on Pendra's book, I'd forgotten.

He was going to be mad when he found out I'd lost them. Maybe I could distract him with a really great science project for the fair. If I could get Pendra's help, we could come up with something.

My stomach churned a little.

An eighth grader, two loud seventh-grade boys, and I were the four students left on the bus after the elementary school kids scrambled off. As soon as we got out at the middle school, the driver slammed the door shut and roared away.

I looked for Pendra in the hallway and saw her bright backpack headed down the hall toward math, flanked by Aja and another sometimes-friend.

Pendra hadn't waited for me at my locker. Instead, there was a note stuck through the vent: *I waited all weekend. I'm done waiting. P.*

I read it twice, my mouth dry as an old book, and then rushed to math. If this was just a misunderstanding, something I could fix up easy, I would. But it hurt.

Could I do it without telling Pendra what had happened over the weekend?

The algebra classroom was freezing cold. Pendra sat in the back, all the seats near her taken. I tried to catch her eye, to tell her I had the book, but she was talking to two of the boys who sometimes rode our bus.

When Ms. Barrow passed out the quiz, she smiled at me. I smiled back automatically, then stared at the paper for a moment. The symbols blurred. There were too many things happening. Too much was broken, or lost. And the questions on the paper didn't look familiar at all.

Calm down. You know this. It's just like swimming.

I took a deep breath and looked again. The first question about simplifying expressions I knew how to do. The second required a bit of prizing apart. The third was a proportional relationship in a graph. That one I understood. I loved graphs. They were like points in space—or stars—relative to other points, and I could see the distance between them on the page.

The distance between seats in a classroom would make a good relationship graph. The distance between Baltimore and Washington, DC. The distance between reality and the river.

I shook my head to refocus and finished the quiz. Kept my head down. I didn't want anyone to think I was cheating. When I was finished and looked up again, Ms. Barrow passed by and caught my eye. She smiled. I was the first one done. That made me want to go back and check my work again, but instead, I started drawing a map of a river on the back of the quiz.

When the bell rang, everyone but Pendra and one of the boys had handed in their quiz. Pendra's face was red with frustration. I left to wait outside, but when she came out, she stormed right past me to her locker.

After math was English, and we got our spelling tests back.

The paper sat in front of me on my desk. I'd missed two words. A double-letter word and an *ei/ie* flip. I knew how to spell. I read all the time. How did I miss those?

I knew how. I hadn't studied because I thought I knew the words, I'd had a lot of other homework, and the house had gotten loud. I spread my fingers across the page, angry with myself. I tried to listen to the discussion of essay structure happening around me.

I graphed the distance between me and everything, and everyone.

Tired of waiting.

Untruths are dangerous for the river.

It doesn't hurt.

I had to work harder at getting things right. And at fixing them if they weren't.

Next period was lunch. I knew I could catch Pendra there.

I grabbed the brown sandwich bag from my locker. Banged the door closed.

"Eleanor?" Mr. Divner caught me first.

Not now! The science teacher split his time between the elementary and the middle school, like Mrs. Sarti. I'd hoped I'd have more time before I had to tell him about the binoculars.

But he grinned. "Ready for science fair posters? How are the birds?"

Oh. I nodded, deliberately vague. *My binoculars were broken and disappeared and haven't been magicked back, I'm so sorry,* wasn't a good excuse. It broke the rules.

He'd lent me that pair of Nikon binoculars early in the fall when I thought I'd wanted to do my presentation on bird migration. Now I couldn't. "I'm probably switching topics, but I still like watching the birds."

Lately, I didn't like it so much, but that had been the truth, once.

"What will you switch to?" He didn't ask about the binoculars. That was a relief. But he still stood in the space between me and my friend.

I stuffed my hands in my pockets. The glass shard was there, wrapped in Kleenex. It fit between my fingers. "Glass, maybe?" I bit my cheek. Dumb idea.

"Oh, excellent choice. Optics? Uses of? Something else?"

Oh no. I'd meant it as a distraction. I was never getting out of this conversation. I'd miss lunch and Pendra both. I started edging toward the lunchroom. No one was waiting to get in by the doors. I'd be lucky if there were any seats left.

"Mr. Divner, it's lunch."

Mr. Divner finally caught on. "Good luck! Glass is fascinating," he said. "Not quite a solid, definitely not a liquid. More something in between. I'm looking forward to seeing it!"

"Okay!" I said brightly.

We had three more days to work on posters. I'd never let a project go so long. I'd planned to figure it out over the weekend, but then everything had happened.

Mr. Divner went one way, toward the principal's office, and I headed for lunch, finally. There were a few seventh graders still going through the line with empty trays, but no one I knew well. Near the window, looking out at the soccer fields, I spotted my old friend Aja sitting right next to Pendra.

Aja and I had drifted apart after she moved, but I knew Pendra liked her.

I took a deep breath and went over. Put the book carefully on Pendra's tray. "I'm sorry I didn't get it back to you sooner," I said. "We had to go out of town."

Let that be enough.

Pendra put her hand on the book and nodded. "Thanks." She half smiled, but then she slid over to give me half her seat too. I relaxed into it, grateful I'd been at least half forgiven. But I wasn't off the hook. Pendra kept talking to Aja. "Eleanor's mom was so mad Friday night." She took a careful bite of her ravioli and chewed so that I'd have a long time in which to respond.

I'd barely gotten my own sandwich—peanut butter, again—unwrapped, and now I blushed so hard I could barely see straight.

Aja leaned in. "Eleanor's dad and my dad fought a lot, but her mom was always really nice. What did you do wrong, Pendra?"

"I'm sitting right here, you guys," I said, calmly even though I wanted to sink into the floor. "She just had a long day."

I looked at Aja pleadingly. She'd lived three houses up the hill from us. She didn't say anything now, but I guessed she knew my parents fought. I'd heard her parents fighting too, sometimes. But not as much.

And Pendra. Why was she doing this? More payback for losing the book? I felt my cheeks heating up with embarrassment. If she was a *real* friend, she'd . . .

Temper, Eleanor. I tried to count to ten.

Pendra blushed. "I didn't do anything. I just wanted to hang out over there. We're at my house all the time."

"She talks about your house like it's magic," Aja said to me.

I rolled my eyes. "It's not."

"The witch ball might be," Pendra pressed. "And Mike said—"

"The old fishing float? It really wasn't . . . Isn't." *Wasn't.* I stumbled over the word. I touched my fingers to the glass in my pocket. Not quite solid. I couldn't feel any magic in it.

Maybe the witch ball would be fixed when we got home. Sometimes house magic was just slow.

"It's just for fish and superstition." I shrugged, hoping she'd let it drop.

"Okayyy," Pendra said. "Fine."

Then Aja turned the conversation to science posters, and specifically to the science of diapers, on account of her new twin sisters. She looked at us expectantly, but I hesitated. After the note this morning, would Pendra still want to work together? Would I be able to without breaking any rules?

Pendra twirled a strand of hair around her finger. "I'm stumped. I was going to do the chemistry of cupcakes. It would have been delicious."

Pendra had the best ideas. But I blinked. She'd said, "was going to."

"But Mr. Divner said someone did that last year. So I was trying"—she glanced at me—"to get someone to team up with. I'm still trying."

I thought hard. Did I want to take the risk? My parents might not like it if Pendra and I had to work together, especially after school now that they'd made a new rule. Suddenly, I was kind of okay with that. "I was thinking of doing something on glass."

Pendra raised her eyebrows. "Like the witch ball?"

"Kind of. More scientific. Still want to work together?"

She grinned and nodded.

I smiled too, a real smile, the kind that made me feel lighter all the way to the top of my head. "I'm glad."

Too soon, the bell rang and Pendra piled up *The Hobbit* on top of one of her other books and checked her tray for her retainer. "I'll see you on the bus."

After a boring soccer drill in gym where I mostly sat on the bench, the final bell chimed. The bus was idling by the time I got changed and climbed aboard. Pendra waved from her seat. She'd saved me a space. I sank down happily.

Two more eighth graders and one of the seventh-grade boys got on board. The driver growled at both of them. "Oh." Pendra put a hand to her mouth. "My science book's in my locker and Mom's already at another school." She jumped up and went to beg the driver, "Can you wait?"

He looked at her for a long minute, then nodded silently and she sprinted off the bus, through the school doors and out of sight. When she was gone, the driver tapped his foot on the brake, looked at his watch, and then slowly closed the door and started to shift into drive.

"You have to wait! You said you would." I was on my feet and standing in front of him before I knew what I was doing.

I'd told the Heron I'd wait too. And I hadn't.

"We're going to be late to the elementary," the driver said. But just then, Pendra came sprinting back, hair flying, and banged on the door. He opened it, but not all the way, and she had to squeeze by. "You kids think you're so special."

Everyone on the bus looked at Pendra and me. I wished I could sink through the bus floor and maybe the pavement beneath. "Thanks," I muttered, all the time feeling the opposite of special. My face was on fire.

But when I sat down next to Pendra, she beamed at me. "You didn't have to do that."

I did. I knew what it meant to be left. "You would have done it for me."

"Thanks," she said, leaning against me and then straightening. A shoulder bump. Friends again. "How did they find a driver who is that mean?" she whispered. "Aja has a nice driver now. Why don't we?"

I shrugged. The driver was sometimes nice to me when I rode with just Mike, and sometimes mean, but he was often awful to Pendra and I hated it. Complaining she talked too much, ate on the bus, everything everyone else did.

"Did Mike have the book?" Pendra asked, pulling me out of my thoughts. I nodded before I realized I'd added another reason for Pendra not to like Mike. Great.

"How did you know?"

"My brothers are a pain, but Mike seems to break and lose things all the time. Remember the binoculars? Have you told Mr. Divner yet?"

"The binoculars. Mike didn't—" I stopped. I'd told Pendra

that Mike had broken them, and Mike had gone along with it. It was either that or tell her they'd disappeared, and how. Pendra had a good memory. "I'm sorry about my mom." *And my dad.*

Pendra shrugged. "It wasn't so bad. You should see when my brothers get in trouble." She grinned wickedly. "*That's* bad. Mom says you should come over anytime. And to not forget about the sleepover."

We'd been planning that for a month. Both our birthdays, cupcakes, movies. I didn't tell her she couldn't come over to my house. I didn't ever want to have to tell her that. But now I didn't want to leave Mike alone the night of the sleepover either.

I pretended like I'd be able to go. I wanted to go.

"It's okay if Aja comes too?" Pendra asked. "You guys were friends before she moved, right?"

I nodded, defeated. We were, until our parents fought and some other things happened. "Sure."

Pendra smiled and unwrapped a brownie and broke it in half. Chocolate and caramel. The rich smell hit me like a wave. She gestured half toward me, but I hesitated. She could turn our friendship on and off. She'd left me a mean note over a book. I wanted to be her friend, but I was feeling cautious still. "I'm all right." My stomach growled, but if I said it, it was true.

When we stopped at the elementary school, a teacher tapped her wrist above her watch and the bus driver glowered at Pendra and me. But Mike and Kalliope climbed up the stairs and sat down in the front row. Mike looked worn out, like her backpack was very heavy.

I thought again about the stories we told to stay out of trouble. The weight of them. What the Heron had said about telling untruths being bad for the river.

Pendra still thought Mike broke and lost things, because of me.

"Mike didn't break the binoculars," I said as the bus shifted noisily into gear. "I lost them."

Pendra's mouth made an O. "I hate it when my brothers blame stuff on me that I didn't do."

I nodded. If she was going to frost me again, fine. Better now than later. "Mike didn't want me to get in trouble, so she went along with it. She goes along with a lot of things. Which is why she gets pushed around."

Mike watched me out of the side of her eye over the seat. Listening hard. Her hair was a mess of curls and tangles and a couple leaves. I was sure we could both hear echoes of our father yelling, "Mary, you should have fought like a boy. You want to defend yourself, I'll show you how."

I frowned at the memory. I'd stepped in the middle of that one too. And the binoculars had gotten broken.

Pendra looked at me strangely. I'd been quiet awhile. "I just don't want you thinking she's annoying," I said. "She's not."

Pendra held the brownie out again, and I took it.

"Delicious."

"Made them myself." She split a piece off for Mike too. And Kalliope.

We ate in silence most of the way home and when we got off the bus, Pendra didn't ask to sit on our dock. I was relieved.

On the neighboring farmland my parents were trying to buy, a dark horse the color of smoke grazed the field. The bay below us was smooth and our house looked untroubled. But Mike and I lingered at the top of the hill.

"You can both come over. We'll work on our poster for the *real* magic of glass," Pendra said. "And if you think she'd be okay, Mike could come for a bit to the sleepover, if you wanted. We're neighbors, it's not too weird." She laughed softly. "Besides, younger siblings have to stick up for each other."

That would mean I could go. I couldn't help but grin. "We'd like that. I would, at least." Mike nodded agreement.

Down in the cul-de-sac, tires squeaked on asphalt. Momma's sedan pulled into our driveway and two doors slammed in quick succession. No, we couldn't go to Pendra's right now. We needed to hustle home instead. "Maybe tomorrow."

When I looked up, the dark horse had disappeared from the farm, unless it had only been shadows to begin with. I shuddered.

Pendra didn't notice. She gave me a hug and spun on her toes. "See you tomorrow!"

The distance between relief and worry was so short. I was caught between the two.

I followed Mike down the hill, counting our steps.

+++

When we got in the door, the tea-tinted stain below the landing had expanded. It looked like a tadpole now, with a fat head and a long, trailing tail.

I tried not to look at it. Mike tried not to look at it.

We looked so hard not at it that Momma gave us funny glances as we set the table. But she didn't look up either.

Dinner was silence and chewing.

Poppa hunched over his plate in a glower. The bank meeting hadn't gone well, was my best guess.

As I pushed my food around the plate, Momma confirmed it. "We can put the house up as collateral if you think it's the best idea." Her voice was soft.

The moment she said the words, the entire room relaxed. I felt the tension go, just like a weather change. Poppa smiled. "You think we could?"

Her forehead wrinkled. "I would have to talk with my mother. She's still on the paperwork."

Poppa's face clouded over.

"But I think I could get her to understand," Momma finally said.

The moment we got up from the table to take the dishes in, I forgot what we'd eaten. The plates said it had been spaghetti with a red sauce.

"My stomach hurts," Mike said.

"Sit down. You'll feel better," I said. Mike sat on the kiddie stool beside the sink and stared at another stain on the kitchen ceiling.

The leaks were spreading.

Forks and knives jangling against the plates, I carried the rest of the dishes from the dining room into the kitchen. I began to put them in the dishwasher without asking permission or rinsing them. We usually hand-washed everything, but we were both tired. Mike stared at me but then helped. We had to figure out how to run the dishwasher, but it was pretty straightforward. Powder in the little box, shut the door. I don't know why we never used it, but I was ready for that to change.

I wanted a lot of things to change. "We need to stop the leaks before they get too big. To help keep the nightmares and Anassa on their own side."

Mike nodded. "If the river comes back."

"I'm pretty sure it will." It was already here. Seeping through. I closed the dishwasher and turned it on. "We'll try after they go to sleep."

I had poster sketches to work on before then. The magic of glass.

Above us in the kitchen, a second small stain slowly deepened in color until it matched that of driftwood.

I wiped down the countertop and tried very hard not to notice.

"It will be all right," Mike said. As if saying made it so.

+++

The sun was still setting behind the trees when Momma tucked Mike in. I heard her telling Mike a story but couldn't make out the words.

She looked in on me. She didn't say anything at first, but she lingered in the doorway. I kept drawing.

"Your grandmother and I didn't talk a lot after your grandfather died. That was probably my fault," Momma admitted. "She means well. But she doesn't get on with Poppa. She bosses him around. Tries to tell him what to do. Especially with money."

"It's her house," I whispered. "And ours too." I surprised myself. That's not what I'd been thinking of saying. But my voice didn't shake.

"I know, and it will still be. He promised we're not going to use it as collateral unless we need to. We think our investment in the development will be enough. We just need to get approved. Though some of the rental properties are starting to leak and now we have to fix those. It's worrying your father especially."

The leaks were my fault. I knew it. I knew what banks did when you couldn't pay a loan on time. Aja had moved because of that. If I didn't fix the leaks, could we lose our house too?

I could stop it. I knew I could.

Momma put her hand on my shoulder. "Don't worry so much, Eleanor. Especially not about what you can't control."

"Okay."

I went back to working on my poster. Drawing different kinds of glass, different glass molecular states, liquid and solid. The lines got thicker and thicker.

My entire life was mostly made up of things I couldn't control. How could I not worry?

Finally, Momma sighed and left my room.

When I was alone, I glanced at the carpet beside my bed, where I very deliberately hadn't been looking for at least twenty minutes. Momma hadn't seen what I saw now: a pool of moonlit water emerging from beneath the bed skirt. Sending out tendrils of water into the room.

“Are they asleep?”

“I think so.”

“What are you doing?”

“Telling a story with pictures.”

“What about?”

“Glass.”

“Like the witch ball?”

“Kind of. Here, let me show you.”

“There are a lot of numbers and stuff.”

“Sure, but it’s still a story. Look: Once upon a time, people thought glass was a liquid. They thought that windows were thicker on the bottom because they were melting.”

“That’s not really a story.”

“It’s a fragment of one. Like dreams are fragments. Want me to keep going?”

“Okay.”

“But no one could agree on what glass was. The local glassblowers talked about glass like it was part water, part canvas, and part brush. And the scientists on the computer drew molecules that didn’t look a bit like glass. They used words like amorphous *and* thermodynamics.”

“Those aren’t really big words. Just sort of.”

“So people argued back and forth about what glass is, and they still do. But I think it’s kind of like magic. A little bit of one thing and a little bit of another.”

“I like how it bends light and traps it.”

"Me too, and I like that there are many ways to think about glass. Just like dreams. And magic."

. . .

"Eleanor, I'm scared."

"I'm not."

"You're just saying that."

"You don't have to come with me back to the river. I can try to fix the leaks myself."

"I'm coming anyway."

"Are you ready?"

"Yes. Are you?"

CHAPTER

THE RAFT

EIGHT

When the house quieted, Mike pushed her backpack beneath the bed. I closed my books and grabbed my pillow from under the comforter.

"We're not going to try to fix the house first?" Mike asked.

I thought about it. "We could patch over the stains. Like with the holes in the kitchen. There's paint in the basement, and foam filler, we could use that. But the problem's coming from the river, so a patch won't stop the leaks forever. Even if we managed to cover them up, they'll stain right up again. They could get worse." No. We had to fix the source.

Mike nodded and maneuvered around the riverlets on her knees, keeping to dry carpet as she slid beneath the bed.

I followed, pushing the pillow in front of me. The hard grip of the paring knife bumped my cheek. A roll of washi tape, a ball of socks, and two sweaters bunched at the bottom of the pillowcase, making it lumpy and awkward.

"The Heron said others help fix leaks in the tunnels beneath the river," Mike said. "Crabs."

"I remember," I said as I squeezed next to my sister. "If we can find them, I hope they'll help us with our leaks too."

"Okay," Mike whispered. She didn't sound convinced.

The underside of the bed was dark, save for the lighthouse's occasional pass. Mike stayed back as far as she could from the water's edge, worried. "The river came without us doing anything. It isn't our fault."

"I know."

"I don't want to fall in again, Eleanor."

Me neither. "We found a way out, we can find a safer way in than falling."

We lay on our stomachs on the dark rug, staring into the water. It was deep, but only a few inches broached the carpet. Then there was a big fall. That I knew. Then more water. Like a sandwich. Or layers of glass.

"Did you know glass remembers?" I asked Mike, trying to distract her. "Even after it's heated and more glass is added to it, it remembers how it was bent and shaped. That adds to the ways it can capture light."

"Even if it's broken?" Mike whispered.

I couldn't answer that one. I watched the lighthouse beam pass over the water. "Maybe the river remembers too. Maybe if we jump in, we'll land by the lighthouse."

Mike reached a hand into the water. Pulled it back, dripping.

"What are you doing?"

"Trying to grab the light beam. It worked for you."

"That worked while we were climbing out of the river. I don't know if it works in reverse." I reached into the water, but the light passed below my fingers, illuminating the bones beneath my skin. Casting a hand-shadow on the bed frame and the torn box-spring cover. Down the hall, our parents' voices grew louder. They weren't asleep after all.

"Put this in your pack?" I pushed the pillow toward Mike, after I removed the ball of socks. They were all odd socks, their mates lost to the laundry. I'd tied their ends together to make a rope. Now I lashed that to one of the bedposts and held on while I slid into the water, feet first.

I got wet, like I imagined I would if I was descending through a rain-filled sky. Then the rope ran out and I fell.

I landed hard, the pebbles of the sandbar cold against my backside. The lighthouse was small and distant, on the opposite shore. Gasping, I tried to pull my breath back inside my body, but it hurt.

Looking up, I saw Mike already descending. From where I lay, her feet dangled in the air, tiny and bare.

She swung, clinging to the rope. I scrambled to my feet. Stumbling on sliding sand and small stones, I lurched forward. My fingers and knees grew dark with wet riverbed.

"I'm here," I shouted, and moved to try to catch her. "You can let go."

She dangled from the rope, looking down. Then dropped the pack. I dodged as it hit the ground with a thump. When I looked up again, my sister had let go too. I caught her as she fell. Both of us rolled backward onto the sand.

Clouds filled the sky. Water rushed past the shore, lapping at the sandbar and filling my ears with whispers. A bird clacked. Reeds rustled. I wrapped my arms tight around Mike and looked for the Heron.

Two ravens, their feathers made from black plastic combs, tended the plants. Several smaller sandpipers shuttled back and forth on the sand.

One dragged a soggy piece of torn photograph from the water and tugged it into the reeds.

For a moment, when the moon broke through the clouds, the river resolved into shadow and gleam: dark waves, bright sandbars, reeds edged in silver, and two sisters crouched on the shore. A raven spotted us and snapped its beak as if to say, "You don't deserve our time." It turned its dark feathered head back to the reeds.

The shoreline grew dark in patches as the moon disappeared again.

"What if more nightmares come?" Mike whispered.

"Then we'll hide. In the reeds, or the water." I looked around. "There are rocks downriver. If we can get there, that might be safer. Stay close." If nightmares did come, could I summon the Heron? Would it answer?

How did you call a bird made of glass and driftwood? Not that I could call a real heron either, or get the one at my window to disappear.

I whistled anyway, just to try.

Nothing happened.

That made sense. Why would the Heron come when we hadn't helped it? When I'd lied?

From the backpack, I pulled two sweaters and dry socks. Mine had stars on them. Mike's had rockets. "Here, get warm."

After pulling my head through the sweater, I scanned the riverside. We were closer to the fast water that kept us from the distant lighthouse on the far shore. More reeds sprang from sandbars along the river's edge, and the rocks I'd noticed looked dark and slick with algae. Safer, maybe, but far. Too hard to walk there. And the current looked almost as turbulent as the middle of the river, which was keeping us from the lighthouse.

Still, the Heron had said the crabs were often found near the rocks. "We have to wade," I said to Mike.

"It's deep."

She was right. I wasn't certain we could make it.

While I hesitated, the reeds shook and the ravens took to the air, screeching. A low whimper came across the dunes and the birds dove at the sand, lifting and tugging something there. Something that cried out.

I ran up the small hill, shouting and waving my arms. The ravens scattered. A few small dreams shivered on the nearby reeds. Dark birds stitched the air, sharp beaks and claws aimed at the ground and the pile of rags there, cawing.

The river was dangerous, and not just for us.

I looked back at my sister's curly head, still cresting the dune, determined to catch up to me. I'd led her back here. I would make sure she got away safe.

But Mike followed me over the rise and began pressing the reeds back, gently. "Don't disturb the dreams," she whispered. Her eyes caught on the rags lying in the shadow of the dune. The ravens circled overhead, slow and watchful, as we neared.

I crouched low, my fingers grazing the rags. They pulled away from my touch and crawled backward and I shrieked in surprise. Towels and rags, all brown and pale cream fabric screamed back. The ravens made sharp sounds overhead.

I fell onto the sand, pushing Mike back behind me. "What is that?"

The rags tried to crawl away, but one of the ravens held a piece of cloth in its beak.

"Is it alive?" Mike leaned around my side.

Waiting until the one bird circled close, I lunged and grabbed the cloth. I wrestled the air for a moment, then fell to the sand holding the fabric.

When I opened my eyes, the pile of cloth was close. I felt its warm breath, fast and panicked. "It's all right," I said automatically. "You're okay."

The rags still gasped but didn't shriek any longer. I laid the rescued cloth down on top of the rest. Watched as the pile slowly pulled itself together. The ravens watched too, swooping occasionally, but I waved at them and yelled until they flew back to the reeds. Mike did the same, shouting and yelling, her voice high and clear.

How could the birds be so mean?

When we'd chased the ravens away and turned back, the pile of rags was gone.

I sat down on the sand, breathless, and stared at the churned-up hill where the rags had been. Then at the ravens watching my sister and me from the reeds.

We'd angered the birds. We couldn't cross the river. Even if we escaped using the lighthouse, we couldn't leave here without fixing the leaks. If we did, our problems would only get worse on the other side. We were stuck.

"We are in so much trouble," I whispered to the night.

No one answered.

+++

Mike and I must have dozed there in the cold sand. I woke, chilly and stiff, to a soft repeating splash coming from the river. A shadow moved toward the inlet, over the water.

I jumped up, pulling Mike with me, and we started to scramble into the reeds, but I stopped when I remembered the ravens.

"Shhh, don't wake them," a voice said. "They hate me."

The shadow drew closer, the splashing louder. A blackboard floated on the water, with a paddle wheel attached to the back. A pale figure stood in the middle of the makeshift raft, its forelegs stepping fast in time with the paddle's turn.

"Come down to the water's edge." The voice was soft and rough.

"No way," I called back. "You come up here." I felt safer high on the sandbar.

"Only for a minute. They'll pull me apart again." There was a grating sound as the raft hit the sand. "I wanted to say thank you."

Mike and I sat silently until the pale figure, muttering the whole way, climbed the dune. It stopped well short of the reeds.

Mike whistled low as the moon emerged from the clouds and illuminated it. "Eleanor, look."

I rubbed my eyes and looked again. A pinto pony stood on the sand, almost as tall as me. On the shoreline, the blackboard raft bobbed, as if ready for a quick exit.

The lighthouse beam passed over the hill and, for a moment, I saw the pony's shanks and neck, its soft muzzle.

All were made from towels and rags. Old T-shirts, socks, and a bit of mop for a mane.

"That's a Chincoteague Pony," Mike whispered. Sand crunched as she started walking toward the creature.

I grabbed her sleeve. "Mike . . ."

I was too slow. Mike met the pony halfway down the hill. As I ran to catch them both, the Heron's shadow passed between the moon and the beach.

Now we were really in trouble.

The pony looked up but didn't bolt. We all watched the enormous bird land.

But, instead of turning on Mike and me, the Heron stalked down the hill toward the pony.

"Dishrag," the bird said, "what have we talked about?"

The pony bent its head as if to crop the rough grasses that poked through the sand. It mumbled something.

"Yes. Exactly," the Heron said. "No visiting the new dreams unless I'm with you." The bird turned to silhouette and stared at us out of one eye. "The ravens won't allow him to get close."

That was the commotion we'd seen.

"These girls saved me," Dishrag—if that was the pony's name—said. "They're nicer than your normal crew."

"They're not crew." The bird turned back to the pony. "They're barely here at all and not helpful."

"We didn't want to be stuck here!" Mike's voice was fierce. "All we want is your stupid river to stop leaking into our house."

Please don't make them angry, Mike. I thought it but kept quiet, proud that she could speak her mind.

The Heron raised one claw to its chest, then put it down, driftwood talons digging into the sand. "And how do you propose to do that?"

"You tell us," I said. "Help us and we'll help you. Please."

"No," the Heron clacked. Its garden-shear beak made a *tsk* sound. "You lied to me. You said you'd stay and you left. I have more than enough to do trying to stop the nightmares from coming farther upriver and monsters getting out. And I don't like lying. So."

The bird turned its back on us and snapped its beak at Dishrag. "Stay in your place."

Then it stalked into the reeds.

Mike watched, openmouthed. "That's not how it happens in stories."

I shook my head. "No, not at all." But we weren't in a story. The river was somewhere between real and dreams. And even though we'd escaped before, we couldn't really leave. The leaks were coming from dream. And if water could get through, what else might? We had to fix the leaks here.

I sat down on the cold sand and rested my head on my knees. There was suddenly far too much going wrong. "How are we going to find and stop the leaks if the Heron doesn't help?"

"Leaks almost always start in the tunnels," Dishrag said. Then he went back to cropping at the grass.

"How do you know?" Mike asked. She edged closer to the pony and reached out a tentative hand to stroke his side. "You're so soft."

Dishrag didn't startle or nip, two things I'd seen horses do on the neighbor's farm. Instead, he nosed at Mike's hand. "I've listened when Anassa talks to the nightmares. They hate the tunnels, at least until they get really old and misty."

"Why? Can you tell us?" I felt a hope glimmer, then die. Dishrag knew monsters. If Anassa talked to Dishrag, did the pony also tell her what he knew?

Dishrag kept cropping the grass. "Maybe."

I thought of the Heron's scolding tone. *Stay in your place.* What was the pony's place? "You're not a dream?"

Dishrag shrugged. "Not a nightmare either. Something in between. I was born here in the reeds, but I can't fly. They worry I'll spoil the others. But I like to see them growing." The pony blew a sad snort.

"But the birds chase you away?" Mike asked. "That's mean."

"They make me stay close to the water. That's where I can help, by moving things around. By taking those who can't swim or fly up and down the river. I can't manage the really deep water yet, though." Dishrag looked at the raft and sighed. "It's a job, I guess. Thank you for saving me." The last words sounded like goodbye and the pony turned and stepped carefully to the shoreline. His raft rocked on the shore as he climbed on one hoof at a time. The large, worn-out blackboard rested on milk-jug floats. A treadmill in the center powered the paddle wheel, which was made from faded old doors.

Mike started to ask another question and I put my hand on her arm. If the birds didn't trust Dishrag, why should we?

"The Heron said crabs worked the tunnels," Mike said.

"Come on, El. It doesn't hurt to ask." She hesitated, though. Tugged on my hand.

I let her pull me to the shoreline. Sometimes it did hurt to ask. I knew from experience. So did Mike.

But Pendra would probably ask, so I could too.

When the pony saw us coming, he began to walk backward on his treads. The raft pitched and rocked. But I caught the craft's mooring line. Held it firm. "Wait. Tell us about the tunnels. Why don't the nightmares like them? You owe us that much."

The birds might not trust Dishrag, but I didn't really trust the birds. And I definitely didn't think that they'd told us everything we needed to know.

"I can show you," the pony said. He looked downriver as if a nightmare might appear around the bend. Or the Heron might scold him. Then he turned upriver and gestured with his muzzle. "See those rocks?"

The rock-pile jetty I'd seen earlier was too far to walk, but not too far for a raft. Getting off the sandbar was a good way to start, anyway. "You mean you can carry us there? Do you think we'll find the leaks that are getting into our house?"

Dishrag blew air from his nostrils. "The crabs can help you with that. They fix the leaks. Build things, too."

Anassa had said something about the crabs when she'd passed us on the river. The Heron had mentioned them too. Now the pony was offering to take us to them, if we trusted him enough to get on the raft.

"There are crabs working on the bridge downriver too, and tunnels down that way, but I don't like going there. Anassa's down there. The rocks here are closer, and these crabs are still helping the birds maintain the river." Dishrag's voice was half whinny, half word. "How will you pay me?"

"Pay?" Mike said, confused.

"We just helped you," I pointed out.

"I said thank you. And I don't work for free. You have to give me something in order to ride. That's the rule." The pony tossed his mop mane and the barge bobbed on the water.

My teeth hurt, I wanted to snap at the pony so much. But I didn't want to startle him or attract the Heron's attention. Mike and I couldn't get across the inlet without the raft and Dishrag's help. "We have money at home," I said, thinking I'd put some in Mike's backpack if we ever got out or came back. "I can bring it next time."

"No good." The pony shook his mane. "You want a ride next time and you can pay, whistle."

Mike fished in her pajama pockets. "I have this." She held out a handful of cereal.

The pony sniffed the offering, then delicately pulled back his lips and—with a washcloth tongue—licked a few pieces of cereal from Mike's palm.

Mike's eyes scrunched shut and she giggled. "That tickles." She wiped her hand on her pajama leg and reached for her backpack. "I have mo—"

I put a hand on her arm, keeping an eye on the pony. "When we get where we need to go, we'll give you the rest."

The pony grumbled but put his hooves on the treads. We climbed aboard.

The wheel began to spin as we found our footing on the raft.

As the boat bobbed slowly upriver, fighting the current, the pony's head sank low. "You've negotiated a fare before. You're as tricksy as the snake."

"Never." I almost laughed until I realized Dishrag wasn't kidding. I stopped smiling. "I just want to make sure we get where we're going."

Dishrag looked mildly offended, but Mike hadn't stopped petting the pony's mane since we got under way. Dishrag didn't seem to mind that.

"I'm glad you're not a nightmare," Mike said.

The paddles spun faster, splashing onto the deck. The river rushed past, trying to pull the raft off course. The pony raised his head and kept plodding on the treads. "I wish I was! Or a dream! But I'm not scary enough or pretty enough. I don't have mirrors and can't make enough smoke to keep up with the herd without disappearing. I can't fly with the flock. And I can't make many dreams, good or bad, because I'm not very good at stories. I'm caught between. It happens to strange dreams sometimes. The herd won't have me and neither will the flock." Dishrag blew cold air from his nostrils and shook his mane. "It's okay about the smoke, really. I'm better with cloth."

Mike stopped petting him, her eyebrows furrowed. "What happens to you if you can't be either?"

Dishrag's head tilted from side to side and his forelock swung. "Don't know. Eventually, dreams grow stronger, and when they're big enough they can't fit through the sky, so they help the Heron guard the boundaries. Nightmares get weaker and fade, until the crabs take them into the tunnels and let them filter through and nourish the river, both. I don't know which way I'll go. But I won't let myself break or give up. Broken things become monsters here. So do people when they forget too much." He sighed. "Sometimes we get to be more. But I'm not very good at much besides moving things around."

I put my hand on Dishrag's withers. The pony's warmth eased the chill in the air. I wanted to reassure him. The thought that he saw himself as a failure when he was this beautiful made me sad. But everything I could think of to say sounded hollow.

But Mike? Mike just threw her arms around the rag pony's neck and squeezed gently. "I think you're wonderful."

If a pile of towels could blush, this one might have.

Dishrag nuzzled Mike's hair, sneezing when the curls tickled his nostrils. Mike giggled. Dishrag whinnied softly. The sound of their laughter caught me up too. The raft spun rudderless on the current. Then Dishrag straightened again and slowed his pace on the treadmill. "There are the rocks, just ahead."

I squinted into the darkness. Closer, the rocks were large and slippery with algae. A border of seagrass swayed around them just below the waterline all the way up to the shore. The rocks glistened like a jumble of black glass in the moonlight, with patches of sand covering flat spaces.

A strange-shaped shadow skittered over the pile and disappeared. Another monster? A nightmare?

What if we had made a mistake going with the pony?

"The tunnel entrances are under the rocks here," Dishrag said when he saw me staring. "The crabs and others use the tunnels to get around and avoid the deep water. A few tunnels used to go all the way to the lighthouse, but those flooded." Dishrag snorted. "So now most use my barge to get up and down the river, and eventually Anassa's bridge will be finished. The crabs don't like that idea much. They think the 'mares should fade through the tunnels like they're supposed to."

"Sounds crowded," I said, watching the shoreline grow closer. "And dangerous."

"Some. If everyone listens to the crabs, the tunnels stay pretty sturdy. The one tunnel collapsed because Anassa convinced a big nightmare to try running through."

Mike frowned. "Why do they listen to her? She's a snake."

"Old nightmares, once they're faded enough, go into the tunnels and through the cracks. That's how you get bad dreams. They're not really big anymore, so they're not that bad. And what they leave behind helps fertilize the river. But Anassa's told the nightmares that if they can get over to the other side at full force, they'll never have to fade. They listen because she's telling them what they want to hear. And with the leaks getting worse, they thought they had a chance . . ." The pony looked downriver again. "That's why the crabs started making everyone get a permit to go into the tunnels."

"Permits?" I was baffled. Poppa had to get permits for work on the properties he managed, sure. But . . . "What kind of permits do you need for a dream river, and who from?"

"The crabs issue permits for everything in the tunnels. Travel. Repairs. Nightmare send-offs. That makes sure no one's creating leaks on purpose. And it keeps the big nightmares away, usually." Dishrag sped up his pace in order to get the raft up onshore near the rocks but away from the seagrass. He was breathing hard when the raft finally ground loudly against the sand. "Nightmares hate paperwork."

The rocks rose dark above the beach, a big scramble of them. Between two big stones, moonlight shone through. It looked like one of Momma's old photographs on the wall in the hallway at home, when the fishing boats were pulled up onshore and the day's haul was spread out on the rocks to dry in the sun, except cold and dark and wet. I shivered. Soft insect noises rose and fell in time with the river's waves. I didn't want to go home. But I didn't want to stay here on the river either.

"Do *we* need paperwork? We're not nightmares any more

than you are," I said to the pony. "We're trying to fix something broken here so it won't leak into our house. We don't want to break more things. Or get stuck here."

Dishrag scanned the rocks. "If most of the crabs are down in the tunnels instead of out gathering fading nightmares, that's a good sign something big is leaking. They might welcome your help. But it might not be your leak you end up fixing. Could be anyone's. Water goes where it wants. So do dreams. So everyone else needs a permit."

I made a face and Dishrag snorted. "You look just like the snake."

"She does not," muttered Mike.

I bit my cheek. "We'll figure it out."

"You can ask the Heron for help," Dishrag said.

"No way am I asking the Heron. You heard what it said. The Heron doesn't care about us."

Dishrag stomped gently on the raft's deck. "The Heron's not all bad. Not all good either. But nothing really is, is it?"

I didn't know. I tried so hard to be good. "The Heron won't help anything that's broken." Like us. Like Dishrag.

"That's not true. The Heron just works at its own pace. It thinks everything through," Dishrag said. "It gave me a second chance, as long as I stuck to the rules." He shook his head like he was driving away a fly. "Though I like the dream reeds still."

Mike, smitten, stroked Dishrag's neck. "I wish you could come with us, beautiful pony."

Dishrag stamped a foot and the raft jerked. "Not beautiful. I need to be terrifying. Or at least frightening. Maybe just discomfiting. Otherwise, I'll never be a nightmare. And no one wants me to be a dream." He made a sound that resembled a wheeze. "You two be careful up there."

We slid off the edge of the blackboard and into the shallows. The pony began to walk backward and the raft slid noisily from the shore. "Why should we be careful?" I spoke louder than I had been. The crickets sawing at the air quieted around me.

"Because you said you didn't want to get stuck here. Don't be in the tunnels when the sun comes up. You'll be trapped, like the crabs and Anassa."

"We won't get stuck. We can use the lighthouse light," I said. "Our ancestors built it so we could get out."

The pony shook his head. "Anassa thought so too, when she first got stuck here. But the light only works at night, and not for anyone who's been here a while. Your great-grandcestor built it to protect the river, not people."

"Is Anassa a Favre, like us?" Mike's voice rose several pitches.

Dishrag shook his head. The raft bobbed closer to the seagrass. "Back before she turned part snake, she followed a Favre here. But she could have just as easily been pulled into the river by a nightmare or a dream. A lot of folks get here that way." Dishrag nodded at the rocks. "The crabs, for instance. They decided to stay. Anassa came back a lot, and then she got stuck. She's been getting madder and more determined to get back out ever since. And she's convinced the nightmares that if they help her, she'll take them with her."

The pony shifted the paddle a little to keep the raft from drifting too far.

"If she could get to the lighthouse, she might be able to climb through, but she can't swim the river, I can't paddle across, and the light bothers her eyes. So she's building that bridge and trying the tunnels." The pony's ears flicked back and forth. "So, be careful."

His nicker echoed across the water as he paddled away. Waves from the raft rolled softly onto the beach and the wind carried his words away.

Now the moon was higher, and the rocks looked darker still. "How do we find the crabs?" Mike whispered.

Mike's backpack slid from my shoulder and dangled from my hands. Dishrag hadn't told us how to do that. And now we were alone on an isolated, rocky shore.

So much for my brilliant ideas. I sat down on the cold sand beside a large stone.

If water stayed where it was supposed to.

If the witch ball hadn't broken.

If I hadn't . . .

"Once upon a time, one of our relatives killed that one bird," I said aloud. All we had was the Heron's word for it, but the Heron hated lies. "And now here we are."

"What if this time, we broke the river because we broke

the rules?" Mike's voice wavered. "What if getting in fights or fibbing is just as bad? The Heron said lying is dangerous for the river."

"I heard what the Heron said," I snapped. Mike blinked and I relented. "What if it was letting Pendra in the house when I wasn't supposed to?" I tried to joke, but my chest hurt like someone had punched it.

Our *if-we-hadn't*s could go on forever. They always did. I threw a small rock into the water. *Plunk*.

"Would you keep it down! We can hear you halfway to the bridge and back. You'll startle the faded 'mares." A shout broke the silence and both Mike and I jumped.

Atop the rocks farthest from the river, a rotund figure stood silhouetted by deep purple night. The moon overhead edged it in silver. On closer inspection, the figure wore a metal shield on their back. They were leading a soft gray shadow on a reed halter with one hand; another hand helped them balance on the rocks, and a third pointed at us. Several more seemed to hang at the creature's side. Metal scraped sharp against the rocks.

I stood up fast, pulling Mike with me. Too many hands. A monster? Had we been wrong to trust the pony?

"A nightmare," Mike whispered.

"Who are you two? Do you have a permit?" The voice was as rough as sand.

We didn't have a permit, and the creature heading for us

looked intimidating. With the water behind us, we had nowhere to run.

I took a step forward instead and met the creature on the sand before the rocks.

Closer up, I saw the creature was an old man, his fingers clawed, knuckles large and red. The shield was actually a covering of gray-blue metal scraps, bound with round rivets, into a shell. His extra arms were metal too.

"I said, who are you?" The sound of the man's voice echoed against the rocks. Beneath his shell, a white and blue-plaid work shirt barely covered his broad back. The shadow he held tethered gave a soft whicker. "Spit it out, then get going," the man said, gesturing to the tether. "I have work to do, as you can see."

Mike edged behind me, away from the faded wisps of the very small nightmare.

"We're looking for the crabs." The words came out in a rush. As I said them, the old man drew closer until I could smell brine and seaweed on his breath. "A pony said the crabs could help us with a leak."

The old man scratched the nightmare behind the ears and the horse pawed the rock. "Crabs are busy folk, worse than usual these days. Patching cracks everywhere. Plus we're always the first to be blamed if something leaks." He drew closer to me. "Tunnels leak! Everyone knows that! We fix them as fast as we can."

I stepped back. "I'm sorry, sir. I meant no insult." But my voice shook. My knee ached from where I'd scraped it the other night. The scab pulled.

The old man huffed and turned to the rock pile, then patted the nightmare again and pointed. "In there, old beauty. The others will show you the way."

The horse condensed, its smoke sides growing smaller and mistier until it slipped through the rocks, tail swishing behind it.

"You're not sorry to go, are you gal," the man said gently. Once the last of the horse disappeared into the rocks, he turned back to us.

Mike's eyes were wide, and I was sure my face looked as surprised. "You just let them go?"

"She's heading through the tunnels, to your side of things. A 'mare's last hurrah, when they get too weak to run the river, is in dreams. They look forward to it, once they stop fighting it."

"All the 'mares we've seen are scary. With bigger teeth," Mike said. She edged out from behind me.

"The young ones are like that. They're dangerous if we have to go in to gather a faded one. Worse now, since they think if they can get out before they fade, they'll never disappear."

Mike's eyes were wider than before. She stepped toward the tunnel. "I want to see where it goes."

The man laughed. "'Mares like their privacy, young one. We help them, but we don't crowd them." He edged my sister away from the rocks. But I could tell he was stalling.

He'd been headed into the tunnels, and now he was keeping us out. And we didn't have time to waste—morning was coming.

My hands balled into fists until I took a deep breath. Stalling was infuriating. But I wasn't going to get mad. Monsters got mad. Not kids. Not me. "Please. We need your help." Tears of frustration pricked at my eyes. Everyone here either wanted something from us or wouldn't do anything for us.

No crying, Eleanor.

Mike edged closer to me again as the old man peered at us.

My eyes welled with more tears. And he laughed. "Crying doesn't get anyone anywhere. Don't be sad, little girl. You just go right back where you came from. Unless you have a permit to be here."

"I am not sad." I was angry enough to melt the old man's shell. I completely forgot about counting to ten. Not for the first time, I wished for eyes that shot flame instead of dripping water.

"You're a crab," Mike breathed.

The old man laughed again. "You got it. Now get going. Crabs are too busy to help you now." He tried to press us back toward the shoreline with his shell. He bumped Mike hard and she tumbled onto the sand.

I reached out and grabbed the crab's plaid shirt. I shoved him. He wasn't going to hurt us too. I lifted a foot to kick at his shell.

"Eleanor!" Mike yelled. "Stop it!"

The crab lay sprawled on the sand, arms and legs waving. Then he flipped himself over and levered up to his knees. "Well, you have some fire in you at least." He glared at me from under heavy brows. "Don't think you can pull that again."

I stared at my hands. I'd never hit anything like that. Mike got in fights, not me. "I didn't mean to," I whispered.

Mike stared at me too. "Your face looked a little like Poppa's," she whispered.

If the shoreline and the rocks could have fallen away just then, and the water come to sweep me away, I wouldn't have fought it.

But the crab chuckled. "Everyone gets mad sometimes. Don't they? I certainly do. Just like tunnels leak. It's how you do it, and what you do after that counts." He held out two of his hands, one metal and one red-knuckled. "Come on."

I let out a long breath for a count of ten. But I didn't take his hand.

The crab continued, "There's good mad and bad mad, isn't there? You've got a bunch of both in there. Most people don't understand. Likely, you'd make great crabs. Come meet the rest of us."

Mike didn't look like she wanted to go anywhere with me right then. I looked at my hands, the ones that had shoved and made fists. I wished them away. "Both of us?"

"Both of you, unless one of you wants to stay alone on the beach and wait for the lady."

"The monster snake-lady?" Mike asked. She took the crab's metal hand gently.

"Aye. Anassa's a chimera. Made of broken dreams, disappointments, bitterness. But still a lady. Crabs are chimeras too. Made of grit and hard work." He tapped his shield again.

Mike, very quietly, and maybe a little disappointed, said, "She isn't very ladylike."

"Whatever she is, she's looking for the same thing we are," I said.

"What's that?" the crab asked.

"A way out of here. But we're looking for a different reason. We need to fix the leaks before she can send the nightmares through or anything else can go wrong on our side."

At that, the crab's eyes widened. "Why didn't you say that in the first place?"

I bit my lip. I wanted to fix so much. Undo so much. *Maybe get things back to normal so that no one would know how bad I was.*

And if the snake-lady who could read my mind got across first, everyone would know exactly how badly I could mess things up. I didn't want anyone to know that.

"Why do you think the leaks are all your responsibility?" The crab leaned in. "You break something important?"

So much for no one knowing.

Up close, his face was as red as his hands. His mouth stretched wide and collapsed in on itself, the way old Mr. Lawton's used to do when he took his teeth out. His eyes were dark and small, and he only had a few strands of hair.

I didn't want to get angry again. But I was tired of taking the blame. I took a deep breath. "We didn't break it."

"But it's broken nonetheless? Funny how that happens. Tell the truth or get out of here."

Oh, this crab made me so angry. More than the Heron had. But I counted all the way to ten this time and didn't push him again. "We didn't break it. The Heron said it was our responsibility anyway. I am telling you the truth."

"Good choice." He turned and began to walk to the rocks, where the nightmare had gone. His work boots crunched on the sand. Mike went with him, after a long look at me. I stumbled, but didn't cry out. When they reached the rocks, the crab held out a gnarled hand again to help steady me over the first rough steps.

I put my hand on his arm and felt strength beneath the fabric. When I had my balance, I followed my sister and the crab into the rocks.

CHAPTER

THE TUNNELS

NINE

The crab didn't look at us as he paced slowly through the shadows within the jetty, his metal shell dragging against the rocks.

Hurry, Dishrag had said, *the sunrise.* And yet, we couldn't hurry. Not unless I pressed him again, and I couldn't do that without angering him. If he was willing to let us follow him, maybe he'd eventually be willing to tell us where the leaks were.

"We can't keep coming back here. We need to fix this now and go back to normal," I whispered to Mike.

The crab muttered as he climbed, as if he was talking to someone else. I kept thinking he was talking to me, and wanting to answer, but when I asked, "What did you say?" he waved me off.

The path through the rocks slanted steeply downward. The crab let go of our hands so that we could hang on to the slick stones as we descended. There was a lot of muttering. Finally I heard, "First, you come here, then the nightmares and Anassa will follow. They'll take us to help build the bridge, or we'll have to hide again. All your fault."

"It's not our fault," Mike countered. She sounded sad and lost. "We fell through."

But I thought about what a crab might want more than anything. "We'll fix the crack, and then? We'll leave."

The crab chuckled. "Smart kid. But you don't have the skills to plug even a small leak." He lowered himself down another bit of sandy trail and sighed. His voice echoed louder in the dark walls that surrounded him, and then us, too, as we followed him. Quieter, he said, "We can barely keep up with them nowadays anyway. If we can't stop it, how are you going to?"

"We have skills," I said. My breath caught as I spoke. The word *skills* ended on too high a note.

The crab looked back at me, his old man's knowing glance telling me he thought I was lying again.

But he'd lied, too. They weren't keeping up with the cracks. They couldn't be.

"Our father builds houses. We've helped him." I lied so hard I thought the sand would collapse beneath my feet.

Mike looked at me and then at the crab. She nodded. "Lots of times."

The crab hissed. "Fine. We've tried everything we know. If we can't stop it, the 'mares will come and break right through. Or they'll take the territory around the cracks, to increase the pressure on the others. Just like our last tunnels. That's it, the river could die, the dream reeds too."

No more dreams at all? I thought of the eggshell egret. "We can help."

But the crab narrowed his small, dark eyes. "I'll have to give you a work permit so you can be in the tunnels. That's going to cost you."

Everything seemed to have a cost on the river. This time, instead of arguing, I held up Mike's backpack. "All we have is in here."

Quick as anything, the crab grabbed the backpack with two claws and rooted around with a third hand. Muttering, he tossed out the rolls of tape and a dry shirt. "Hey!" Mike said, running after one of the tape rolls before it disappeared down the dune.

The crab's red hand emerged from the bag holding my paring knife. No. I needed that.

The look on my face must have been enough. The crab chuckled. "This will do." He put the knife between his teeth and hummed. Then he pulled a piece of red plastic ribbon from inside his metal shell and tied it to Mike's pack. The ribbon had the word *permit* stenciled on it.

I'd frozen. I wanted to yell, to grab back the knife. "I need that back," I finally said. It sounded hoarse and weak.

"You don't even know how to use it," the crab said. "A kid like you could hurt herself with a knife." With a long look that froze me even more, he whispered, "Or someone else."

"She would never," Mike said. "You just made her mad. That's all."

The crab squinted at me. "We'll see." He knelt on the sand beneath the rocks and then tapped at the ground with his claw.

With a screech, sand fell away as a thick metal hatch swung up. A light flickered from below, orange in the shadowy night. "James," a soft voice called, "it's worse again."

Near the deep center of the rock jetty, the crab ducked into the hatch. "Come on, Sheila and I will show you." He put on his metal shield and climbed down the hatch. It barely fit, and it scraped along the sides of the walls. "Everyone's been trying to fix the tunnels as best we can, but these new ones are difficult. And there are so many of them. But now you might help."

I didn't like the thought of going down that hatch at all. I especially didn't want Mike going down there. We'd be under the river, practically.

But I didn't want her staying alone up here either.

We moved toward the hatch together and peered down to where James had finished descending.

"Everyone?" I squinted.

From below, James coughed. "There are three of us here. We each got stuck in dream a long time ago. Called ourselves crabs because we didn't like guests that much. Now and then is nice, but you can't be welcoming now and then and chase people away the rest of the time. Confuses everyone." In the tunnel's shifting light, his metal shield gleamed.

"Come on, if you're coming," the crab called gruffly.

We climbed down the metal rungs of an old ladder, following James's lead. Me first, then Mike with the pack.

The damp air grew colder the farther down we went. The rungs became slick, then slippery. A quiet *drip drip . . . drip* patterned the air. The brine smell was even stronger down here. I tried not to breathe too hard. Banged my shin on a bar when I slipped.

The echoes of Mike's and my feet bounced off the walls, which felt cool and rippled with light and shadow as if they were made of dark, water-toned glass. In places, mud, woven reeds, and thin veins of glass patched the walls and seemed to be holding. We heard a soft splash ahead.

I knew what we had to do. We'd find our leak in the tunnel. Figure out how to patch that, too, and go home. Before sunrise.

But when I reached the bottom of the ladder, I saw entrances to more than one tunnel. The network of passages James and his friends maintained was vast. My heart sank. There was caution tape strung across one of the openings. A danger sign. The collapsed tunnel.

There could be so many leaks here, and none of them going to our house. How to fix the right one?

Come on, Eleanor. I just had to, that was all.

A shadow skittered sideways. Several hands reached out to steady me. A gentle smile, a slightly younger face than the elder crab. Too many arms, some with metal pincers at the ends, caught Mike when she slipped.

Claws. Pincers.

I turned to push Mike back up the ladder, away. But her face had already lit up, looking at the old man's shell. "More crabs."

"Of course," James said. "At your service."

In the tunnels, the shells and extra arms seemed more logical. They helped ease passage against the curved walls. They helped the crabs float in the waterways. The woman who had steadied me held out a bit of seaweed-wrapped fish. "You must be hungry."

Mike looked at the morsel doubtfully, but before she could say anything, I took it and put it in the pack's side pocket. "Thank you. We'll save it for after."

James looked at me sideways. "You excel at being the good one, don't you?"

I didn't know what to say. I'd pushed him. He'd fallen. "I'm not good. I just try to fix things," I admitted. I said it low so Mike wouldn't hear. "I try to keep us from breaking too many rules."

"Like I said," the crab James muttered. I felt more eyes turn toward me, staring. Mike moved closer to my side.

I shifted, embarrassed by the attention. Couldn't be much time left before moonset. "The cracks?"

The smallest of the crabs pointed at the openings to several tunnels made of glass bricks, tightly woven and sealed river reeds, and long stretches of clear panes, so the light seemed to ripple. I could see the shadows of fish moving in the water outside.

"Some tunnels have a few cracks, some have many." She rolled her vowels like wave-turned sand. *Sheila*, the old man had said. "The passages we use to start the dream reeds growing aren't so bad. The tunnels that filter faded nightmares through to reality have to be tended regularly. The ones that feed nutrients to the river, too." She gestured to each opening in turn, then nodded us toward a narrow, damp tunnel lined with glass bricks.

No part of me wanted to go down that passage. My feet arched, ready to run the other way. My hands reached for the ladder. I wanted to hear the sound of the river in the open again, not in the tunnel echoes.

I imagined I heard the nightmare's hooves on the tunnel floor. Where had it gone?

I tried to cover up my panic, for Mike's sake. "Are there many big leaks?"

"We've sealed off the collapsed tunnels and the bigger leaks as best we could. We're worried about a few more spots, too, but this one is the most urgent. Several big cracks started appearing the other night."

This tunnel could be one that was affecting our house. Maybe not the one under the bed, where the river had broken through, but the one in the kitchen? The leaks in the neighbors' houses?

I pulled the tape and socks from Mike's pack. The foam from the pillow too.

"Eleanor, why did we say yes?" Mike whispered. "What if we can't?"

"Shhhh," I said. "We will."

Sheila's eyes twitched in my direction, but she didn't stop moving. Mike dragged her feet.

"If the river gets in the house much more, no house magic can fix it. And then how long until Poppa notices?"

My panic rose again. I didn't need Mike slowing us down. I started to pinch Mike's arm. Then I remembered. My temper. I couldn't lose it again. Not with Mike. Not with anyone. I let go fast, and the marks my fingers had made on Mike's arm faded quickly, but they never should have been there in the first place.

Just like Poppa.

"You didn't hurt me," Mike said. "You're okay."

But I really wasn't. I didn't like this me.

Mike tugged up my sleeve, revealing the place where she'd pinched me at Gran's. It was barely visible now. "You're okay," she whispered. "We'll be okay too."

Maybe saying it made it so this time. We linked hands and followed the crabs together.

The light from the bigger tunnel began to dim, just as Sheila pointed at a crack low in the wall, where water was swirling and gurgling. The wall had hairline breaks around the larger crack, like a dropped eggshell. "Here."

A wave of guilt hit me as I knelt. Had I made the breaks in the river worse? Anassa seemed to think I had that power.

And twice tonight I'd lost my temper because we needed to get something done. At home, every time I lost my temper, things got worse. When Poppa lost his temper, things broke.

If you can't control your temper, Eleanor, you'll be just like him. Momma had said this so many times.

My throat closed up again. I'd been so worried, and impatient, and then, I'd just—Mike tugged on my sleeve. "Eleanor, here." She handed me a rag. Pushed my hands toward the crack. "We can fix it."

My sister, pointing me at something I could do? James believing that there were good and bad ways of being mad? That helped more than anyone telling me to count to ten. I focused on the tunnel wall.

The tide came in and the water level in the tunnels rose. The water pressed into the cracks. Worse, if I put my ear to the glass, over any one of those hairline fractures, I could hear echoes of voices. Momma and Poppa still arguing. That was good, actually. It sounded like they were in the kitchen. This was the right leak.

But I also heard Pendra fighting with one of her brothers. The cracks led to more than just my house.

At one place in the tunnel where woven reeds made a filter, I thought I heard snoring. Through the dark glass, I saw a shadow moving gently into a distant room. From the soccer posters on the wall, it could have belonged to Pendra's brothers. I saw the flick of a faded smoke tail. I backed away.

Nearby, another crack grew and I could hear the nightmare splash softly across a floor.

The break was already sending the river into reality—into my house and more than my house. Into others all along the development.

This was going to ruin Poppa's plans. He would be so angry.

How do you patch holes in dreams? In families?

Mike pulled out more tape and an extra roll of socks. Damp air weighted the cotton almost as soon as they were out of the pack.

I squished one sock in my hand and then pressed the blue-and-yellow fabric into the crack. I kept stuffing, my fingertips pressing farther and farther until only the cuff stuck out from the wall like a strange plant.

While I held one edge, Mike layered tape over the wall. Zigs and zags of striped washi tape, a layer of the half-roll of packing tape I'd managed to grab.

Some peeled away, but the rest stuck. For now. The voices sounded muted, at least.

"We need sturdier tape. More time," I said. We had neither.

Sheila came and looked at our work. "That's better than shell bits and sand and seaweed." But already the tape was bubbling. It wouldn't hold forever, just slow the inevitable.

I coughed, trying to get the nervous tickle out of my throat. "We can try again later. We need to get better supplies."

Sunrise had to be soon. We would have to come back.

We knew where the leak was now. We could go home and get more tools.

But we hadn't fixed it. Not even close.

"What will you do in the meantime?" Mike asked Sheila.

Would Mike and I be trapped here one day like Anassa or the crabs? Would we hide in tunnels? Try to avoid the terrifying horses?

I touched the cold metal shell beside me with a fingertip and tried to imagine what it was like to be one of the crabs.

"We'll keep trying. The tunnel will be unstable, but, worse, the nightmares will come if we don't," Sheila said. She turned to lead us out of the tunnel and her shell scraped the wall. "We'll keep helping the faded 'mares across. Besides, there aren't many other places left to go. The nightmares have the whole downriver now."

I'd failed to help them. I'd failed to keep the water out of my own house.

But she didn't sound angry. Her voice echoed thoughtfully against the walls. "There are a few stretches of river farther up, maybe. And the lighthouse side, if we can make it across the river. Those are still safe." She looked up the hatch. "The moon's setting. You need to hurry."

I remembered what James had said. That they'd become stuck here too. But instead of trying to break the river, they'd begun to work on the tunnels.

Instead of turning into a monster, they tried to help fix things.

I hugged Sheila, patting the cold metal shell. "Do you remember before the river?"

She squeezed my hand with a metal claw, then Mike's. Shook her head. "Not really." Then pushed us toward the stairs. "Hurry."

"We'll be back, I promise." I meant it. If they could help, we could too. But we weren't going to get stuck.

When we climbed out, James was waiting. His face was contorted.

It took me a heartbeat to realize he was smiling. "Thank you. Come back, all right? Anytime."

"But we didn't fix anything." The words squeezed from my throat.

"But I think you will," the crab said. He looked at me for a long moment. Pressed my hand in his. "You are the only ones who have even tried."

Mike crept out of the rocks first, toward a shoreline already beginning to tint mauve.

James held on to my sleeve for a moment. Tugged at it until I looked at him. "You aren't as bad as you think. No one who tries is," he whispered. He slipped my paring knife back into my hand.

And then he disappeared back down the tunnel, and I was left standing in the rocks, trying to hear what he'd said over again. I'd failed to help, and this crab still liked me. I didn't understand.

✢✢✢

By the time I reached the shoreline, Mike had whistled so much, her lips were dry and she sounded like she was spitting. No raft came to carry us over the river.

The lighthouse beam swung across the water, slowly. As it moved toward us, it seemed to flicker, then catch. In the predawn light, it looked darker somehow.

"I thought Dishrag would come back," Mike said. She stared into the shadows downriver. "I hope he's not in the reeds again."

"We'll go the way we did last time."

Ponies were unreliable. Mike needed to realize that. Especially if she didn't want to be trapped here.

I tugged at her. "Come on. Step there."

The light passed over my feet and I jumped on top of it. It tugged and pulled, just as it had before, and the lighthouse's single glass eye stuck and didn't move. The beam pulled taut, all the way to the fishbone tower.

We were leaving them here, the crabs and their tunnels. Just as we'd left the Heron. But this time, I didn't want to leave as badly as I had before.

"We're coming back," I promised the empty shore.

The beam beneath my toes felt cool, not warm. It wobbled again. My sister was halfway out over the river. The flicker threw her to her knees. She whimpered, afraid.

"Mike, I'm coming! It's going to swing a little." I climbed up on the beam and felt it stutter into motion. Not the smooth arc of before; a feeling of stuck gears. The beam moved slower. In the tower, the lamp flickered. It grew brighter for a moment, then dim.

The water turned darker. I grabbed Mike by the backpack and pulled her along. "Let's go fast."

We were climbing up the slowly spinning beam when the lighthouse went dark.

For a moment, all I knew was air and darkness. I still had Mike's pack in my grip and I hung on.

We fell into the river with a splash.

The moon was a sliver over the lowest sandbar. The river rose and fell around us, the lighthouse drawing farther away as the current pulled us downstream, toward the bridge. "Swim!" I yelled, then coughed, as river water flooded my mouth. I spit it out and looked at Mike. The backpack was floating, and she held on tight. "Kick hard!" There was a small piece of land downstream of the lighthouse on that side. We might make it.

But the river moved fast. My calves began to ache and cramp. *Don't panic. Breathe.*

Mike's fingers slipped off the backpack as it sunk lower.

All I wanted was to hear the beat of the raft's paddle and a nicker from a washcloth muzzle.

No such luck. The river made a sucking sound as it drew us toward the bridge. The wind shifted and I heard Anassa laughing up there.

"Come this way," she yelled. "I'll help you get home. You can get as mad as you want around me, whenever you want. And you'll never have to worry about falling into dream again."

I kicked harder. Mike did too.

The clatter of wings in the air above us made tiny ripples on the river waves. Then I was lifted by my pajamas out of the water, with Mike beside me. I struggled, trying to get away, thinking about what the ravens had done to Dishrag. What if the birds made us stay here?

Even as I thought it, they lifted us both, and our pack, dripping, above the river.

"You broke the light!" The Heron flew lazy circles around us. "We could hold you here until the sun comes up. Drop you back in the river. There would be nothing easier. We need any help we can get here more than ever."

The wind had shifted and I could no longer hear Anassa's shouts, but I could see her on the distant bridge, watching.

"We will come back to help," I said. "I promised the crabs already." The moon was almost down, even from as high up as we were. "We'll fix the light before we leave. Put us on the ground."

But the flock flew low over the water, listening to the Heron. They flew low enough that we skimmed the river with our toes. Low enough that a washcloth pony, lying in wait in a bit of sea kelp, could spring up and grab first me, then Mike from their claws with his teeth.

We lay, stunned, on the raft as black and gray birds dove and swirled around us.

Dishrag galloped on the treadmill and the paddle wheel flew around. River spray drove the birds higher up in the air. Meantime, we sped across the river, breathless, as the sun came up. Mike and I dripped wet puddles on the blackboard. "How can we pay you?" Mike said. "We don't have anything left."

"Maybe you can pay me back with stories." The pony breathed hard as he drove the raft toward the lighthouse. Behind us, the birds circled like a dark, fluttering cloud. "Scary ones."

Nightmare stories. I understood a little more. "You want to be scarier so the 'mares will take you in."

Dishrag nodded. "Of course. But also you looked like you needed a hand. Or at least some horsepower. And I owed you." He stomped hard on the treadmill. "See. This is why I fail at being a nightmare."

Mike leaned on the pony. "I don't think you fail at anything."

The barge drifted for a moment. Then the pony picked up more speed. We reached the lighthouse before the moon disappeared behind the sandbar. The horizon beyond the lighthouse glowed pink.

Hurry. We'd promised the crabs we'd come back. We had to get the right supplies to fix the leaks and now the light too. And we couldn't get trapped here. At least not yet. Though I had to admit, battling nightmares and monsters? I might be really good at that. And it was easier than not breaking rules at home.

But we weren't ready to give up on home just yet.

We scrambled up the rickety wooden-crate staircase that ringed the fishbone lighthouse. From here, the different fish our great-great-grandmother had used to make the lighthouse were more obvious. Whalebones—the big vertebrae discs from the spine—made up most of the base. Then came ribs and even some heads and fins from different fish. Everything looked big and pale. Our predecessor had wound these bones together and bound them with glass that glittered in the last of the moonlight.

Above, the lighthouse lantern had burned out, its bulbs broken. The jars of fireflies had tipped on their sides and grown dim. The witch balls still glowed with moonlight, but they weren't strong enough to make a beam on their own.

Near the shoreline, some stray garbage had washed up. I saw a broken computer screen half floating, half scraping the sand. The lighthouse's bulbs had glowed without a power source here, why not a screen? I raced back down the stairs and grabbed the screen, then lugged it up to the top of the lighthouse. With Mike sitting on my shoulders, we lowered the screen into the lens. Then we righted the firefly jars with a stray fishbone.

Mike watched the horizon for sunlight as I waited for the lantern to glow again. The fireflies lit up first, pulsing slowly, then the moonlit witch balls, then, finally, the old computer screen, cracked and dented, turned on with a slow increase in light. Would it be enough? I wasn't sure.

"Hurry, Eleanor." Mike pointed at the sky, which was distinctly pink now.

Walking carefully on whorls of fishbones away from the lens, Mike and I reached the ladder. We climbed to the hatch and pulled ourselves through just as the sun broke over the water, spilling pink light. The hatch slammed closed behind us.

I thought I heard laughter. But it was only Momma yelling that we were going to be late.

CHAPTER

FLOODS

TEN

If there was ever a morning to sleep in, Tuesday was it.

But Mike and I rushed to peel off our damp clothes, hide as much of the evidence of our journey as possible, and clean off the smell of brine and tunnels. There was no time to shower.

The river had stopped leaking from beneath my bed. When I looked back at my room, there was nothing to give away my secret. But the feeling of relief ended when I went downstairs.

The leak wasn't gone. It hadn't grown. But it wasn't gone. Mike saw it too.

"We just have to do better next time," Mike said as I grabbed a snack bar. Outside, mist curled from the lawn and hemmed our house in. I couldn't see the top of the hill.

Momma stood in the driveway, struggling to right the mailbox that had gotten knocked over. Pulling my coat tight, I hurried out to help her.

"There was a squall," she said. "A fast one."

The storm had been pretty specific. Just a toppled mailbox. But I went along with it, because I wanted to talk to her. "Momma, do you ever—did you ever—" What could I ask her? *Did you ever battle nightmares*? Ever try to keep dreams from leaking through to reality? "Can I help you?

She looked up and brushed her hair back behind her ear. "The way you and Mike help me is to go to school. To do well there. And to not bring any trouble home. We'll get through this if you help me. Just like that. And by not being late for your bus. Go on."

"Momma . . ." I fidgeted with the strap on my backpack. "Did you ever have anything really strange happen in the house?"

Her face clouded, then she looked confused. "Strange?"

"Like with the witch ball? Or a river?"

She shook her head slowly, as if a memory tugged at her. Then her gaze hardened. "Nothing like that. Childhood dreams, but nothing comes of those." Then she snapped to. "Don't miss your bus. Go on. I can't drive you today."

One look at her face made me not want to ask any more questions. Her eyes were like paperweights, heavy and still, though she was smiling. She kept it up until the neighbors drove past.

Mike ran ahead of me to get to the top of the hill and out of the fog. She disappeared when the wisps of cloud closed behind her.

I sped up, watching her gray shadow fade. When I broke through the fog at the top of the hill, Pendra waited, her hands on her hips. "I had to work on our science project all by myself last night. Why didn't you at least check in?"

"Sorry!" I hated letting her, or anyone, down. "I have some sketches done. Let's figure out the rest on the bus."

Pendra narrowed her eyes. "You okay? You've been . . ." She waved her hand in the air.

I'm on a quest, I wanted to say. *Like in our books.*

But how could I say that to her? She'd think I had gone over the edge.

She'd tell her mom. Or, worse, she'd want to come along.

There were a lot of things I couldn't tell Pendra, but this was the hardest. "I'm fine," I tried.

"You forgot to call. You're losing things. And your clothes are . . ." She raised her eyebrows at my outfit.

I looked at my clothes too. I'd gotten dressed with my hair still wet. Skirt, T-shirt, jean jacket. Sneakers. My bare legs were covered with goosebumps.

"You're not fine, and you won't tell me why not. El—" Pendra turned to my sister. "Mike, if Eleanor won't tell me, you will, right?"

No. I glared at my sister, willing her not to say anything.

For once, she listened. "Nothing's wrong. Eleanor was up late working on the glass project. I helped."

I couldn't even feel relieved, because that would show on my face.

Pendra's frustration sure showed. Her eyebrows tucked together to match her frown.

She looked at my bare legs, at the bruises and scrapes. I put one leg behind the other, trying to disappear the worst of it. Stood there in the trailing fog like a spindly bird until the bus heaved itself to a stop in front of us and let out a bus-size sigh.

Pendra sighed too, adding a long, meaningful look, but she got on the bus and settled down with me. I showed her what I'd drawn the night before. The distraction worked. "Look at what you did! You're good at this."

She opened up her notebook and pulled out a long, clear stick from a pocket folder. "Dad brought it home from the laboratory for us. It's called lampwork." The thin straw looked nothing like glass to me.

"If this is going to work," Pendra said, "we can't just tell everybody glass is one thing and then another. We have to make it real for them. We have to show them."

"Right. But we can't get anything hot enough to turn molten in a classroom."

"No, but with this?" She waved the straw. "We can give them a good idea."

"I don't see how." The lampwork was hard and inflexible but not brittle. "It doesn't look like glass at all."

She put it back in her notebook. "I'll have to show you. And these?" She pointed to the molecular sketches I'd done before Mike had come to my room. "We'll use these to show the class."

"Thermodynamic properties? With a single piece of plastic?"

Pendra rolled her eyes at my doubt. "It's not plastic. It's lampwork. Plastic would char if you tried to heat it."

I laughed. "How are we going to heat this?"

She got that smile on her face. "I'll find a way."

The stops flew by, but we finished talking about the poster before the bus reached the elementary school. Then Pendra stared hard at the top of Mike's head, just visible over the seat. She turned back to me. "Why are you mad at me?"

I sat up straighter, surprised. "I'm not."

"I just . . ." Pendra looked at her hands and a lock of hair fell into her eyes. She tucked it behind her ear. "I wish you could confide in me. You never tell me things anymore."

"I tell you a lot of things," I said.

"But not important stuff. Like the witch ball. Like—" Pendra lowered her voice and tilted her head in Mike's direction. "House magic."

I groaned. "It isn't—"

She held up a hand. "See, you're doing it again. I heard what Mike said, and I know she's a kid, but Eleanor, I also know you've got something you're not saying. I share everything with you. Tell you all about my brothers' annoying—"

"It's not the same," I burst out. Then shut my mouth hard. "It's not really magic."

Pendra got a look on her face like she'd lost a prize at the library fair. The bus screeched to a halt and Mike and Kalliope got off. Mike didn't give me a backward glance, but from the set of her shoulders I knew she'd been listening. She was bracing for trouble. *Oh, Mike.* I watched her go, trapped under Pendra's gaze.

Before, when Aja had lived next door, she'd asked a lot of questions too. When I didn't answer, she'd gotten mad, then distant. And then she'd had to move.

Now she'd wave and say hi, but she was Pendra's friend, not mine.

I didn't want to lose another friend, but how could I do what Pendra wanted? I couldn't even find the words to describe what was happening.

If I did, my fears might come tumbling out and not stop. I chewed my lip but couldn't come up with a solution.

I just wanted things to be normal. Not trouble.

Maybe I should have stayed on the river fixing leaks after all.

The bus started up again and for the short ride to the middle school, I said nothing. Pendra finally shrugged and when we got up to exit the bus, she put an arm around my shoulder and squeezed. "It's okay, I know you'll tell me sometime. Maybe for my birthday." And then she jumped off the bus and headed inside to homeroom.

I paused in the entrance hall thinking, *No, never.* I couldn't break that rule, even if it left me by myself again.

+++

By second period, when Pendra slid into the seat next to mine as Mr. Divner started to take attendance, she seemed to have dropped the subject of magic.

She smiled at me and we both ignored Bevan and Mark, the boys from the bus. They sat behind us, loudly declaring that they were going to give science fair presentations on the physics of farts.

Mr. D smiled. "That's a good idea, actually. Biology, properties of gas? Go for it."

He ignored their grumbling and slowly worked his way around to us, an eye on my sketches. "What have we here?"

"Glass magic," Pendra said with a cough.

So she hadn't let it drop after all.

"Why glass can act like a liquid sometimes and a solid others," I said after missing a beat. "Thermodynamics. Not magic."

Pendra's turn to wince, but she nodded. Mr. Divner chuckled.

"Also, I accidentally lost your binoculars," I admitted to Mr. Divner, trying to slip in the unpleasant fact.

Mr. Divner frowned. "After class, we'll talk, okay? You need to be more careful with school property."

"I know," I said. *Someone* should have been more careful at least. But relief washed over me. I'd been avoiding that conversation for a while.

"Okay, sell me on your theme," he said, with a glance at the back of the class. "Make it good."

Pendra pulled up a screenful of glass technology on the computer. "Glass was used in the late nineteenth and early twentieth centuries to insulate and alert. It kept electrical signals flowing instead of running to ground at pole points. Glass lenses magnified light for signaling purposes." Then she took the lampwork straw from her bag. "And we can melt these to show other properties of glass."

Our teacher narrowed his eyes. "Like what?"

"Like change and memory," I continued, nervous. "Even after it's heated, glass remembers where it's been. When you pinch or fold heated glass and then put it back in the fire, what's been done doesn't magically melt away. Instead, that becomes part of the way the glass captures the light."

I pressed my lips together, expecting an argument. But Mr. Divner was listening. This was kind of fun. "And how glass can be beautiful and useful at the same time. It can flow into shapes, so there aren't many seams, and can trap air and light." *And maybe it could catch other things too.*

"What makes glass flow and gives it memory?" Mr. Divner asked. "What makes it a good insulator? If you want to get past 'magic,' you've got to show me the science."

Pendra caught my eye and whispered, "Trap." I laughed.

"We don't do materials science until next year, Mr. Divner," she said.

The seventh graders sitting near us and working on their posters on the floor clapped theatrically and cheered.

Our teacher sighed. "That doesn't mean you aren't allowed to find something out if you're interested. Especially for extra points at a science fair. Look up *amorphous solid* if you're curious. Okay, you two. Approved. Go ahead."

I knew *amorphous* already. "Between here and there. Oh! Like glass is somewhere between solid and liquid. Not really one or the other, sometimes both."

Mr. Divner moved on to the next team. But I was already thinking about what he and Pendra had said. About what I'd said too. Sometimes solid, sometimes liquid. An insulator. A means of protection.

Between here and there. Like between real and dream? I had a lot of fragments from the broken witch ball, and the glass feather, and the tunnels were made of glass too. Could I use the glass shards from the witch ball in the cracks somehow? I couldn't imagine melting glass in the tunnels, but we'd tried so many other things. Maybe it could work.

"El!" Pendra waved a hand in front of my face. "Where'd you go?"

It would have been so easy to tell her then. At least a little. But I didn't.

When water seeped under the classroom door, I was busy sketching. I didn't see the leak until my sneaker was wet and Bevan screeched and picked up his dripping poster board. "Gross!" shouted my classmates.

The paper had a water stain on it almost all the way across.

Oh no.

I got up and trailed the class into the hall, where everyone was gathering around the washrooms. My heart sat in my throat. Had the river followed me here?

The linoleum floor was slick with water coming from the girls' washroom. "Just an overflowed sink," Mr. Divner said.

"Good," I might have said out loud.

Pendra gave me a strange look. "What's good about that?"

I kept quiet while Mrs. Wunner, the assistant principal, came downstairs and then went inside the washroom to check the sinks and toilets. But she came out shaking her head. "Not an overflow," she said. "It's coming from inside the wall."

Then the plumbers came.

"The elementary has a big leak too," one of them said, his Baltimore accent thick with annoyance. "But that one was intentional. Some kid said she was responsible. They've got her in the principal's office; they're calling her parents. Some people's children . . ."

Oh no. I had a sudden idea who that was. But I had no idea how to help her.

At least they wouldn't be able to reach Momma easily. I'd taken care of that with some magic of my own at the start of the year.

Maybe I could find Pendra's mom and help clear things up first.

+++

But instead, it was Mrs. Sarti who caught up to me. She made a fast pivot in the stairwell and caught me gently by my elbow. We stood for a moment on the empty stairs as the class change chimed. "Eleanor. Can you come with me? I'll write you a note."

A sudden press of students going up and down swirled around us as I struggled to find a reply. All of a sudden, I didn't want to go with her. A backpack caught my shoulder. Elbows jostled us but then as quickly as it had come, the crowd was gone up to lockers and classrooms. "I have lunch now." That wasn't a yes or a no.

Mrs. Sarti nudged me upstairs. "Something happened at the elementary. A small water fight that got out of control, maybe. We can't be sure, but Mike's claiming it's entirely her responsibility and won't say who else was involved. There's no real damage, but Eleanor, we can't reach your parents. I have Mike in my office until we can sort it out. She says she's feeling sick, though. Wants to go to the nurse. Can you help?"

I nodded. "Of course. I'm sure there's an easy explanation."

I was pretty certain there was no such thing.

One last glance back at the water pooling on the floor outside Mr. Divner's classroom and I escaped.

As I walked through the halls past the seventh-grade lockers with Pendra's mom beside me, an awful quiet broke before us like a wave running in front of a boat. The few classmates heading slowly to lunch that period stopped talking and watched us pass. In our wake, murmurs of "What's Eleanor done?" rippled against the lockers. I could hear it, barely.

At the end of the row, Pendra leaned a shoulder on her locker, talking with Aja. She waved but then very deliberately didn't look or whisper. But I knew she was curious too.

By the time we reached the office Mrs. Sarti shared with the assistant principal, my skin was hot with embarrassment. I wished I could turn into a small sparrow, the kind that sometimes got stuck in the lunchroom and then had to be let out through a window.

Mike sat in a chair by the desk, kicking her feet. Her sneakers flashed green and white, then back into shadows, then out again. Her blue shirt was splattered with damp spots. *Oh, Mike.* "What happened?"

"I tried to stop it, Eleanor," she whispered, her eyes still on her swinging feet. Then she looked up, face puffy. "I couldn't stop it."

I crossed the bright room, feet scuffing the ornate, worn carpet that had been placed over the simple pile rug. Past the desk cluttered with plants and pencil holders and an old-fashioned telephone with lots of buttons.

Two were blinking white.

It felt like it took forever, but I was by her side in four steps. I dropped my backpack by the chair and put an arm around her. "It's okay," I said. "I know you tried."

She breathed deep. "Someday," she whispered.

"Shhhhh."

Mrs. Sarti frowned, confused. "Can you tell us what happened, now that things are calmer?"

Mike shook her head. "There was a leak in the bathroom and I wanted to see if I could fix it." She shrugged. "I made it worse."

"But why wouldn't you call for help? What really happened?"

The guidance counselor didn't believe my sister. Would Pendra's mom believe me? Could I use the same lie we told the night before?

"Mike's been helping our dad," I said. "Maybe that's it. She thought she knew what she was doing."

Mike's head bowed and I saw her glare at me through her hair, but she nodded. "I just wanted to try."

Mrs. Sarti made a small noise through her nose. "That's something we need to leave for adults, Mike."

"I know. I'm sorry." Mike's voice was perfectly contrite. But her eyes were angry.

"You're lucky I was here. The school won't file property damage, but we still need to speak to a responsible family member."

Mike looked hopefully at me.

"Eleanor doesn't count. And we've phoned on both your parents' numbers. Sent emails." Mrs. Sarti sighed. "With this plus the other items on your record, if we don't get in touch with someone, we'll need to call in a report."

She splayed her fingers in the traditional half-shrug pose of adults stating there was nothing more they could do.

Ohhhh, Mike.

I balanced between frustration and fear. An official report from the school? That was bringing trouble in the worst way.

Breathe, Pendra had said. A deep breath. I tried it and had an idea.

"Momma will be home later. She might have forgotten her phone. Just this one time can you let Mike go back to class and talk to them this afternoon?" *And not file a report?* I didn't smile. I knew this was serious.

Mrs. Sarti held up a finger. Mouthed, "Wait." Then she ducked behind the gray divider that separated her office from the assistant principal's. I could hear them murmuring.

They'd left the door to the hallway wide open. Mike was eyeing it carefully. How hard would it be to just walk out? To run? Mike was probably entirely capable of doing that. Even Pendra might if she thought it was the right thing to do. I was rooted to the floor. Waiting on adults. Hoping to convince them things would be all right.

"What would you do if we could leave?" I asked the mess of red curls, which was the most I could see of my sister. I sat down on the chair next to her.

She lifted her head and smiled. "I'd go to Gran's," she said.

Gran's? We'd only been there once, and she hadn't really wanted us. I stared at Mike and thought about it more. Gran might not remember any more about the river than Momma did, but at least she wouldn't yell at us for bringing trouble. At least, she hadn't that one time.

Mike swung her feet and I swung mine too, thinking. Two pairs of Converse All Stars: turquoise for me, green for Mike. My socks looked like the tops of No. 2 pencils, all scrunched up, and I'd pulled on a pair of leggings from my locker under my skirt. Mike had on plain blue socks that barely peeked out from under her jeans. She didn't smell like river water anymore. She smelled like hand soap.

Finally, the assistant principal and Mrs. Sarti came back around the other side of the divider.

Just as they did, I whispered to Mike, "Don't worry, maybe getting in trouble won't break the river too much more."

Tears began to roll down Mike's cheeks and drip onto her jeans. *Plunk.*

I felt awful. But it worked.

Mrs. Wunner bent close and touched Mike's shoulder, forehead wrinkled with concern. "Aw, honey."

"Girls, we just need to call *someone*. An adult. Now, not later. If not, I'll have to do an official home visit and . . ." Mrs. Sarti stopped because we all remembered what had happened when she'd visited our house unofficially. "Do you have another number I can try?"

"Just the one you have on file," I lied. I'd filled out that file. I'd magicked the numbers. But I did know one new number by heart. "We could try our gran?"

It never hurt to ask, right?

Mrs. Sarti smiled, relieved. "Always a good problem-solver, Eleanor. We can try that."

Not really, I thought. *I make problems. I don't seem to be able to fix any at all.* But I smiled. "Thanks. I hope we can reach her."

Mrs. Sarti picked up the big black phone and put it on our side of the desk. I pressed the numbers I'd memorized. The phone rang and rang while the white lights continued to blink.

My heart kept beat with those rings. When Gran finally picked up, it nearly stopped.

"Hi, Gran," I said.

Would she recognize my voice? I waited to see.

"Eleanor! What's wrong?"

A good sign. I tested my luck a little further. "A misunderstanding at school, and Mike—well, they need to speak to an adult before they can let her back into class. And Momma's busy. Do you mind?"

There was a long pause. I've never wished so hard for magic in my life. *Please, Gran. Please don't ask too many questions.*

"Of course, Eleanor. Who am I to speak to?" she said loud enough to be heard beyond the phone's handset. Mrs. Sarti's face brightened and she began to reach for the phone. Meantime, Gran whispered, "And what should I say?"

My love for a person I'd only just met expanded like a sail filling with wind. She would help us.

But I couldn't answer in front of Mrs. Sarti and the assistant principal. "They're right here, I'll pass you over."

"I'll just say you all are never in trouble when I'm around, and that she can call me anytime." Gran laughed. "This is probably all a big misunderstanding."

I couldn't help it—my breath escaped in a big *whoosh*. "Love you, Gran," I said.

I didn't wait to see what she'd say back.

I handed the phone to Mrs. Sarti and stared at Mike's feet. They began kicking faster while Mrs. Sarti explained the situation. The assistant principal went back to her side of the office.

My feet swung in sync with Mike's. Finally, Mrs. Sarti paused and listened.

Then she answered again. "Oh, of course, just a small incident.

No, no, we can get Mike a dry shirt and get her back to class. Of course. Kids just want to help so much these days. I understand, and I'm glad to have your contact information. I look forward to meeting you in person too."

And then she set down the phone and beamed at us. "There. Not perfect, but better. Mike? No more waterworks?"

Mike nodded. "I promise."

Mrs. Sarti smiled at us. "Good. I'll take Mike back over to the elementary school and Eleanor will still have a few minutes for lunch."

My stomach growled in anticipation, but as Mike and I parted ways, I didn't feel hungry at all. I hoped I'd done the right thing.

Back at my locker, Pendra waited for me, an apple in her hand. Aja was already gone. "The bell's about to ring. What was that all about?" She ducked, trying to look in my eyes. "What's with all the flooding? Did Mike . . ."

"It's nothing, Pendra, okay?" I didn't feel like talking, but I took the apple. I needed to think about the consequences of calling Gran. About the magic I'd done—which was mostly fibs and lies. We were safe. Mike was all right. But more rules had been broken. I needed to think about how I'd tell Momma.

Pendra's face clouded over. "This is just what I mean. You never want me to know anything anymore. You don't trust me."

Please, Pendra. It wasn't that I didn't want to tell her or that I didn't trust her. It was that I wanted everything to be normal. And I wanted to be able to tell her that.

Saying made it so, sometimes. "It's all right now. My grandmother helped us."

Pendra smiled and eased up a bit. "I'm glad you're okay."

I leaned against my locker in the quiet Pendra left in her wake. Closed my eyes and saw the river flowing. The cracks getting bigger.

The shards of glass in my pocket were cool against my fingertips.

CHAPTER

THE ROCKS

ELEVEN

Pendra didn't take the bus home with us, so Mike and I walked down the hill to our house quietly, each thinking our own thoughts. At least, it looked like Mike was thinking her own thoughts. She scuffed her shoes on the blacktop.

"You're going to trip," I said, sounding grouchier than I meant it. She didn't answer at first.

The sky behind the house was dark green and the bay had turned that particular steel blue that could only mean another storm was on its way.

"Remember when Poppa helped you with homework?" she finally said. "And read to you? You told me he sometimes read to you."

I smiled. "Yeah." He'd helped with math sometimes, back when I was in elementary. It had been fun. We'd sat at the dining room table and he'd made the numbers make sense on the page.

"Maybe I could get him to help with homework. Maybe that would fix things. Kalliope's dad helps her."

I slowed as we got closer to the house. "Wait until Momma says he's not stressed at work anymore."

Both the car and the truck were in the driveway. Momma and Poppa both home early, when they'd been planning on being out on property calls all day. That looked like trouble.

I was glad I hadn't eaten more than an apple. My stomach turned to stone. The messages the school had left went to a wrong number, but the emails? I wouldn't be able to get to the house computer in time if Momma was home.

When I slowed my steps, Mike did too. "What's wrong now?"

"Nothing," I whispered back. Nothing we could do anything about unless I could get to the computer in the kitchen.

I'd fix things with Mike later.

Rain began to pepper down in stinging, urgent drops.

We hurried to the stoop and when I opened the front door, a staccato of curses rolled from the den in Poppa's deep voice.

"Troll," Mike whispered.

"Shhhhh," I hissed. I dragged at her jacket. "He's just working on the land deal. He'll be better soon. Momma said." If

Poppa was in the den, we could probably get to the kitchen. "Maybe there are some cookies left. Are you hungry?"

"He's always doing deals," Mike said.

The office door creaked and we froze in our tracks. Mike's backpack hung from her fingers, ready to hit the floor.

"You were supposed to come with me to the appointment, Simon." Momma's voice. Fiercer than I'd ever heard her. "It was important to try to talk this through. For all of us. For the girls too. What if the school wants to talk about Mary again? What about my mother? She's going to have questions before she signs over the house."

My fingers on the door handle, my sister and I caught between inside and out, ready to run if we were in trouble. But Momma kept talking. She must have been standing by the cracked open door.

"We have to be better at this. All of us."

Poppa's response was muffled by the room. The door clicked shut again.

Mike and I slid our drenched shoes off and set our bags down slow. We slid through the dining room as quietly as we could.

Mike was the one who noticed the new stain on the dining room ceiling. She stared up, openmouthed. I pulled her away to the kitchen, fast.

"You get some cereal, I just need to check a thing," I ordered her. But she was looking up at the kitchen ceiling stain. "Mike!"

Her head snapped down and neither of us looked at the ceiling again. She went into the pantry and I sat on a stool in front of the big screen. I had Momma's email open and Mrs. Sarti's messages deleted before Mike peeked back in from the pantry.

"No cookies left," she said, her arms wrapped around a box of Cheerios.

I heard the office door creak again and I dimmed the screen.

"What are you doing, El?" Mike asked.

"Some house magic," I whispered. I closed Momma's email and opened another window: a nature video about the bay.

Just in time. Poppa rounded the corner. His face was drawn and grim. He looked as if he'd been pacing.

Pacing was trouble.

Mike jostled the box of cereal and it hit the floor with a rattle. Then, slowly, the box tipped over and spilled its contents in a fan across the floor.

She made a soft sound and dropped to her knees, reaching for still-rolling Os. I slid off the stool and down to the tiles to help her. My shoulders tightened, preparing for yelling, or worse.

But Poppa laughed. "Oh, Mary. Fumblefingers."

He got down on the floor with us. Picked up a Cheerio and popped it into his mouth.

We stared at him. Then Mike's face broke into a wide grin. She tilted her head back and popped a Cheerio into her mouth too.

Momma paused in the doorway. Then she chuckled softly. "You look like a monster down there, Simon, crushing Cheerios with your knees."

A pause. Mike crunched a Cheerio. For a minute that was the only sound in the room.

Then Poppa laughed, and Momma laughed with him.

The room seemed to lighten. Mike and I looked at each other, unsure of what to do.

Momma nodded at us, encouraging. I stilled, watching, smiling.

Mike tossed another Cheerio in her mouth and crunched it, then coughed and sprayed cereal crumbs across the floor. She looked down, then began sweeping it up with a hand.

Poppa laughed a deep belly laugh and patted Mike hard on the back. "Don't choke, Mary. Girls, my God."

But he was still laughing. And so was Momma.

Mike stepped away from them both and went to get the broom, whispering, "Sorry."

Her eyes shone and I could hear her coughing in the pantry.

"See? I get along with them just fine. Right, Eleanor?" Poppa said, but he was looking at Momma.

"Of course you do." Momma nodded. She looked toward the pantry. I did too. Where was Mike with the broom?

Poppa stepped on crumbs. They went *pop!* between his shoe and the tile. "Even when they're clumsy brats." He laughed again. Momma laughed too and it was a brighter sound now, just above her normal pitch. I heard Mike suck in a whistling breath in the pantry.

There was no time to count to ten. Frustration hit me like a wave. No one had stood up for Mike. But I could and she'd hear me and she'd know I was on her side. "Mike's not clumsy. She's just a kid." I said it louder than I meant to.

I swept the floor with my hand, picking up more Cheerios. The floor was nearly immaculate now.

"What did you say?" A low murmur. No more laughter.

I looked at Mike peering around the corner of the pantry. Held her eyes. Then I looked back at the floor. "We're just kids. We're not perfect." I said it as calmly as I could.

"You are not by any means perfect," Poppa replied somewhere above my head, his voice deep and getting deeper. I wasn't looking, but when his frame blocked the ceiling light, a halo formed on the floor around me. "You are far from it."

"Simon." Momma stepped forward. Poppa's arm swung, pushing her back.

"I. Am. Talking," he said. "To my eldest daughter." Each word was sharp and separate. "You have no respect. Stand up when I talk to you."

His words came faster. I stood slowly as Mike scurried past and out the kitchen door. I heard her feet on the stairs.

Good.

I raised my eyes and looked right into Poppa's darkening face. It was suddenly very close to mine, his eyes black, his breath sharp from lunch.

"Don't you sass me. Don't you do it. There are rules for how a family should behave and you can't follow any of them."

Yes. I'd heard that before. Not new, so it didn't hurt as much.

I held my breath and blinked until my eyes stopped prickling. Heard Mike's door shut upstairs. I wouldn't cry.

"Say something, Eleanor."

I bit my lip. Saying something easily turned into talking back. Which was against the rules. I'd already broken that one, though. I could see that in my mother's frown. With the witch ball broken, and the trouble with school, how bad would this be? In my hesitation, I angered him more.

"What do you *say*? Are you *listening*? You are worthless, the both of you."

"Yes, sir," I said finally. A river roared in my ears.

"Simon," Momma said, but I could barely hear her.

Beneath my sock feet, a small piece of Cheerio pressed sharp and dry. I tucked my toes to try to pick it up. I ran through the list of rules I'd broken today, trying to pick out the smallest one I could offer.

Above my mother's head, the kitchen water stain began to bead. Droplets curved like glass in the light.

"Yes, sir, *what*?" he asked.

"I am sorry I talked back." Each word a breath, each breath a hope it would be enough.

His face came closer to mine. I could hear his breathing as well as my own. I didn't blink. Didn't cry. He waited, looming. He took up all the air around me.

"Simon!" Momma shouted. Then, in a calmer voice: "Please."

And, fast as anything, Poppa wasn't in my space anymore. Wasn't breathing my air. He stepped back and pushed Momma hard into the wall. "Garbage. All of you."

He stomped out of the kitchen. "I should send you both away." Slammed his office door.

In the empty air he left, I stood still as the Heron had on the river. I felt tears press against my eyes now and willed them to turn hard, like paperweights. Slowly, I moved my head enough to look at my mother.

She leaned against the kitchen wall, fingers pinching her left ear. "Damn you," she muttered. Eyes closed.

I took a step forward. Her ear bled, right where her gold hoop had hung a moment before. I pulled a tissue from my skirt pocket and held it out. "Momma." My hand shook, but only a little.

I'd tried to help, not hurt.

The earring made a noise like a marble as it rolled on the kitchen tile, its metal circle still clasped.

Momma opened her eyes. She pushed my hand away. "You had to ruin everything, Eleanor. Damn you. Damn your temper."

She had meant me. "I'm sorry," I said fast. I meant it, more than anything. I was a container of regret. It wouldn't make anything better, it wouldn't fix Momma's ear, but maybe she'd hear me. I wished I could seal up my mouth and change time as easily as I'd erased Momma's emails, so I would have never said anything.

"Go to your room. Don't do anything else wrong. Now."

She said it fast, like she was holding her temper in. Like a good person did.

I turned on my sock feet, the Cheerio piece still mashed beneath my toes. Then I raced for the stairs, beneath the water stain, and up to the landing, past where the yellow starfish suncatcher swung.

By the time I reached my room, Mike was waiting with both our backpacks by her feet and yelling echoed up from downstairs. From the office to the kitchen, then to the hallway, Poppa was roaming the house, pointing out wrong things.

Mike shook like a reed on the river. "I'm so clumsy," she said. Snot ran from her nose.

"You're not. I'm worse," I said, trying to make her feel better. "I can't keep my temper."

Below us, in the kitchen: "They're your problem. You fix it." Then a crash. A long pause. "Another leak? How is this happening? Sarti called me to say his ceiling was leaking too today." He sounded more baffled but also more than angry at the last question. I hoped he wouldn't blame us for that. I hoped he'd never find out.

We shut the door to my room tight, without turning the lights on.

Everything inside my room was in order and lit by the setting sun: books on the shelves glowed, dolls against the walls looked like they were made of flame. The seams and folds of the carefully made bed shone.

But when I looked beneath the bed skirt, there was no river. Nowhere to go.

A door slammed. Then the truck roared to life.

Rain smacked my windows as headlights spun past the glass. Good, he was going.

Damn you, Eleanor. The words flowed in my memory like water. I tried to brush them away. Had Momma and Gran fought like this?

I would be better. I wouldn't let anyone get hurt like that again. Or I would fix it.

In the quiet of my room, Mike whispered, "Can he really send us both away?"

"He won't," I said. "I messed up, not you. All of this happened because the agreement with the river was broken. The school, the leaks, the flooding. He'll blame me. Not you. Unless we fix the leaks fast. Then maybe everything won't be so bad anymore."

"But it wasn't your fault, Eleanor," Mike said. "He broke the witch ball. And our real parents got lost a long time ago. Remember the story? Someday, they'll come back for us."

They won't, Mike. They aren't. We have to rescue ourselves.

I bit my lip. The river hadn't appeared, and it was getting dark.

Downstairs, Momma began to slam drawers and tidy up.

+++

When Mike and I ventured back downstairs, Momma was still tidying. Her ear had a small Band-Aid over the hole. It looked like it had when she'd had an infected lobe a year before. That was one of the reasons I wasn't allowed to pierce my own ears yet. Now I didn't want to, ever.

"Can I help?" I asked in a whisper, then louder.

"Just tidy your room," she said. She meant stay out of the way.

Damn you.

"Your father's had a rough day with neighbors complaining about their roofs. And your Gran called. She wants to come to dinner Friday."

Momma sighed heavily, as if this was all my doing too. I wished I could disappear into the wall. It *was* my doing. I'd phoned Gran. Now she was coming to dinner. Momma would hear all about school. And Gran would learn all about me and probably wouldn't want to see us anymore.

I thought I'd been fixing something—my own kind of magic—by giving the school Gran's number. But even that led to more trouble.

On the landing, Mike tugged at my sleeve just as the sun went down. "It's back." She pulled me toward my room and I saw the glimmer of water beneath the bed.

The events of the last hour faded. We'd never escape the river. But at least if we were on the river, we wouldn't have to watch Gran turn away too.

Damn you, Eleanor.

"You said you thought you had an idea how to fix the leaks?" Mike asked.

"Shhhh Mike, Momma will hear."

I had said I had an idea. *Idea* being the most important word. Not a plan. Not even a true scientific hypothesis. Just a guess. Some of the tunnels had been made of glass bricks. What if somehow the shards of glass in my pockets helped patch the cracks? What Mr. Divner had said about glass's properties echoed in my mind again.

It couldn't hurt to try. We had to do something before all of the houses leaked and Poppa realized what was causing it. But I didn't know whether I wanted to get Mike's hopes up yet by telling her. I looked at the water pooling, dark against the carpet.

Tidy your room, Momma had said.

"Okay. Only for a little while, just to help the crabs."

I slid beneath the bed, pushing both backpacks ahead of me, and Mike followed. We lowered ourselves down the rope. The moon was purpling the shoreline, so we had plenty of time to avoid getting trapped in the river. But Momma would be up to tuck Mike in at some point, and Poppa would come home . . .

"Maybe we can ask Gran to come to the river." Mike interrupted my thoughts when we landed hard on the shoreline, near the rocks. "Maybe she knows more than Momma about all this."

I couldn't imagine Momma on the river. She would hate it here. But Gran? Maybe she'd been here, done this. We'd seen the map.

There had to be a way to ask her.

I began to wade toward the shore and the tunnels.

Smoke rose over the jetty, curling into the night. The sand below the rocks was pockmarked with hoof-holes. My stomach turned. What had happened?

And coming around the jetty, near the place where James and Sheila had bid us goodbye, was an unmistakable figure, walking all in shadow. I saw the snake's head first, then the garbage-bag dress. I turned, but there was nowhere to hide. Nowhere to run.

I heard the now-familiar beat of paddle wheel against water and Dishrag's raft appeared on the horizon. Would he arrive in time to get us away from the monster?

"Lie down," I told Mike. "In the water behind me. So she doesn't see you."

"Who?" Mike hadn't spotted Anassa yet.

But Anassa turned toward the sound of Mike's voice, smiling. Before she reached the shoreline, Anassa was laughing at the sight of us—of me—trapped on the churned-up sand between the river and the rocks.

"Hello there. Back so soon? Or are you already stuck here?" she said, her tongue darting in and out. "Why not come with me? Back to the bridge, downriver. I'll find a 'mare for you when we get there."

She stopped and listened to the sound of the paddle wheel splashing closer. "Or you could ride the barge with me."

"The bridge is the last place I'll go," I said before I could stop myself.

She laughed more. "I can read your heart. You have nowhere else to go. The Heron doesn't like broken things. You've seen what it does to the dreams that don't measure up. Tosses them away. That bird will do the same to you."

Behind the snake's head, a curl of smoke rose through the rock pile. The monster's knitted-plastic-bag dress rustled as she moved closer to the shore.

When Mike opened her mouth to speak, I took her hand, wove my fingers in hers. She closed her mouth and we stayed silent, together.

Anassa hissed. "If the Heron doesn't throw you away immediately, it will use you up to save the river and THEN toss you away. Like poor Dishrag. Like the crabs." She looked out over the water, then pursed her thin lips. "And you can't win, unless you get out. I'm getting out. Once we take the lighthouse and all the tunnels, we'll be able to cross over into the real and everything will be better."

"We can patch the cracks and keep you from crossing over," Mike whispered. "We can stop you."

Anassa laughed. "Don't you understand? Your boundary is broken. Your being here weakens dream, your being *there* weakens reality. No one wants you in either place, lovely girl."

She responded to Mike as if she thought it was me talking. Maybe I could keep Mike safe, at least.

I stood my ground, the evening breeze dampening my face. Waved Mike down so that she stayed out of sight. "I can fix things."

"You cannot. Even when you try, you break things, don't you? Too much anger all bottled up in there. Staying in dream will show everyone what you really are. There's nothing left for you to do but come with me," she said. "The nightmares have raided the tunnels." She patted her chest and the plastic dress crackled beneath her hand. "You should come with Aunt Anassa. We can be friends, Eleanor. You can be useful, powerful. That part of you everyone tells you to hold? I can teach you how to really use it. It's what you're good for."

Mike's shoulders drooped. I felt the words like a punch to the stomach.

But overhead, the Heron circled, screeching. A flock of birds chased dark horses out of the rocks. Their hooves splashed in the river, moving fast.

Maybe the battle had not been lost if the birds were still attacking; Anassa had only wanted me to believe it had been. What else was she lying about?

"You're wrong," I shouted. "Go away!" The flock of birds startled but swooped lower.

Anassa glanced up and shrugged. "Your choice." She walked into the water up to her ankles. Whistled. "But." She paused. "I know you, Miss. I've seen your type before and I know your heart. You're a monster too. Just a little one. But you'll grow."

Dishrag pedaled closer and my stomach ached with the realization that the pony was not here for us.

"I'm not a monster." My voice sounded weak.

"The Heron knows what you are. That's why it won't give you another witch ball. But I'll help you get what you need. I'll show you plenty of things to get mad about." Anassa climbed on the barge with a great groan. She pulled a dirty washcloth from a pocket in her bag dress and gave it to the pony in payment. "Back to the bridge. The girls will be along."

Dishrag snorted and began to work the treads of the barge. Whispered, "They won't. They aren't that dim."

Anassa laughed. "They will, because they're that smart."

"What do you mean?" Mike said before I could stop her.

Dishrag pedaled the raft away as fast as he could go, but I heard the snake's hiss.

"Because I have this." She held up a turquoise glass sphere, slightly cracked but taped over. "I found it in the garbage." Moonlight brushed the surface of the witch ball, making it sparkle. "One last chance."

Was that a way out for us? That ball didn't look *too* broken.

While Mike and I stared at the fishing float, the raft began to move faster.

Then Dishrag and Anassa disappeared into the mist by the bridge.

+++

Mike, shivering from lying on her belly in the river, began digging in the packs. She pulled out a change of clothes—sweatpants and a shirt that were too big for her. "Should we chase her? Try to get the witch ball? Maybe fix it up?"

"No. I don't think so." Every muscle in my body wanted to swim after the barge and shake Anassa until that witch ball fell out of her hands.

Mike stared at me. "Why not? It's our way out of here for good, Eleanor."

"Because," I said, "she wanted us to come with her right away. She was telling lies to get us to come with her."

"Not about the witch ball, though." Mike's voice wavered. "Eleanor, if there's a way to stop the river from following us to school, I would do anything."

"Me too." But something bothered me. The circling birds had followed the raft downstream like they were chasing the last of a straggling group away. "She was trying to lure us away from here for a reason. Come on."

I pulled my sister closer to the rocks and tried to find the hatch that led to the tunnels.

Deep hoof-holes also pitted the sand around the hatch, as they had on the shoreline. But the hatch itself was shut tight.

I knocked on it, then banged against the metal with my shoe. "It's us, Mike and Eleanor. James?" When I wore myself out with trying to get the hatch open, I sat down in the sand.

After a long moment, the hatch cracked open and a young crab peered out. She held a blade made of the same metal as her shell. "If you are with the nightmares, you'll never get through," she said. "I'll seal this tunnel forever."

She wasn't much older than me, I knew from before. And yet she was fierce and brave. She'd beaten the nightmares back.

"We aren't with the nightmares," Mike said.

After a hitch in her breath, and two false starts, she said, "I am glad to hear it. Sorry for this." She put the blade away, tucking it carefully behind her shell.

"What happened?" I asked her.

"James and Sheila were taken, defending the dream reeds and the tunnels." She looked out over the jetty. "They fought until I was able to seal the entrance and keep the nightmares out."

"The three of you made a stand here?"

She nodded. "The two of them on top of the jetty. Me in the tunnels."

"That means the tunnels are still intact? The nightmares didn't take them?" My hope rose for an instant when she nodded. "But where are James and Sheila?"

She nearly sank back down in the tunnel and I worried she'd lock us out. Stranded in the open. I wasn't sure whether we'd be safer in the tunnels or on the river.

Finally she spoke again, her voice like sand rolling softly underwater. "The 'mares caught them out in the open."

The thought of one of those horses bearing down on me on the beach was too much. I tried to squelch my panic. "Dead?"

She shook her head side to side. "Not that I saw. The 'mares can't get through our shells, but they can drag us off." Her voice cracked. "I don't know if I'll ever see them again. And the tunnel is leaking worse than ever. So the 'mares will come back, and I can't—not by myself—" The tunnel lid began to close again.

"Wait!" I called, putting my hands between the lid and the sand. "What's your name? We'll help. We want to try something different."

In the moonlight, the crab looked skeptical. "Last time . . ."

Last time we hadn't helped and we might have made things worse. We might have even shown the 'mares where to attack. "I think I understand better now. The river and the tunnels need magic to keep everything on the right side. We weren't using magic. But I think we can." I held out the pieces of the broken witch ball but kept the Heron's feather in my pocket. "What if these still have enough magic in them to patch the cracks?"

The young crab narrowed her eyes. "Maybe." But she lifted the tunnel lid and crawled down the ladder to let us inside. "Zöe," she said as she climbed down. "That's my name."

I could see the river light glint off her metal shell as she disappeared. Then we followed her. Our steps echoed against the repetitive *drip drip drip* that water makes when trying to sound its way into unfamiliar, empty spaces.

As we walked the silent passages, Zöe began to hiccup. Mike patted her shell, then took one of her hands. "They'll be back."

"I'm so frightened," she said. "I promised to guard the breaks until they're fixed, but I don't know how I can, not alone."

"It's going to be okay," Mike said. "Somehow, some way . . ." But Zöe tucked inside her shell and scuttled sideways.

Mike looked at me sadly. "I wanted to help her feel better."

"I know." I squeezed my sister's hand. We followed Zöe along the tunnels to the crack in the wall. It was much bigger now. Water pulsed against the crack and was sucked away, across the barriers.

Now that I stood in front of the break, I didn't feel anywhere near confident in my guess, but guesses were all we had. I pulled one of the pieces of the witch ball from my pocket and stuffed it into a narrow part of the crack. Water lapped at our ankles.

A clicking on the edge of the tunnel was shell striking glass.

"The tide's coming up. The 'mares will be back soon to try again," Zöe said, still tucked in her shell.

On the other side of the crack, I heard a kitchen timer go off. Sounds of people watching television. My heart raced. We couldn't linger. We couldn't leave either.

The glass shard stuck where I placed it, but water continued to pulse around its edges. The young crab groaned and started to scuttle back the way she'd come. Mike pressed against the wall to avoid her but I shook my head, and my sister stepped forward and gently trapped the crab in the tunnel. Zöe's shell would scrape and crack the walls unless she wanted to bump Mike or me.

She looked at the cracks. "We should leave here before the wall collapses or the 'mares come. There's nothing to save any longer."

But Mike and I didn't budge, no matter how much we wanted to. Finally the young crab dropped her claws.

The washcloth pony had said he needed scary stories to help him become a nightmare. And the Heron had said that stories were recycled on the river, like everything else. "Maybe stories can work like magic. Mike, tell a story."

"I can't think of one."

"Sure you can. Once upon a time . . ." The glass sparkled and seemed to stretch in the crack. But then it hardened again beneath my fingers. "Mike, try it."

"Once," Mike said, "two girls fell into a river." The glass shimmered again, blue and turquoise against the damp moss and cracked tunnel. Then it stretched to cover the small edge of the crack, flowing into place like hard water.

"Keep going," I whispered.

"I can't come up with anything more . . ." Mike looked worried. The glass stopped expanding.

Thinking fast, I whispered, "The river carried them far from home. They were frightened. But then they found an island, where dreams grew." The blue glass expanded to fill most of the larger crack and two more hairline breaks. Its color had thinned to light blue with shadow behind it, but it held. I couldn't hear sounds from the other side anymore.

"It's working!" Mike cheered.

"Shhhhh," said the crab. "Let her finish."

"And the two girls came back to the river now and then to make sure their friends were safe and to help fix the cracks, but they couldn't stay because they had school and tests. And soon they were able to sleep in their own beds, and to hide under them too, without any rivers appearing."

The wall sealed. A blue glass seam thickened across where the crack had been. I stared at it. Had the leaks stopped on the other side? I would have to go home and find out.

Zöe tapped at the seam. "It will hold." She wrapped all of her arms around Mike and me, the metal ones, the regular arms, in their soft sleeves. "I've never seen anything like that before. You do know what you're doing."

Mike opened her mouth to object, but I stilled her with a hand. "We're learning." We'd done something. We really had.

But Zöe glanced down the tunnels. "There are many more cracks," she said. "This was just the worst one."

My happiness faded. "Many?"

She nodded. "It's why we stayed here. But this will keep for a while. Until my family returns, or someone else comes to help."

I turned away from Zöe. I didn't want to leave her alone here, but I did not want either of us to have to stay permanently. Not with Gran coming to dinner Friday, and our parents fighting so much.

But then again, I didn't look forward to going home much either.

"You won't be alone for long. They'll get away from the nightmares." I handed the crab more pieces of glass. "For more of the cracks."

She smiled sadly. "I can manage," she said.

"We'll come back to look for James and Sheila," I promised, feeling terrible and surprising myself. Mike stared at me, open-mouthed. I wanted to fix things. But coming back again? I didn't want to get trapped here like the crabs. I would have to find a better way.

The young crab hugged us again, tighter this time. "I know you'll help. You are the best thing to happen to the river in a long time. You helped patch an impossible leak. The 'mares haven't been able to come any higher because the Heron's flocks have been fighting them off harder than ever the past few days."

That was why we hadn't seen the birds. "We can't stay now, though," I said. "We can't miss school." And sunrise.

Zöe scrabbled the tunnels with us as far as another ladder to another hatch hidden in the rocks. Mike and I peered out, looking for nightmares. We climbed out onto the rocks and then down to the sand.

At the shoreline, the lighthouse beam sputtered and caught, then dimmed again.

"That doesn't look very steady," Mike said, remembering the last time, when we'd fallen off the beam.

It didn't look steady at all.

But up and down the shoreline, neither Dishrag nor the Heron was anywhere to be seen.

"We have to run, Mike. Faster than last time. Can you do it?"

My sister looked at me and bit her lip. "Okay," she said.

She grabbed my hand and we each put one foot down on the beam when it swung around again, stopping it, though the pressure made small tears in it like it was tissue paper.

"Very fast," she whispered.

We pushed off from the beach, the light spinning across the river, and scrambled up it as fast as we could go. My foot punched through a thin part of the beam once, but I struggled out. Mike nearly fell into the waves more than once, but I kept hold of her hand and we clawed our way up, getting light splinters in our fingers. They burned long after we'd reached the lighthouse deck. The light flickered like an old screen once but never blinked out. Our fix held.

As we caught our breath, I looked out over the river. Flocks of birds cast dark shadows on the far shore. On the bridge, now and then lit by the lighthouse beam and constantly loud with construction, several nightmares moved, and crabs too. Could James and Sheila be there?

Anassa was nowhere to be seen.

But in the tunnels, things had gotten a little better, maybe because of us. "We made the river stronger, I think."

"You did it, Eleanor!" Mike threw her arms around my waist. "We fixed something."

And as we climbed back through the lighthouse hatch, I laughed, realizing that we really had.

Just one small thing. But it was a start.

CHAPTER

LIKE GLASS

TWELVE

Wednesday afternoon, Pendra and I worked on our science presentation at her house. On Thursday, after a slow day at school, we got off the bus and went back again to practice our speech. The river at the bottom of the hill and the sky over Pendra's house were matching shades of storm gray, but there was no breeze.

Being at Pendra's house was easier. When we were home, Mike and I kept checking under the bed. No matter how many times we looked, the river didn't reappear. The leaks had slowed at our house and at the other houses. Poppa wasn't yelling on the phone as much. But we couldn't figure out how to get back and help rescue the crabs. We tried to focus on our work instead.

Both days, Mike followed me to Pendra's. She sat quietly on Pendra's bed, doing third-grade math problems and yawning.

I stifled a yawn, but it was too late. They were contagious. Pendra yawned also. "Stop it, you two! Or get some rest."

She was right, we were both exhausted from lack of sleep.

Mike and I packed up our bags and headed down the hill before Pendra's parents got home. We ate the cheese sandwiches Momma had left us for snacks, and then Mike helped me finish the poster with my blue and green watercolor pens for the glass.

"Maybe we fixed more than the one leak," she said to the paper.

A car's brakes squeaked as it pulled into the driveway. "Shhhh, Mike." No talk of tunnels or monsters. Not around our parents.

We heard the door downstairs open and shut. "Girls, did you eat?"

"Yes, Momma." Mike's coloring was so careful, staying inside the lines. But no one came upstairs.

A heavy silence filled the house, from our father's office, through the kitchen, and up to our room, but nothing more broke. Nothing leaked.

Finally, Mike slid off my bed and went to put on her pajamas. "Maybe we fixed it all," she said. "Maybe everything will be all right."

I heard her whisper *someday* as she shut the door behind her.

When I looked beneath my bed, the carpet was still dry. "Maybe someday soon," I echoed to the empty room.

+++

The next morning was Friday. Presentation day. Grandma day. Sleepover day. Pendra looked over my final drawings on the bus approvingly.

"We're going to have so much fun tonight." She nudged me. "Mike too. Mom has five kinds of cupcakes for us to share."

I nudged her back, relieved. If Mike could come, I wouldn't have to think up an excuse to stay home. I didn't want to leave my sister. Not now. Three seats ahead, Mike and Kalliope laughed over a comic book. She hadn't heard what Pendra said, and I hadn't hinted at the possibility before. Hadn't wanted to get her hopes up. Or mine.

I'd tell her later.

The bus crossed the bridge over the swollen river. Below the gray pilings, water lapped at the tall reeds edging the shore. Then we rolled onto the highway and off at the next exit, just like usual.

Overhead, clouds pressed down on us like a clamp. We dropped the little kids off, and the driver grumbled about the weather a lot, but we made it to school on time.

No notes stuck to my locker, no leaks in the bathroom. Things were looking up.

In second-period science, Mr. Divner kept the Weather Channel on. The screen showed a fist-shaped storm moving up the coast. Not a true sou'wester. Not a hurricane either. But the storm was coming in at high tide on a full moon. On the television, a fisherman talked to the weather woman, worrying over storm surges. "The wind's going to blow right up the bay," he said.

I knew that meant trouble. Mr. Divner did too. "The harbor and its rivers flooded a lot during a hurricane like this back in 2004. So we're keeping a close eye on it. I know the district science fair is scheduled for this weekend, but if we need to, we'll postpone. You'll give your practice presentations today as planned. If you can't present at the fair, this will be your grade."

"What?" one seventh-grade boy said.

"Mr. Divner, that's not fair," Aja protested.

"Yeah," Pendra agreed.

Mr. Divner shook his head. "You can't fight the weather."

I wilted. I'd been looking forward to the science fair since last year, when we went to watch the seventh grade present.

Then I'd worried if the leaks that seemed to follow me everywhere might show up at a science fair.

But we'd fixed the leaks. And I'd started looking forward to the fair again.

Now it might not happen. Served me right.

When Mr. Divner turned off the lights so Aja and her partner could do their presentation, everyone quieted. Aja had slides and graphics. Her partner dissected a diaper and explained the layers. Lots of gross stuff.

Pendra and I had drawings on my carefully lettered poster, slides, and the lampwork glass. It would be all right. Not everyone had to present the same way.

"Okay, Eleanor, Pendra. You're ready?"

We both nodded. Mr. Divner waved us up to the front of the room. I propped the poster up while Pendra and Mr. Divner put on safety glasses and took the classroom's small butane torch from the supply closet.

Everyone waited, shifting in their seats and whispering. The poster fell down and I propped it back up, embarrassed.

Can't do anything right. Anassa's voice. My father's. But I wasn't going to listen today. I tugged at my sleeves and studied my shoes until I was ready to look at everyone again.

Pendra returned. "Ready for some magic?" I smiled broadly and my classmates quieted, some starting to smile back.

Mr. Divner nodded encouragement. And Pendra, beside me, glowed in front of the class. When she started talking, I relaxed. We'd practiced. This would be fine.

"Glass can be a lot of things," she began. "Brittle, hard, molten. It takes a ton of sand—tiny pieces of quartz—plus limestone and soda ash and a bunch of heat to make it." She held up bags of each from her father's lab.

The class door opened. Mrs. Sarti peeked in. Pendra blushed hard. But Mrs. Sarti handed a note to Mr. Divner and left.

He read it while we waited, standing in front of the class, then he frowned and wound a hand through the air. "Keep going." But the way he looked at me, I could tell it was trouble.

Please don't let it be Mike again. She'd promised.

Pendra elbowed me. My turn. I tried to focus.

I lifted the piece of lampwork from where I'd put it on the desk. "Molten glass needs to be heated up to two thousand degrees, which we can't do. But lampwork behaves nearly the same way. It's a good way to show you why there have been debates about glass being a liquid or a solid for a long time."

Mr. Divner had cleared off an area just for us, near his desk, and put a fireproof mat down. He lit the torch and turned it so that the tip of flame flickered orange and blue.

I put on safety goggles, too, and I got out protective mitts . . . oven mitts, really. Blue, with a compass rose on each one.

I pointed my mitted hand where I wanted Mr. Divner to put the heat.

When the orange flame hit the lampwork and made it glow, it softened and flowed until it bent into a new shape.

When Mr. Divner pulled the heat away, the lampwork grew solid again.

We did it four more times until the glass straw was bent into a rosette. "From solid to liquid and back again."

Once I got into the flow of the words, I had a really good time. It was like telling a story to Mike. The class was listening. The whispering had stopped. No one coughed or made a joke.

Pendra picked up where I'd left off. "Glass molecules aren't organized like other solids," she said. "They don't repeat regularly like diamonds or wood molecules. Regular structures make most things resistant to change. Especially between liquid and solid states. But the rules for glass are different."

I remembered the glass shard flowing into the crack in the tunnel. Sometimes the rules were *very* different.

Pendra nudged me again. "It's a bit like magic, right, Eleanor?"

My turn. Almost done. "Right!" She'd made me promise to keep that in and now it made me laugh. "Except when it's not. Glass's structure is just more irregular than other solids." I pointed at one of my sketches. "But it's not as varied as a liquid. That's why some people think of glass as neither a liquid nor a solid. It's something in between. One of the terms for that in-betweenness is *amorphous*—which means having little or no form. Like a dream, sort of. Real and not real at the same time. Liquid and solid."

Pendra held up the cooled glass rosette. The class applauded. Mr. Divner gave us both the thumbs-up. Something inside my chest uncoiled. I'd done a thing right. I beamed at Pendra and she grinned back. Not *I*. *We'd* done it.

As I went back to my seat, I looked out at the meadow and the parking lot just beyond the windows. I saw a dark truck and a blue sedan parked side by side. Moments later, Momma walked past the science lab windows and up to the main entrance. Her clothes and makeup were perfect. Her heels went *click, click, click* on the sidewalk beneath the echoing awning.

Poppa followed, wearing a sweatshirt from his development company, looking as if he'd been fished out of a meeting. Neither looked happy.

Oh no. What had Mike done now?

The class bell rang, and Mr. Divner stopped me as I headed out the door. "Eleanor, you'll need to go to the guidance office."

The lampwork glass rosette cooled in my hand.

Nothing was ever enough.

+++

With Momma, Poppa, Mrs. Sarti, and Assistant Principal Wunner all crammed into Mrs. Sarti's office, there was barely room for me.

When I entered, I sat in the only chair left, next to the desk. I didn't see Mike. My mouth was dry as sand.

"Eleanor," Mrs. Sarti began, "the contact form for families . . ."

Oh. This wasn't about Mike making trouble.

This was about me.

I focused on Mrs. Sarti's mouth, not her eyes. Her lips formed words like "administrative issue" and "suspension."

I absolutely didn't look at Poppa, though I could hear him breathing.

Mrs. Sarti kept talking. I could see the small hairs on her cheeks. ". . . We've had students adjust—or try to adjust—the form. Forge signatures. You name it."

I held my breath. I was going to be sent away for sure.

"But Eleanor's one of our best students," she finally said. "And I wanted to see if we could get this straightened out. It looks like one of you may have filled out the form incorrectly. These numbers are different from the community directory."

Mrs. Sarti opened a manila folder and pulled out a sheet of paper. Handed it to Poppa. "Is this your signature?"

Outside a flock of birds landed in a tree. They were noisy and the tree seemed to blur with all the feathers. When the tree settled down, I could no longer distinguish leaves from wings.

Poppa's jaw clenched. He looked at the form as if he'd never seen it before. In truth, he hadn't. I'd magicked it. Or tried to.

My spells never worked. Not really.

"Of course it's my signature," he said. I tried to keep my face as expressionless as possible, but my chest tightened around my breath. There would be so many consequences.

"And yours?" Mrs. Sarti passed Momma the form.

"Yes, this was clumsy of me." Momma blinked slowly. Her ear still had the Band-Aid on it, but the bandage was flesh colored. It was hard to tell what had happened, but I could still hear *Damn you, Eleanor.* There wasn't any bandage for that.

Momma kept talking. Her fingers were wrapped tight around her chair's armrests. "There are so many forms at the start of the year, things get confused. I'm sorry you had trouble reaching us. It won't happen again." Her smile was a perfect composite of embarrassment and dizzy overworked mom.

I almost admired her magic, but I didn't feel the same kind of relief I'd felt when Gran said she'd help. I knew there would be a price for this too.

"We were lucky to be able to reach Eleanor and Mike's grandmother, who could smooth everything out." At Mrs. Sarti's words, Poppa turned a sharp intake of breath into a sneeze. "And we're glad to have the third number on file. But if you'll correct the form and give us more than two points of contact now, I would appreciate it. For emergencies."

There was no call sheet I could use for what was going to happen at home tonight. I felt sick.

Poppa hadn't said anything since *Of course*.

At the moment, his eyes were focused on Mrs. Sarti's desk. His hand jumped on his knee like he wanted to knock things off the top. Mrs. Sarti and the assistant principal couldn't see it.

But I could.

The class change bell rang, and Mrs. Sarti relaxed. "That's really all then. As long as you're doing all right, Eleanor? You've seemed a little scattered lately."

I beamed. I knew the answer to this. "Everything's fine, Mrs. Sarti. I just need to get to math."

Poppa's hand stopped jumping. Momma relaxed her grip on the arm of her chair.

Mrs. Sarti smiled thinly, but she nodded. "I'll write you a pass."

I smiled right back. My mouth closed like a trap around my tongue before I could say more.

This time, even with all the coming consequences, I felt like I'd worked real house magic. Maybe I'd fixed things enough to avoid too much trouble. For a moment, I hoped.

But on the way out, Poppa leaned close. "You come straight home. Be on your best behavior. Your gran will be there. Do not make trouble." The way Momma looked at me, I knew he meant it. I shivered.

I'd have been better off staying on the river with Anassa.

+++

Still, we didn't go right home, Mike and I.

On the bus, I sat in the second-row seat, alone. Pendra had gone with Aja to see the soccer game. "Us against Cardinal Bishop Academy," Aja had said, her eyes sparkling. "My brothers are playing. Fields are soaked, they're going to be a mess." She sounded like she couldn't wait.

I would have loved to go, but I didn't dare. I didn't want to jeopardize being able to go to the sleepover any more than I already had.

"See you tonight!" I called. *Hopefully.*

In my ears, I heard the beat of hooves, the crash of waves. But we'd fixed the river. The sounds were just the rain on the school's roof.

"See you tonight then! You and Mike!" Pendra sounded like she couldn't wait, either, though she'd already turned toward the fields.

"You know it!" I smiled as brightly as I could. Maybe saying so would make it happen.

The bus pulled away and I watched the school disappear out the window. The rain pocked the glass. And I sat alone until the elementary school, when Mike and Kalliope got on, and they sat behind me.

Kalliope kicked the back of my seat the whole way home. I said nothing. When we finally got dropped off, it had mostly stopped raining.

Mike and I walked out on the public dock, far from the house but close enough to see when Poppa came home. We sat in the drizzle, our feet hanging over the edge. The water looked gray and churned up. We couldn't see the riverbed.

"They know," I told her. "That I switched the contact numbers. They know about Gran."

Mike stared at me. Then she leaned her head on my shoulder, her curls tickling my chin. My fleece jacket felt warm where her head was. The wind chapped my cheeks and hands. I leaned back.

"It will be okay," I whispered. "I promise."

"If we get a witch ball, will everything be better?" she whispered back.

The river was very high, breaking in big splashes against the dock. "Maybe someday."

"What happens if we don't go back?" Mike said.

I couldn't tell if she meant back home or to the dream river. I didn't answer. I needed to think.

"What happens if we live under the bed?" she added.

I tried to think about the way families worked. About apologies and being sent away. About how stories held things together but lying pulled them apart.

"Eleanor, what happens . . ."

"Shhhh."

It was hard work, thinking with Mike thinking too.

The sky darkened more and the river kicked against the dock, rocking us.

A shadow passed overhead, enormous wings, long stick legs trailing the air behind. I didn't look up.

When the bird circled and landed on the shore, then walked out to the edge of the shallows, I still didn't look at it. *You've seen what the Heron does with broken dreams. It will use you up and throw you away.*

I threw a mussel shell at this heron, without looking.

"Once upon a time," Mike whispered.

"Once upon a time, there were two girls who went home and faced consequences." I pushed myself to my feet.

The heron levered its body close to the water, its neck flexed like a snake. The shadow of it on the gray waves looked like ripples. A drop of rain splattered my neck. The bird gave no sign of having heard me.

Brushing my jeans off, I waited for Mike to stand. Poppa's car was still not in the driveway. But as we crossed from the public dock to the house, Momma came out the front door. "Girls, to your rooms. I have to cook. You're soaked. And you have thinking to do."

Thinking was all *we were allowed to do.*

We took our shoes off outside the door, then came in. The foyer sparkled already. But there was a bucket on the floor. The ceiling of the landing was dark and the drywall was starting to bubble. Momma caught us looking. "It's everywhere." She sighed. "And it's making your father very stressed. You should have thought of that before the trouble at the school."

We didn't look at the ceiling or each other anymore. But oh, I wanted to run. Where, I didn't know.

Mike scuffed her feet all the way down the hall, leaving drag marks. I went into the bathroom and soaked a washcloth, then pressed it to my face. Mike, in her room, whimpered. Then she slammed her door and locked it.

"What is it? What happened?" I whispered.

Were there leaks in her room now too?

Mike didn't answer. Poppa's truck's brakes squealed on the driveway.

I turned on my heel and walked back through the shared bathroom, then into my room. I closed my eyes, but I knew what the room would look like when I got there. Even without looking.

I let it hurt for a minute. Then I opened my eyes.

My room was neat as a pin.

The dolls were in their boxes in a row against the wall. The drawing pads were stacked up, the pencils put away. My nightstand had been cleared.

That was the worst part. The table was empty. So were my shelves.

All my books. Gone.

Consequences.

House magic took things away too. Especially when the rules were broken. Now I understood Mike's reaction. On my desk, there was a brochure for a school in Connecticut, where everyone wore dark blue uniforms.

I crawled under my bed. Nothing remained there either, except a single pillow. I put my head on it and listened to Momma and Poppa talk downstairs. Their voices echoed up through the floor.

"I told you, there's no reason to send either of them away, Simon. They're in their rooms. They've been punished," Momma said. "We'll tell them we expect better."

"They have no respect. No discipline," Poppa countered. "Eleanor especially. I don't have time to deal with the disobedience. The lies."

Today, I wanted to be sent away almost as much as Poppa wanted me to go.

But then Mike would be alone. I didn't want that.

The carpet was rough on my cheek. The bed frame felt like a cage, not a shelter.

"Don't cry," I whispered. "Don't you do that again, ever." My cheeks were summer-sand hot.

A cell phone rang. A soft pulse like waves through the floor.

Poppa's hello loud in comparison. Then a long silence. Finally, "Thank you. I'll fix it. Of course!" Then a crash.

"Your phone!" Momma said. "How will you—"

"The bank wants more paperwork. The seller's talking about backing out of the deal. We need more time. Dammit." He began pacing and didn't stop.

"You need to calm down before my mother gets here," Momma said. "She can help."

I held my breath for the entire silence that followed—*ten-nine-eight-seven-six-five-four-three*—until Poppa's office door slammed. *Two-one.*

Tears cut tracks down my cheeks and dampened the carpet below me. I had never been so mad at myself. Another rule, broken.

The bells on the bed skirt jangled softly and Mike crawled under the bed too. "My stuffed animals are gone," she whispered. "I don't know what else."

Behind her, the light in my room was dimming, too early. The storm was getting worse.

I held out my arms and Mike crawled into them. "We'll get them back. I promise." Then: "Someday."

CHAPTER

DINNER RULES

THIRTEEN

For a long time, beneath the bed, I hoped the river would come and swallow us both. But it didn't. The carpet stayed dry. The light didn't return.

So we gathered ourselves up and crawled out from under the bed, still damp from the rain. We smelled a little like brine.

I leaned my ear close to the air vent. Below, two voices in the kitchen, both female. Taut like plucked strings.

Motion out the window: A yellow cab pulled away from the driveway.

Gran had arrived.

"Mike, hurry. She's here." Mike's hair stuck up at angles, but she brushed off her T-shirt and jeans while I tried to calm her hair.

She paced while I pulled a dry dress over my head.

"Eleanor! Mike!" Momma called up the stairs with a lilt.

I couldn't do anything about our wet hair or puffy faces, but I thought we looked pretty good, given everything. We walked down the hall together, past the empty wall, the yellow suncatcher.

Momma waited, tense, at the bottom of the stairs. "Where have you been?" she asked. Then she whispered as I passed, "I needed things to be perfect."

I nodded. "I'm sorry, Momma. We lost track of time. Homework."

But Gran had overheard. She reached and gathered us until Mike and I were pressed tight in her arms. "This is all the perfect I need, Moira." I could feel her smiling over my head. Had Momma not told her anything?

"They look like they've been playing in the riverbed," Momma protested.

My face grew hot. How I wished that were true. When we pulled away, Gran's dress had two damp marks.

Momma's face reddened. "I'm so sorry."

"It's quite all right. We're old friends now." Gran winked at us. My throat unclenched, making it easier to breathe. But Momma looked even more uncomfortable. *You had to ruin everything.*

Down the hallway, the space around Poppa's office had grown so quiet, it smothered any small sounds near it. Mike stood as close to me as she could without actually touching me.

I tried to count to ten for calm. Said a spell: *Please don't let me break any rules.* There were so many ways this could go badly. Old ways and new ones.

When I had a chance as Gran and Momma walked into the dining room, I looked up at the landing ceiling. The water spot hadn't dried or faded.

Nothing was right.

+++

Momma and I brought dinner out—a perfect lasagna that came out of the oven at the exact right time. A green salad. We sat, me and Mike on either side of Gran, then Poppa and Momma on either side of us at the round oak table. I waited for someone to say something.

Poppa's eyes were darker than dark, shadowed by his brows. Finally, he lifted his water glass and toasted Gran. "The property is doing really well. We are looking to expand the development. Growing what you gave us." But his hand clenched at his side and he saw me notice. He stuck his hand in his pocket. His nostrils flared.

And then he began talking. All the quiet he'd held in earlier came out as words. They were calmer words than that afternoon's, certainly. I wasn't surprised by that. Poppa was always nice to people outside the house. He spoke about the land purchase, about the properties he'd invested in downtown. About the opportunities created by the highway and the river. "Good commuting from here. Why the area's so popular. Imagine it's only going to get better."

Momma nodded and started to serve everyone dinner. Gran lifted a finger to ask a question. But Poppa was on a roll. It didn't really matter what he spoke about—though he was carefully avoiding the urgency with the bank, and the leaks. What mattered was that he didn't stop. He didn't ask questions. He didn't pause. "The land permit's tied up with the sale, very complex. Still, we know what we're doing now. If we didn't, there would be a whole lot of trouble." He slapped the table. "Instead, we're creating a legacy for the girls."

"Yes, Simon, I . . ." Gran said.

I crossed my ankles and then wrapped one foot almost back around again, twisting the part of me hidden by the table into a tense snake. *Please don't hate us.*

But Poppa hadn't stopped speaking. His enthusiasm for the project bubbled over.

Gran sat up straighter as the talking went on. Mike slouched until I untangled my feet enough to kick her ankle, gently. We knew how this kind of dinner went. We had to pay attention just in case there were questions. To show respect.

Usually, eventually, he'd have to pause for water. That would give Momma a chance to shift the conversation. The table would relax.

I half hoped he'd eat some dinner soon. The cheese was congealing over Momma's lasagna, but it still smelled delicious. If he didn't eat, we really couldn't start either. Mike's stomach growled.

But if he stopped, Gran might bring up the call from school or our visit to her apartment. Or anything else that might bring trouble. Eating seemed optimistic. I didn't really know if I'd be able to swallow my dinner anyway.

On he went. As I watched him, I realized with a sinking feeling that I talked with a similar speed when I was nervous. I'd almost done it in class during our presentation. Was Poppa nervous?

Finally Gran got up and went to the kitchen. She returned with a plate of cookies—thick chocolate icing on top of vanilla wafers. Not like ones Momma made or from the bakery Poppa went to. Mike and I looked at each other, confused. Adults were hard math sometimes, and we hadn't eaten dinner yet.

"I bought these downtown. Would you like one, Simon?" She held out the plate.

Miraculously, Poppa took one and popped the whole thing in his mouth. He chewed. And chewed.

Gran smiled.

Momma breathed, "How was your afternoon, girls? Mom? What's new?"

I took a bite of lasagna and chewed, staring at the tablecloth. *Please don't mention the meeting, Momma.*

"Pretty good." Mike eyed the cookies but Momma shook her head. "We're going on a field trip up the Sassafras. I'm going to try to find another witch ball to replace the broken one."

I kicked her under the table. She was going to get a bruise if she kept talking.

The minute I thought that, I felt worse than ever.

But it was too late. Gran turned to her, eyebrows raised. "You were asking about those the other week too."

Was that it? Maybe our opening to ask Gran later about the river and the agreement, once Poppa had left the table? I wanted to hug Mike. She was brilliant.

"Girls," Momma cautioned. She shook her head. "They're suddenly very interested in glass, of all things."

But Gran kept talking too. "What happened to the fishing float I left here? The really old one? It was an heirloom." She looked at Poppa strangely. "Valuable."

Momma coughed. "More lasagna, anyone?" She hadn't touched hers yet. No one had, except me, and that bite was stuck somewhere high in my throat. It was the worst feeling.

Dad still chewed the cookie, but his face had grown tighter, his brows lower. He finally swallowed, took a noisy gulp of water, and smiled. "Interesting."

"The cookie? They're Bergers. An old favorite of Moira's," Gran said. She smiled. Poppa didn't. "I'm interested in what the girls were saying."

"And you've heard it. Pass the salt."

If Gran hadn't been there, this would have been when Mike and I found a way to excuse ourselves. But Gran *was* here. I knew there'd been a fight between her and Momma, and then she'd stayed away. I didn't want her to stay away. And I didn't want to leave her at the table.

Mike passed the salt. Poppa shook it all over his dinner, as if to teach it something.

"Simon, please." Red splotches colored Momma's face and neck.

"We're glad you could come." He didn't look up when he spoke. Just lifted his fork to his mouth and pointedly took a bite as he finished his sentence.

I tried to swallow. What would Gran say?

She didn't look at us, or Momma. She smiled placidly at Poppa. "Moira seemed open to me spending more time with the girls. I enjoyed seeing them last weekend."

Poppa paused, then said, "Moira could have just sent the paperwork. I think you're really up here to see how the property is doing. Our investments. Asking about that ridiculous fishing float is just a distraction. The property is doing well. We'll take good care of the house. You can relax, sign the property over if you want, or don't and go right back to Alexandria."

"Poppa, she's not distrac—" I started, my voice shaking like I was mad. And I was, a little. But Momma put a hand on my shoulder and squeezed. Hard. I closed my mouth.

Gran's jaw worked and she closed her eyes for the barest moment. Almost as if she was counting to ten. Then she opened her eyes and looked at the ceiling, near where the water stain was the barest shadow. "I can see that, Simon. But I was also invited."

Poppa stood up, his dinner barely eaten. "The cookies were delicious."

He stayed standing, until Momma rose too. Gran looked equal parts angry and unsettled. Mike and I watched her, trying to hold her with our gazes. *Don't leave. Don't sign.*

But Gran held her seat. She turned back to us, trapped in our chairs, and left Poppa standing. "That sounds like a good field trip, Mike. When is it?"

Mike's mouth worked like a fish until sound came out. "Two weeks."

"Ah! I'll be traveling. You must write me how it is."

Poppa was trapped. He had to decide whether to sit down again, or leave. His dinner cooled on the table, one bite eaten. I couldn't take my eyes off of it. Couldn't eat my own.

Finally, he stomped away from the table and Momma, released like a string had been cut, sat down again. She frowned at Gran. My mouth ached from smiling. Mike's eyes were shining. More arguments. Just like before. But very different now.

Gran's face gave nothing away. She hadn't left, though.

It was Momma who was furious. She looked at the three of us like we were all conspiring. Suddenly, my lasagna became fascinating.

"I think this was a mistake," Momma said.

Gran frowned. "Moira, I would like to help. If there's any way other than the house."

Momma's smile hardened as she looked at Poppa's office door. "We are fine, Mom. Everything is fine."

After a few long minutes of silence where Mike and I picked at our food but didn't eat it, wet tires squealed on the drive outside. A horn honked. Gran, still seated, blinked.

Poppa's door opened. He walked through the kitchen and into the dining room. "I called you a cab to take you back to the train before the weather gets too much worse."

"She just got here!" Mike protested. She reached out and grabbed Gran's sleeve.

Gran slowly unwound Mike's fingers. "Sometimes it's best," she said. She didn't say what was best. "Walk me to the door?" She nodded at me too and I was suddenly freed from my chair as if by magic.

Momma hadn't said anything about the school forms I had forged or the meeting at school. And Gran had somehow skirted all the house rules. But the house was expelling her anyway.

Mike and I walked with her to the hall to get her coat. I wanted to tell her I would remember what she did and said at the dinner always.

"I'm sorry," I whispered instead. "I didn't mean to sound so angry."

Gran squinted at me. "Angry?"

"She gets mad like Poppa a lot," Mike said helpfully. I couldn't look at either of them.

Gran knelt so she was at eye level. "That wasn't angry, Mike, and Eleanor's not at all like your poppa. You didn't do anything wrong. Either of you."

I wanted to believe her. I wanted Mike to believe her too. But I didn't want to risk saying anything that could break the magic of what she'd said. I smiled. "I can get your coat."

"Your interest in the witch ball," she whispered as I opened the closet door. "And your science project on glass. Are they related?"

She'd called it a witch ball this time. Not a fishing float. I nodded. "A little. I always liked it. Glass is a bit magical." Was that enough? Would she say something now?

Mike leaned closer, watching Gran carefully.

Gran laughed, a soft, dusty sound. "I think it's magic, too. And the floats—they catch the eye, don't they? I used to have such dreams." Her voice drifted off as she looked back at the dining room.

Mike's mouth hung open. Dreams. But she didn't remember? A wave of disappointment swept over me.

Did adults really not remember the river? The Heron had said our family had kept the agreement for generations. Gran had to remember something.

To keep her from noticing my worry, I reached into the closet for her coat. The air inside felt damp. A sleeve of her coat also. I looked and saw a new damp patch on the wall. Another leak. In a new spot. I bit my lip to keep from groaning.

We hadn't fixed anything. And Gran didn't remember.

But Mike wouldn't give up. She nudged me. So I couldn't give up either. "What kind of dreams, Gran?"

"Oh," she chuckled. "Good dreams. Nightmares. All tangled up together. We had a story about a fisherman that my mother used to tell, back when the family still worked the river, and some of the bay too. But it's all very foggy now. Except when I draw and paint." She reached into her coat as I held it out to her. Pulled two envelopes from a pocket. Pressed them into my hands. "For you two. My phone numbers besides the house."

The floor creaked. Poppa and Momma came into the hall together. Gran handed Momma a thick envelope. To my surprise, Poppa smiled broadly when Momma took it. She rubbed the paper between her fingers.

I slid my envelope and Mike's into my skirt pocket.

Gran smiled again at both of us. Mike and I smiled too. Gran spoke first. "I'd like to have the girls down to stay with me for a weekend. They can take the train. Especially if you need a break, I could help."

A visit to Gran's, as soon as possible. Yes. If we could avoid getting stuck on the other side of the river. She could help us find a new witch ball.

Poppa's frustration with Gran, his nerves, faded away as he held the envelope. "Where is your next adventure?"

"Venice," she said. "Next week."

I felt the lightness ebb from the room. When Gran left, we'd probably be in trouble either here or on the river, unless she were nearby. I asked the question. "For how long?"

Gran's smile faded. "Two weeks. An artists' workshop. Part of the fellowship. There will be some glassblowing, Eleanor. I'll tell you about it. And I'll keep an eye out for more fishing floats. The real ones. Not the store ones."

But Poppa made an *Oh, of course* gesture as my heart fell.

Momma's face darkened. "Why tell them now, then? Why get their hopes up and then go away?"

"I hadn't thought that it needed to be sooner," Gran said.

I hoped we didn't need anything sooner.

Momma seemed to be about to say something, but she didn't know how to. Her mouth opened and closed. Outside, the cab honked again.

Gran's raincoat was red with big flowers on it. She slipped on a pair of boots and tucked her shoes in her purse. I took her paper-soft hand and tried to think of something important to say that wouldn't break house rules.

"Gran," I whispered. "What happens if there are no more witch balls?"

"Don't you start, Eleanor," Poppa said. "It's just a bauble."

But Gran's face flickered worry and concern. Then she smiled. "Then we make more. They're good for catching more than just fish."

Momma bit her lip and her eyes softened, as if she was trying to reach something far away.

"Moira!" Poppa said, tugging her hand, hard, like he would one of us. Drawing her back.

Momma's face hardened. "Goodbye, Mom," she said. She patted her mother on the shoulder. "Thank you for this."

"We'll try again sometime," Gran said without looking at Poppa.

Momma nodded. "Say goodbye for now, girls."

We hugged Gran as if we might not see her again. I smiled as brightly as I could, hoping that's what Gran would remember, not the awful, uneaten dinner, but us, and her promise. Mike followed my lead.

"You're sure you're all right?" Gran whispered to us before she let us go.

What would she do if I said that we weren't? That we were frightened? That there was a river in our bedroom and nightmares chasing us?

What if she could read my mind, like Anassa claimed she could? I wished somehow she would. But then she would see how angry I really was. How angry everyone was.

Adults were unpredictable.

And there was no right answer. Only something in between right and wrong.

"We are fine, like I said," Momma answered for us. She shut the closet door without noticing the new leak, then took Mike's hand and pulled her out of Gran's reach. I followed my sister's steps. Momma put her arms around both of our shoulders. "All fine."

"Call me if you need anything," Gran said. "Like I said." She looked at Poppa one more time and shook her head. "Moira. Please."

"Thank you, Mom, for coming all the way up when you didn't have to," Momma said. "We are fine." She held the door open and watched Gran leave.

Mike and I waved silently from the frame of the doorway as the taxi pulled away.

When she was gone, Momma turned to us, her face composed and calm. Poppa held out his hand for the envelopes Gran had given us. "I'll keep those safe for you."

I started to scowl and quickly pulled myself together. "I thought I could keep them." *In my room, in my pillow.*

Momma pulled the envelopes from my hands. "I'll keep them," she said. I could feel where the paper had been.

Poppa grumbled but didn't argue with her.

Finally, Momma said, "Your behavior before and at dinner was not appropriate, no matter what Gran said. But the trouble with the phone numbers? That's far worse." She pursed her lips, not waiting for me to speak. "You've made things very difficult. Put added pressure on everyone at exactly the wrong time. Your behavior this afternoon, also. You're grounded for the weekend. Both of you. So you can think about how you can do better."

No. That was extreme. Trapped in the house for the weekend.

For the sleepover.

I looked at Momma, pleading. But she shook her head.

Mike squeezed my fingers as Poppa, returning to his office, said, "You should have thought about consequences before."

+++

In the small echo of our bathroom, Mike and I brushed our teeth side by side.

Grounded. It had happened before, but not when I'd wanted to be far from home so badly.

Mike padded to her room. I washed the salt off my cheeks before I went back downstairs again.

Momma sat at the dining room table, her head in her hands. For a moment, I watched her quietly. So quietly that she jumped when I moved and the floor creaked.

She put her hand over her mouth. "Eleanor, you scared me." Angry.

"So sorry, Momma." I leaned my hands on the table. I was sorry. For everything.

She looked at me, at eye level. Put a hand over mine. Her fingers felt warm, and her pulse beat fast, like a bird's. "It will be all right," Momma said. "The bank is working with us. The deal will go through, and your father's crew is fixing the houses that need repairs. I'm sorry about Gran, though. I wish . . ." Her voice trailed off. "She's just unpredictable."

That wasn't it at all. I started to argue but remembered what happened the last time. Momma looked at me expectantly, waiting for me to say something. So I did. "The fishing float was valuable, right? Is it magic?"

I was taking a risk. I knew it.

She tilted her head. "Eleanor, it was just a bauble. Like your father said. Don't fill Mike's head with any more stories, please."

"I'm not." *A lie.* "But stories help. Tell me a story about the witch ball."

"I've heard enough about that thing. It was something I kept long ago—I don't even know why, really. And now it's broken and it doesn't matter anymore."

It does matter. It matters more than anything.

But arguing with Momma risked my being grounded for longer, or worse. The brochure on my desk was a clear consequence.

"I need you to be more helpful, Eleanor. I have enough to manage without you and your sister making up stories and phone numbers and bringing trouble." She said it like she was torn between being angry and some other thing.

I swallowed my questions. My arguments. "I will, Momma." I paused. "I promise. But the sleepover. We've been planning it for weeks. Pendra's waiting."

"I'm sorry, that's out of the question. Not with everything that's happened." All the rules I'd broken, she meant.

She patted my hand. “It’s going to be all right. We’ll make it all right, I promise.” She smiled at me, finally. “Just work with me, okay?”

Her face was creased with lines of exhaustion. I wanted to hug her. So I did. She stiffened for a minute, then hugged me back, holding on for longer than usual. I wanted this Momma so much.

Much more than the one who said, *Damn you*.

“I’m sorry, Momma.” I couldn’t say it enough.

“That’s my girl,” she said. “Go on up to your room.”

I climbed the stairs slowly. Ignored the awful yellow suncatcher. Walked past the wall of square shadows where there had once been so many photographs. I put my hand where the others had been. Great-Gran with Gran and Momma. A bunch of men with beards by a wagon. A crowd around the huge arched husk of a whale, down near Cape May, where Gran had gone as a child. Photos older than that. A cottage by the river. Five young girls seated in a low, wooden boat. Every one of them a sailor, until Momma.

I touched the photo of Momma and Gran again. They’d stood side by side, the dock rickety even then in the background. No other houses, just the farm, and a dark horse pacing the field.

The outlines of the missing photos hid so many secrets. I tried to remember if there were any photos of the fishing nets, or the floats.

No quest is ever that easy, Eleanor. Pendra would understand. But Pendra was having a birthday sleepover with Aja and not me and not Mike because we weren't allowed to go.

In my room, my sleeping bag sat at the end of the bed, waiting like a promise. In Mike's room, she'd unfurled hers and added it to her nest of blankets. She'd stuffed more blankets below her bed.

"Why?" I asked, pointing.

"So nothing can get out from under there."

I tucked her in, then walked toward my room, hands in my pockets, pressing my fingertips to the remaining glass chips. The last pieces of the witch ball. It hadn't been magicked back and the photos hadn't either. I touched the bare wall where the pictures had been.

House magic wasn't working any longer.

I heard her door squeak and turned to see Mike peering from her room.

"Stay in bed. I'll come get you later," I hissed. "The leaks aren't fixed. We have to find a new witch ball instead, or help fix the river another way." Like the Heron had said. I hadn't wanted to listen. "But not yet."

Mike pulled back into the shadow of her room until only her profile showed beside the doorframe. "I don't want to go. I don't want to get in any more trouble or get trapped on the river."

Me neither, Mike. "I know. You can stay here. I'll go."

I knew who had a witch ball—Anassa. I could try to get that first.

Mike darted from the room and stood on her toes, getting her face as close to mine as she could. She held both my sleeves and whispered, "No. No, no. I don't want you to go either. Neither of us. If you go, what if you don't come back?" Her eyes went wide and she clutched my hand. Wove her fingers through mine. "Stay."

The house was quiet. Listening. "Go back to bed, Mike," I murmured. "I'll see you in the morning. I promise."

When she didn't budge, I pushed her gently. "Go."

I watched her retreat into her room. Footie pajamas. Curls wild.

Her door squeaked closed again and I leaned against the wall and listened to my heart beat slow in my ears.

A creak on the stairs. From the landing, Poppa's anger-muted voice. "Eleanor. Why are you keeping your sister up? And what did you say to your mother? She's very upset, especially that you keep bringing up that glass ball."

I turned for my room. I didn't want to fight with him, and he was fishing for a fight. The first step would be for me to disagree with him. I wasn't going to do it.

I heard his shoes on the carpet, his hand caught my shoulder. "Always so innocent. *Whatever did* I *do?* You know well and good this is your fault. Sneaking around. Lying. Being manipulative. Bringing trouble."

He didn't know the half of it. But I didn't answer. Sometimes it was better not to.

"You gave your friend's mother more reason to worry about us. Your grandmother's nosing around too. You interrupt. You provoke. I expect you're proud of yourself."

I couldn't meet his eyes. He wasn't right, was he? I'd tried so hard to fix things. Furious tears burned my eyes. I would not start a fight.

He saw my weakness. "We'll send you away, and you'll deserve it." Then he smiled, one corner of his mouth turning up. This made me angrier.

Spells and anger. I wasn't very good at either.

"Maybe *you're* the one who should go away," I said.

Maybe the ravens would come and carry him off. The nightmares.

Maybe someday our real parents will come. Maybe Mike and I could stay together. That's what I meant.

But he heard it differently.

"Who would people believe? You?" He laughed.

Downstairs all was quiet. Momma didn't say, *Simon, stop.* He continued. "*They'd* split you and Mary up. Whatever happens then, *you'll* deserve every bit of it. Ungrateful garbage. Did you think your gran would save you? No one's ever tried to save you."

Spit struck my cheek. Poppa's hand gripped my shoulder harder. I couldn't shake free. I let myself hang there, at the end of his grip. But I held his gaze now. I didn't look away.

He stared at me for a moment, his mouth tight around words he wanted to yell. If I moved, if I said anything, he would strike. Instead we watched each other, eyes unblinking. Then he swung me hard against the wall anyway. "Who would even bother trying."

I slumped there, below the shadow of a broken frame. Closed my eyes against the coming blow. I tried to force myself to relax. Things hurt less that way.

But the blow never came.

Down the hall, a door slammed.

I opened my eyes to shut doors all along the empty hall.

I didn't want to get trapped on the river. I didn't want to stay here. I didn't want to do what the Heron wanted me to do. I wanted everything to be fine and normal, for just one night. Instead, nothing was normal.

In my room, I ran my fingers over the rolled sleeping bag, then stuffed it into my backpack. Already, a tendril of the river reached out from beneath the bed skirt.

I dropped a pillow on it.

Mike was safe in her room; it was my room that had a river problem. She was safer tucked in her own bed than hiding somewhere dark, telling stories.

Lifting my comforter, I punched two pillows into what I thought I'd look like sleeping on my side.

Maybe if I left, the river would leave everyone alone. Even for just one night.

Maybe I could celebrate my birthday, and Pendra's too, instead of worrying about my family, for once.

Maybe I could just pretend everything was normal and it would be.

I leaned on the wall by my door until Momma climbed the stairs. When their bedroom door clicked shut again, I snuck down the dark stairwell, moving through the house like a shadow.

The basement hatch door tried to squeak on its hinges, but I only opened it a crack and slid through, scraping my arm and my backpack on its edge.

The wind pushed against me as I shoved my way out of my house and toward the river. The ground there was marshy and slick, but it wasn't pinpointed by streetlights like the driveway and the road.

One of my sneakers got stuck in the mud, but I pulled it free. The air cooled as I climbed the hill all the way up, past two houses, to where the bluff began near Pendra's house. Her lights were still on, and the downstairs lights too.

The sleepover was only getting going, probably.

I wiped my eyes with my sleeve. Took a deep breath and practiced saying, "Hi!" with a smile in the dark until I could do it without my voice cracking.

I was just going to be a little late, that was all.

CHAPTER FOURTEEN

SLEEPOVER RULES

In the Sartis' foyer, a bucket slowly plinked as water leaked from the ceiling.

The cracks still weren't fixed here.

I shucked my damp jacket and pulled my backpack back onto my shoulder. Tonight I wasn't going to think about the river.

Pendra's older brother Mo leaned on the door, texting. He'd let me in without a word. The family golden retriever barked on the stairs and then lurched forward to lick my hand.

"Eleanor! Hi!" Mrs. Sarti stuck her head into the hallway from the living room. "Sorry about the mess—all this rain!" She waved her hand. "The girls are upstairs. Is Mike coming?"

I shook my head. "Our grandmother came for dinner. Mike decided to stay home." I wasn't lying, not exactly.

Still, I felt the tug of wanting to be home, in my bed. And never wanting to go home again. *Garbage.* That was me.

I tried not to get trapped in the foyer with Mrs. Sarti. I didn't want to talk with her about this or anything right now. Especially not about how things were at home. Or Mike.

"Oh! How wonderful. Your grandmother seems lovely," Mrs. Sarti said. "I'd love to meet her in person."

Too bad she's going to Venice, Mrs. Sarti. "I'll let her know!"

I stopped, looking up the stairs, caught suddenly between here and there. Only now that I stood inside Pendra's house did I realize I hadn't brought her present.

"Go on," Mrs. Sarti said. "They're watching a movie."

The rules for sleepovers, Pendra had said back when we'd first planned this, were simple: No sleeping, lots of sugar. Presents.

I'd been invited to sleepovers, but I'd always had a reason to stay home. And I'd laughed at her rules. Everyone knew them.

Now I'd already broken one.

At the top of the stairs, I turned right and heard laughter coming from Pendra's room. They were watching an old movie, one with robots and a dog. Aja had claimed one of Pendra's two beds with her purple sleeping bag and she and Pendra were draped across it, watching on a propped-up screen.

"You're late!" Pendra cried over the movie chatter. "To your own party!"

"But I'm here!" I cranked out a smile. My house was in another world, far from here.

I set down my backpack and sleeping bag with a sigh. Pendra scootched sideways to make room for me on the bed, nudging Aja over in turn.

Aja grumbled but didn't protest too much.

On the table by the bed there was a yellow plate with cupcakes and cupcake-shaped spaces decked with crumbs. In one, velvet cake showed beneath thick raspberry-colored icing. "Your mom lets you eat up here?"

"Just tonight. I have to vacuum later." Pendra shut her eyes and scrunched her nose. "You know how much food is in my brothers' room?"

Aja laughed and I shook my head. "I don't think I want to know."

The cupcake looked delicious, and I was suddenly famished. I peeled back the paper and took a bite. My teeth tingled with how sweet it was.

The movie ended while I chewed.

My mouth was still filled with crumbs when Pendra said, "Let's do presents now." She started to slide off the bed.

"I don't . . ." I nearly sprayed cupcake all over Aja's sleeping bag, but I caught myself and ended up breathing in.

No one wants cupcake up their nose. I coughed until Pendra patted me on the back.

Just for a moment, I wished I'd stayed home.

Finally I could make words again. "I left your present at my house." Late. No present. "My pajamas too." *Great job, Eleanor.* I was doing really well at this sleepover. And Aja was here to see me screw up.

Pendra surprised me, though. "You're good for it." She lifted a small box. Passed it to me. "We can open them together later if you want."

The box was lighter than I expected. "Absolutely." I wasn't going to open anything on my own. I tucked it in my bag.

"And you can borrow pajamas—there's a pile of T-shirts and shorts on the drawers in my closet." She waved in that direction and I slid off the bed and went to find an extra pair. Why couldn't I get it together enough to sneak over here in the right way?

Back at home, no one knew yet what I'd done. Everyone was sleeping, I hoped. And the river? Would hopefully stay put.

But as I opened the closet door, the light switched on automatically. Down the back wall, a small line of water darkened the paint. When I grabbed a pair of shorts that were on top of a chest of drawers, I traced the leak down to the floor, where it eddied beside the dresser. I shut the door and leaned against it.

Just like at school. Was the river following me, like Mike thought?

No. It was just a leak. From all the rain.

The Sartis' house grew noisier as Pendra's other brother came home late and pounded up the stairs. The dog barked until someone shushed it. Back at my house, Mike was huddled in her comforter, the house silent around her.

Aja and Pendra laughed from the bed. "Come on, Eleanor," Pendra said.

I almost went home then. Back through the rain and into the house to check on Mike. To make sure the river wasn't under her bed.

But I knew in my heart that her bed wasn't where the river was.

I'd left. I'd walked away from everything. I'd tried to have a minute of my own. And the river had followed me.

It followed us, because, like the Heron said, the river was partly our responsibility. And all of it—the leaks at school, the ones at home, the leaks in the other houses too.

My coming to the sleepover had made things worse. No matter where I went, the river would follow until I fixed it. And if I wasn't careful, Pendra and Aja would find out. But I knew, once the others fell asleep, I'd be going back into the water.

I changed quickly into Pendra's shorts and put my jeans in my backpack, where I could reach them. Aja turned on another movie just as Mrs. Sarti came upstairs with three bowls of popcorn and more cupcakes. Chocolate this time.

Mike would have loved those. Any other night, I would have loved them too. Tonight, they tasted like mud.

At Mrs. Sarti's urging, we piled pillows on the floor to watch the next movie. As the screen flickered and characters faced their challenges bravely, I snuck glances at the crack between the closet door and the carpet. I couldn't help it. My skin crawled at the thought of water creeping across Pendra's floor.

But out of the corner of my eye, I caught a glimmer from beneath Pendra's guest bed. The one Aja slept on.

I risked putting my chin down on the floor and looking more. There wasn't a lot of water yet—only about the size of a serving platter—but it was growing. I could see the lighthouse beam flicker as the water rippled.

The river was here.

"Where'd you go, Eleanor?" Pendra asked. "Sleeping?"

I looked up. "Not tired," I said, but I yawned and Aja and Pendra laughed. I blushed, but they didn't ask any more questions. We finished the movie in quiet—cartoon monsters, a floating airship—the screen's light flashing over our faces in the dark.

This was almost fun. It would have been fun, on any other night. I caught myself laughing a couple of times without thinking. Then I remembered.

The movie ended and the screen went gray. No one moved to turn it off. Aja snored softly, her head at an angle against her arm. Pendra's eyes closed, too, and she drooped against her pillow. I kept myself awake by pinching the skin on my hand and by imagining waking up in a pool of water and having to explain it to Pendra. By the time my friends' breathing shifted and slowed, my hands were red and blotchy, but I hadn't drifted off.

The bedroom was dark, save for the dim blue screen. The rest of Pendra's house was quiet.

I eased from my sleeping bag, trying not to make a sound. The harder I tried, the louder everything seemed. Finally I worked my way free.

Grabbing my backpack's strap and dragging it with me, I slid beneath the bed.

The river had grown.

+++

Beneath Pendra's guest bed, boxes and books jumbled. Some teetered on the edge of the river. One had fallen and was floating away. Dust thicketed everything. I stifled a sneeze. Even the muffled catch sounded so loud.

There was no bed skirt below the low metal bed frame. Everything could be seen and heard if someone looked in the right spot. With the noise I was making as I scrambled under the low frame, I hoped no one would wake up.

A floorboard squeaked. My heart thudded against my ribs. Darkness all around me. Strange noises. This wasn't my house. This wasn't my bed.

But this was almost certainly my river. At least part of it.

And there was no other way to stop the river from coming through. I had to go back in.

If I did, and if I retrieved the witch ball from Anassa and brought it back home, everything would go back to normal.

If I kept my family's agreement, no one would know how much of this was my fault. I'd brought Pendra home that day,

I'd broken the rules, the float had smashed, and the river had come.

Aja murmured and rolled over above me. I froze mid-crawl. When I heard no more movement, I slowly pulled myself forward and tucked my legs and feet under the bed. Once more, I lay beside the river. I looked down into it.

The carpet—peonies on a green background—itched where my pajamas had scrunched while I crawled. I inched forward and touched the water. Pulled my fingers back, dripping.

I couldn't move enough to pull my pack over my shoulders, the bed frame was so low. Instead, I leaned over the edge of the river as if I was going to take a drink. I watched for the lighthouse beam.

The first time I'd tried to catch the light beam from this side, it had slipped below my fingertips. I didn't know if I could do it now, but the river was certainly getting stronger. Maybe the magic was spilling over. Pendra would say that it never hurt to try.

The beam swung, small on the strip of river beneath Pendra's bed and I reached into the water and grabbed for it. My fingers, cold from the water, grew hot when they touched the light. It slipped through my fingers like before, but I twisted my hand fast and the beam caught on my pinky and thumb, stretching thinner and thinner. I stared at it for a moment, dumbstruck. It had worked. "Mike," I whispered. "Oh, you'd love this."

But Mike wasn't here. Just me. I wrapped the beam around my wrist and pulled tight. The line of light fought me the way a hooked fish would. I rolled back and, with one hand, tried to reach for something to tie the line to. If it would tie. I wasn't sure about that.

I'd found a spring, close enough above my head, which seemed like it would hold the line taut for me when a hand grabbed my leg.

In the narrow light of the lighthouse beam, Pendra stared at me, her hair tangled and her face sleep-marked. "Eleanor. What are you doing?"

The words wouldn't work in my mouth. For a solid minute, my hand gripping the light beam hard, I couldn't tell her.

Among the things you should never do when sleeping over at a friend's house is crawl under the bed when everyone else is asleep. That's probably the third- or fourth-most-important rule.

Another rule: Keep any large bodies of water at home, or at least out of sight.

Pendra pulled herself under the bed, and I made room for her. She stared at the river flowing beneath her bed. At my hand, holding a beam of light taut between the springs of her bed and some unseen object far below.

"Magic," she whispered. "I knew it. Where are we going?"

"What?" I said. "No. *We're* not going anywhere." A memory tugged at me of someone who'd followed their friend to the river. Anassa.

"Of course we are. You're going. So I'm going." Her whispers were sliding away from wonder, into normal, *No-isn't-an-option* Pendra. How could I explain any of this to her?

"It's dangerous. And scary."

Her eyes lit up. Exactly the wrong thing to say. "How do you go? I've never had anything this weird happen ever. Come on, Eleanor!" She tugged on my backpack. "How does it work?"

For a moment, just one moment, I wanted to push on her shoulder and shove her out from under the bed.

This was my river. Pendra would make it hers, too, somehow.

Or she would get stuck.

Or she'd find a way to help.

And I didn't want her to. I wanted to do this myself.

But I wanted to get the witch ball more. And no one stopped Pendra, ever.

"I don't know where this leads. I've never—" I didn't want to say that I'd only gone from beneath my own bed, though it was true. "We could fall into water or onto rocks. Or something could find us." I shivered. "It's not . . . safe down there."

Pendra tried to tug on the light line just ahead of my hands. Her fingers passed right through it. "It's not real."

"It's real. It's magic."

Her face lit up.

"But you can't use it. You'll fall." I wasn't sure if she would, but I didn't want her to. "There's a big drop. It's like being inside a bubble, a little. I hate the fall. Also—"

Pendra lifted the line behind me. "It feels like fishing line now. What happened?"

I shook my head. "Magic, maybe."

"Well." She made a pushing motion with her hands, palms out. "Get going! We don't have all night." Her eyes shone with excitement.

"You're not coming." I wasn't giving in. I wasn't that selfish.

"I am. This is my bed. My room. You can't tell me not to." She had a point there. "And we'll wake Aja if we keep arguing."

Just like Pendra to jump in, without having any idea of where she was going or how she'd get back. No, that wasn't true. With the light tied, we could climb out. If it didn't snap from being tied in place for too long.

I hoped it wouldn't.

I pulled my pack awkwardly up to my shoulder, wriggling into it within the confines of the space beneath the bed. When I was ready, I closed my eyes and grabbed hold of the light. If she followed me, that was her fault. Not mine.

"Okay." I pulled myself over the edge, into the water. The light was warm on my hands but not hot anymore.

I inched down, hand over hand, until I was hanging in water and air, the line holding me so I didn't fall.

I felt Pendra's weight on the line behind me. "Wait," I called. But she didn't hear me.

With a sound like glass snapping or a rope breaking, the beam of light broke away from the bed frame and Pendra and I swung fast into the night sky and then the river. Pendra falling faster, below me. But neither one of us let go of the light.

Pendra yelled in half laughter, half fear all the way down. Every nightmare in the area would know we were there.

Anassa would know too. Great.

Pendra landed with a splash near the lighthouse and quickly made it to shore. I swung to the lighthouse stairs and scrambled down, the beam of light shredding in my hands. Slowly, as I watched, the beam dimmed.

I didn't have time to fix the light again.

In the dark, I heard the splash of a paddle wheel. Saw the raft, with Dishrag at the helm, drawing close.

Pendra's eyes were the size of coffee cups. "How did you make this?" she asked me. She brushed wet sand from her pajamas.

"Make what? I didn't make anything," I said.

"I made myself," Dishrag said when he was close enough. He looked at Pendra for a long moment, then twisted his head toward me. "Where are you heading? Where's your sister?"

I watched the pony carefully. He'd helped Anassa escape back to the bridge before. But he'd helped us too. Whose side was he on?

Pendra looked back and forth between us.

"If you're not going somewhere, you've given up already," Dishrag said, leaning forward until he could nudge my hair with his muzzle. "You'll get stuck here. Or there. Both of you. You'll forget what you want."

I stared at the pony, forgetting Pendra was there. *Was that what happened to Momma? She got stuck?* What about Gran? "The crabs too?"

Dishrag snorted. "I heard, thirdhand, that the crabs forgot where they came from. Decided they could make do here. Birds like to gossip. But it's important not to give up."

"What about other adults?" I hadn't seen many, aside from Anassa and the crabs. But I wondered. Gran didn't remember much. Momma not at all.

Dishrag said, "Adults think of this place differently. When they think of it at all. Even those who helped the river once. They're too busy for it. So. They forget, or get stuck. Don't you do that."

"We promise," I said for all three of us. Pendra, Mike, and me. Pendra wasn't getting stuck; she was getting out of here as soon as I could manage it. And hopefully Mike would never have to come here again.

Dishrag pawed the treads of the raft. Nervous. "Your presence has been requested on the bridge, by Anassa. And the Heron's asking for you too."

The pony was working both sides of the river. I frowned. But Pendra didn't understand.

"Those people—Anassa and the Heron—already know we're here?"

"You fell. Everyone saw. And those who couldn't see, heard." Dishrag nickered.

I looked at Pendra. She blushed and began pacing the shoreline. "I didn't think. I was scared." She didn't look at me.

I was amazed.

For the first time since I'd known her, Pendra didn't know what to do. She always knew what to do.

But now, walking a strange river, I was the one who had to choose.

To the Heron or Anassa? The reeds or the bridge.

Dreams or nightmares?

I couldn't stay in between any longer.

"Come on." I tugged on Pendra's sleeve, wishing she'd stayed asleep in her room. Wading out a few steps into the water, I grabbed the edge of the blackboard raft and held it steady. "Hop on."

She hesitated. The night breeze pushed at her pajamas and made them ripple around her legs. Her hair, braided and wet, barely moved. "It's cold."

I lifted my pack. "I have a sweater." I wasn't that cold. I was warm, actually. Somehow, knowing what I wanted to do and deciding to do it made everything feel warmer. I passed her the backpack.

Pendra put my sweater on. I looked out over the river and at the stars and the deep purple sky. Mike and I weren't going to save ourselves by patching leaks. We'd wind up as stuck as the crabs. We needed a new agreement for our family. I needed to fix what I'd helped break.

I brushed the pony's mane with my fingers. "We go to the bridge. Take us to Anassa."

Dishrag began to tread backward immediately.

Something nagged at me. "You didn't ask for payment."

The pony shook his head and his mane shook too. "Anassa paid."

That I didn't like at all. "I pay our way." I said it fast, before I had time to worry about what I could use to pay with. I hadn't even brought any Cheerios. If I paid, then I got to tell Dishrag where to go and Anassa didn't.

Pendra handed me the pack. I rifled through it while the raft moved closer to the bridge. Not much inside the bag to pay a pony with. The present Pendra had given me. A pair of jeans. No money.

The other shoreline came close and the feet of the bridge grew broader as we moved downstream. Nightmares ran dark along the river's edge, steam rising from their backs. One bit at another, until it collapsed into smoke. Seated on the raft, watching, Pendra gasped. "What are those?"

The paddle wheel plowed the river and Dishrag's pace didn't slow. But the pony's towel neck twisted to keep the 'mares in sight long after we'd passed. "They move so beautifully."

I tried to imagine Dishrag running with the herd. I couldn't see it.

"What keeps you from being one?" Pendra asked.

The pony breathed mist into the night. "I can't hold smoke together enough to form a body. I need better stories to bind my shape, or I'm stuck using old towels for the rest of my days. I need mirrors for eyes, not whorls of cloth. But the stories are the most important. Scary ones. No tired, old tales."

"How do you know?" Pendra asked.

"My cousins are nightmares. They told me. But that doesn't make me any more of one."

I dug once more into the backpack and came up with my birthday present. The neatly wrapped box had mirrored paper and reflected the moon. It caught Dishrag's eye before I could stuff it back in the pack.

"I'll take that," the pony said.

"No," I said. "That's mine."

But Dishrag leaned over and picked it from my hand with careful cloth teeth.

Pendra glared at the pony and then at me. "That was for you."

"Give it back," I said.

Dishrag shook his head and spoke around his gritted teeth. "You've got your ride. You'll need something to fend the barge away from the bridge with, unless you want to go straight into her nets. There's a barge pole tied to the deck." He gestured twice with his chin. The river's lily pads and reeds gave over to wide sandbars and fast-moving deeps. We hit an eddy and the barge began to spin. Stars wheeled overhead and Pendra looked dizzy.

But I frowned and kept my footing and my focus. "Give it back." I held out my hand for the box. "That's Pendra's gift."

"Eleanor," she said. "You need this. I'll get another one."

I couldn't make the pony give back the box and take us around the bridge trap. Not both. I gave in and searched for the pole. I found it lashed to the deck with a thick grass line. The pole was wooden and stout.

Any other time, it would have made an excellent staff for a quest.

A gnat made of knotted string buzzed close to my face and I chased it with my free hand. Its high-pitched whine made me swipe at my ear. When it was gone, I held the pole with two hands and sank the end of it into the river.

The current pressed against the pole and tried to take it from me. When it caught the clay river bottom, I fought even harder to hold on. "I need help," I finally said with effort.

Pendra moved to my left and together we bent our knees and leaned back, steadying the pole.

"All you have to do is say you need help." She grinned. The raft slowed and Dishrag began treading backward. We moved the pole forward and hit a rock. I could feel the wood skidding over the submerged, uneven surface, the vibration in my hands. My fingertips felt like they'd turned into bees.

Slowly the barge stopped spinning.

"Thank you," Dishrag said, teeth still clenched on the ribbon of the box. "It's nice to have help."

The pony tried to bite at his haunch, chasing a gnat. Probably the same gnat that had annoyed me. The box dropped from his teeth and Pendra scrambled to pick it up. She held it out between us. The pony said nothing. Pretended like he wasn't even looking, though occasionally, his eyes would roll sideways toward the box. The mirrored paper was torn. The boat began to drift again.

"That's Dishrag's now," I finally said with regret. "Can I have a look at what's inside, at least?"

The bridge grew larger and darker. I could hear shouts far above our heads.

Dishrag whinnied softly. "Inside?"

Pendra looked boggled. "You've never seen a gift before?"

The pony swung his head side to side. "I thought the outside was the present."

"Do you want . . ." I said slowly as the bridge loomed closer, shrouded in mist. The spans looked like the backbone of a fish rising out of the water. ". . . what's inside?"

As Dishrag shook his head, the air turned thick with smells: rotten eggs, motor oil, old tuna fish. A sweet odor hung over the rest, like icing.

"Ughhhh," Pendra groaned. She nearly dropped the box.

But Dishrag dipped his head to retrieve it. "Just the outside."

Oh! Dishrag wanted the reflective wrapping paper—which was like a mirror.

Now I understood.

Pendra grabbed for the box, confused. I pulled the paper off and gave it to the pony, then gave the box to Pendra. "How's that?"

As Dishrag ate the paper, the current caught the raft and we began to spin again. I pressed the pole into the riverbed. The river grew as stagnant as the air, algae a luminescent green on the surface. Some of it dragged up with a sucking sound when I lifted the pole. Gross.

Pendra stared at me. "You're different here."

I felt different. The water was dangerous and confusing but not as much as home. I could fix parts of here. At least, I was learning how. I didn't have to stay out of the way here. "I've had practice, that's all."

I hoped she wouldn't have to build up practice, too. Priority one was getting the witch ball back. Now. Priority two was getting Pendra out.

The shadow of the bridge patterned the water ahead.

Gnats and bigger flies buzzed a low chorus and bit at my ankles. Dishrag twitched his ears and his skin danced as he tried to shake the bugs off.

The barge struck something solid. *Thunk*. Pendra wobbled and fell to her knees. Another *thunk*. I kept my footing. In the moonlight, sharp corners and long lines in the water became points of boxes, edged in silver, silhouetted and deeply shadowed.

We were moving through a garbage run that thickened the closer we got to the bridge. And the bridge was acting as a net to catch the garbage. I used the pole to fend off the biggest pieces of flotsam. By the time we were next to the bridge, I was drenched in sweat.

The bridge's broad arches created darker shadows on the water, salted with the reflection of a few sparse lights that draped the bridge above. The structure stretched three quarters of the way across the river before it ended in a pile of garbage.

As we drifted closer, I could see more crabs working to press the trash into cubes. They piled these on a raft that floated near the bridge's end, manned by stranger creatures than I'd seen elsewhere. Shadow-shapes and half-beasts. Spiders and crabs working together to build the bridge.

"We recycle here," the Heron had said.

The whole bridge was made of the kind of garbage that house magic cleared away most mornings. In the water, a cracked television screen floated, an old mailbox post. Game cartridges. A torn book. Mr. Divner's cracked binoculars. A broken baby chair that looked like one of my favorites.

But there were other pieces I didn't recognize. Pendra pointed. "That looks like my old magic oven set," she said. "My brother wrecked it." And there was more too. The bridge had objects from all over. An entire span was made of beer cans. We didn't have any of those in the house.

"Why are they building this?" Pendra asked, her head craned back at a painful angle.

"To get across the river to the lighthouse, all of them at once. Most cannot swim the deepest part. The nightmares will evaporate, Anassa will drown. I can take one or two, but they want to go—"

"In force," I said. Dishrag pawed the treads in agreement.

The garbage piled up at the end of the bridge still wasn't enough to reach the lighthouse. Not yet. But with every piece swept downstream, Anassa and her nightmares were getting closer. No matter who stopped the leaks, or how many were stopped, without an agreement on the other side, she would gain more access. I couldn't let her do that.

I spotted her trap then. A net made of six-pack plastic and garbage bags, floating just beneath the surface of the water. It looked like normal garbage, but there were wires running up to the bridge. Most garbage didn't have strings attached. I had Dishrag angle the raft to go around it, but in a way that made it look from above like we were headed straight for the trap.

"I'm here, just like you asked," I said.

Anassa turned, her plastic-bag dress rustling, her eyes red beneath lids set deep in her snake face. She was big enough that I could see her scales flaking and scarred where the birds had grabbed her.

"I'll lower a rope," she said. "Stay where you are."

For a moment, I did put the pole down and stop the raft, I was so used to following orders. But this was a monster who'd set a trap for me, telling me to do something that would make her life easier.

I held the barge pole at an angle, water dripping off it, and pushed the raft farther down the bridge, toward a row of nets. Why hadn't I told the Heron about Anassa having a witch ball of her own? It could've brought the birds and helped me. Or gotten it itself.

Who has ever come to save you?

I shook Poppa's voice from my head. I would save myself.

I hadn't told the Heron because I hadn't trusted the bird. Just like Anassa had said. And I'd wanted to get the float for myself. That way, I wouldn't owe the Heron anything.

Above, snake-headed Anassa could no longer see the raft, although we could still see her. "Where'd you go?" She tossed garbage off the bridge near us. "You don't want to come up? Are you going to give up on the last witch ball?" The trash rustled when it hit the bridge and floated on top of the oil-slick water.

Anassa held the glass bauble up over her head and the light caught it. Turquoise blue, with a taped crack.

Pendra gaped. "That's—" *a witch ball*, she mouthed silently.

"I know. And I need to get it." I'd fixed the crack in the tunnels with stories. Maybe I could fix the witch ball, too.

I found the yellow netting on the backside of the bridge and grabbed hold. "You can't come, Pen. It's too dangerous."

I can read your mind, Anassa had said. *I can see your flaws.*

I didn't want Pendra to hear what Anassa had to say about me any more than I wanted her stuck here.

"I can help, though. I can cause a distraction while you climb." Her voice sounded small, distorted by the rush of the river.

That would be useful. "From the raft?"

"Yes." She nodded. "I won't leave the raft." She looked frightened enough that I believed her. The thought of Pendra, afraid, nearly made me more afraid. But I didn't have time for that. The moon would set if I waited too long, and we'd *both* be stuck here.

The raft lifted beneath my feet with the next wave. I dragged the net closer with the barge pole. The raft turned slightly and banged against the bridge.

"You promised to help fix the river, didn't you?" Anassa shouted, looking for me. "And here's your chance. Where are you? Are you a liar? Too afraid? Do you not want to help? I'll tell everyone you are a liar and you don't keep your promises."

I did keep my promises. Always.

Anassa made me so mad. I was about to answer her when a spray of water cascaded up over the bridge and hit Anassa. Dishrag had sped the paddle wheel up while the raft was pressed against the bridge footer, the resulting wave swamping Anassa, barely spattering me.

Anassa flailed her arms and wiped at her face, spitting. Then she moved to the edge of the bridge and started throwing things at the raft. Pendra handed me a pole and I climbed the netting up the other side.

Pendra, taunting her, shouted, "You can't swim, you can't fly, you big baddie, go cry." Her voice carried on the wind. Anassa roared at her.

While Anassa was bent over the bridge, shouting at the raft below, I scrambled to the top and pulled myself over the edge. "I never said I would help *you*," I said to her quietly. "Why are *you* lying?"

She straightened and turned to face me.

Keep calm, Eleanor. Count to ten.

I couldn't remember what order the numbers went in. I felt my cheeks flush. The river roared in my ears.

"Yes. I need you," Anassa mused. "More than I knew. Maybe you're one of those who can tear a hole so big in the river that we can all get out for good."

"That's not true," I said, even though the Heron had said it was.

"But it is. You break things. You're the worst of all your family, worse than your father." She spat the words and I felt them like a punch in my chest. She saw me react and her mouth spread in a wide smile. Her tongue jutted out. Once, twice. "I can see just how terrible you are, Eleanor. If you help me, I won't tell anyone. Better. I'll help you forget. When you forget, you'll be normal, like you want so much."

She offered the glass sphere, flat in her palm.

"I won't help you," I said, but my voice sounded quieter, even to me.

"I'm certain you will. You'd do anything to get back to normal. To keep from being trapped here. Maybe you'd even betray a friend." She looked over the bridge again. At Pendra. "I'll prove it. Let's see what you choose: your future? Or your friend's?"

When she lifted a piece of sharp metal in one hand and held both that and the witch ball over the bridge's edge, she grinned at me. Her tongue flickered. The metal was big enough to slice the raft and sink it. Big enough to seriously hurt Dishrag and Pendra.

"Choose," she said.

I stood on the bridge and felt like I was falling.

She shifted the witch ball and the light caught my gaze. "Will you choose? Or will you just stand there?" she shouted. "Your future or hers? Selfish girl."

"I am not selfish!" I rushed at Anassa, without thinking. Without trying to reason any longer.

The snake-woman began to laugh as I barreled toward her.

Below, Pendra looked up at me. "Eleanor! Watch out!"

Anassa tossed the witch ball and the metal shard at the same time, away from herself. They seemed to hang in the air as I pivoted. I could only catch one. The shard gleamed sharp in the air.

I lunged and knocked the metal aside with my pole. It rang from the contact, over Anassa's laughter, and then spun into the river, away from the raft.

The witch ball fell past the edge of the bridge, out of reach. The witch ball gleamed like a tear in the night. A bright piece of moonlight.

"You didn't deserve it anyway." Anassa watched me. With a tiny *pop*, the last witch ball hit the bridge span, then the footer below.

Glass reflected stars as pieces of the sphere fell into the water and began to sink. Some gleamed on the bridge footers. A few shards fell on the raft.

"That was mine!" I rushed at her.

"It was never yours," Anassa said, dodging me. She turned her back on me and started to move away, too fast to catch. "I hope you enjoy being a monster here more than I do."

I heard Pendra shout.

Below, the nightmares pacing the river turned and rushed the bridge while others swirled around something on shore. One leapt over the side and down, landing on the raft.

"You can't fix the river," the snake hissed over her shoulder. "And you're not as strong as I thought. But you can still help us break it, Eleanor. You're so good at breaking things. Help us. Everything will be so much easier if you do." She held out her hands to me, empty this time.

Pendra and Dishrag struggled to knock the nightmare off the raft. Their voices echoed up in ripples. "You won't take this raft." "Watch out!" The nightmare menaced them, its long teeth gleaming and sharp behind its pulled-back lips. The 'mare lunged and grabbed Pendra's braid in its teeth.

I'd lost my temper. I'd lost everything.

The raft swung below me, about to break away.

I jumped down to it.

CHAPTER

HOMECOMING

FIFTEEN

I fell past the bridge and landed in the water beside Dishrag's raft, close enough that, once I surfaced, I could grab the paddle wheel and pull myself up. The trash-filled water's slimy grip let me go and I dragged myself onto the barge, gasping.

A few pieces of the witch ball sifted far out of reach through the water beside the raft. I tried to grab them anyway and missed. The pieces of glass and mirror on the blackboard beneath me I scooped up and stuffed in my pockets.

Garbage clung to my hair and to my clothes. I swiped at it until a nightmare's hoof crashed down next to my head.

"Watch out!" Pendra shouted. She sounded terrified. I rolled away. That hadn't felt or sounded like smoke.

Pendra held a barge pole, like the one I'd used up on the bridge. She swung it around and I ducked low.

"Careful!"

She was trying to clear the 'mares off the barge so that we could get away. She'd almost cleared me off too.

Meantime the 'mares bit at Dishrag, pulling pieces of cloth from his flanks and neck.

A 'mare came at me, too, its ears pinned. Its mirrored eyes glinted starlight. Dishrag bit it on the flank and pulled it away. Smoke oozed everywhere. Another nightmare crowded Pendra near the edge of the raft.

It was trying to push her into the water.

"Pen!" I swung my own barge pole and caught the nightmare true in its neck. The horse disappeared in a dark cloud.

The two remaining 'mares fought hard to avoid the water, but we pushed them off and they sank deep when they couldn't find their footing, until the river bubbled and smoked.

From the shore, I could hear Anassa shouting as she rode away.

I pulled the piece of mirror out of my pocket and gave it to Dishrag. "Payment," I said. I hoped it was enough. "Finally. Anassa's not the only one who can pay."

Dishrag nickered and leaned to my hand. "We'll see," he said. A soft muzzle picked up the mirror. He closed his washcloth eye and his shiny-paper eye. "I'm thinking the bridge attack is a pretty good scary story. One that's all mine," he said. He opened his eyes; one was a mirror now.

We'd driven the nightmare herd away for now. But I could hear Anassa up on the bridge span, laughing. We hadn't won for good. She would finish the bridge, they would capture the tunnels, and the lighthouse—and I'd helped them by breaking the light.

I had no witch ball to bring home to keep the nightmares and Anassa on their own side of the river. I had no way to keep Mike safe or to get us out of trouble with Poppa and Momma. I'd failed completely.

But the moon was setting over the darkened lighthouse. The beam my ancestor had made drooped down the fishbone wall and coiled like a dimming snake at the tower base. We couldn't cross that way, and we couldn't swim.

"Will you take us to the lighthouse," I asked the pony. If Dishrag still worked for Anassa, I would find out soon enough. He'd said he would never take her there. That he'd never been able to make it across the deepest part of the river.

But the pony kicked in his traces and began to paddle. Pendra poled while I pushed away garbage until we were in dark, clear water. Then the current grew faster and the boat spun wildly again.

"Together!" I shouted, and Pendra and I both used our poles to steady the raft while Dishrag paddled as hard as he could. The river tossed the raft, but we didn't stop. Sweat poured down my face, burning my eyes. The lighthouse blurred in the distance.

Then the raft shot out of the current. The river slowed. We were on the other side. The blackboard ground against rocks and Pendra and I tumbled to our knees, our poles skidding into the shallows.

The pony's towels had come unwound around his hooves and he couldn't move. But he looked at us and nickered. "Go now. Don't wait."

We pulled ourselves up the rocky shore as the moon set. Across the river, pink light sparkled. "Hurry," I said, looking back once at the raft and the pony slowly folding himself back together. "Thank you," I whispered. Then I tugged on Pendra's wet sleeve.

We had to get back to Pendra's before Aja woke up and noticed us missing. Before we were stuck here forever. And then I had to sneak back into my house.

We scrambled up the wooden steps, Pendra following me, curiously quiet. Just as I opened the lighthouse door, she grabbed my shoulder. "You have to tell me exactly what's going on."

I took her hand from my arm. "I don't."

"But this is magic! You're on a quest. Is Mike too?" She looked at the lighthouse, the rickety stairs we'd just climbed. "This is made of fishbones!"

I reached for anything to tell her that would stop her questions. I didn't have the answers she wanted.

"It's a dream, Pendra. You're dreaming." I yawned carefully. "It's really late."

"Eleanor! This isn't a dream!" She sounded frightened, not angry. "Please tell me."

"I can't," I said, and led her to the hatch. "Just follow me."

I climbed up and through, until my head bumped the bed frame. In my own bedroom.

Oh no. The lighthouse led to only one place.

Back home.

+++

Pendra emerged from the river beside me. She looked around, confused. "This isn't my room."

"It's mine," I whispered. This was bad—Poppa had banned Pendra from the house. "You have to go home. My father will kill me if he finds you here."

Pendra, wide-eyed, nodded. "That wasn't a dream, was it?"

I shook my head, knowing she could tell when I was fibbing. "Not like a normal dream, no."

"And those horses?"

"Pen, I'll tell you later. You have to go back to your house." I'd go with her to get my sleeping bag and be back here in no time. We crawled from beneath the bed and she followed me into the hallway. I paused at Mike's door, feeling relieved. I could tell her what happened, and we would figure out something. We always did.

My relief was short-lived.

When I cracked Mike's door open, I saw a lumpy pile of blankets on her bed. The kind of pile that we'd make when we were hiding beneath another bed.

In an instant, I was in her room, sweeping back her covers.

I didn't want to see those pillows, all white and punched into shape. But no Mike.

Had she been magicked away? Sent away? A trail of socks, pencils, and tape led from her door to mine. No. She'd heard who had the witch ball as clearly as I had. And now she was missing. Would she have gone to the river alone? The nightmares on shore had circled something. I'd thought it might be the crabs. What if it was Mike?

Outside, it was still dark. We'd made it in time. The gray clouds rolling in kept everything dim a lot longer. That might give me more time to get everything put right again.

But Pendra waited in the hall. "Hurry." I pulled her down the landing and through the first floor, until we were out the basement door again.

No one had woken upstairs. We'd done one thing right. I hugged her goodbye. "I'll get my sleeping bag later," I said.

"You're not coming? Why?"

Upstairs at her house, a light went on in the hallway.

I shook my head. "I can't. Pen, I have to find where Mike's hiding. She wasn't in her bed. Please let me go."

Would she listen? Would we still be friends?

"All right," Pendra said, and I could see she was troubled, but I couldn't linger to fix it. And at least she didn't demand that I do what she wanted. "I'll see you in school on Monday. Good luck."

If I was still here on Monday and not stuck on the river or sent away myself.

She watched me, bleary eyes squinting a little in the predawn light, mouth skewed to one side. Then she rubbed her nose and turned on her bare heel and began to trudge back up the hill.

"See you Monday," I answered, then eased the basement door shut and tiptoed back upstairs, barely breathing at all.

I checked my sister's room once more, but Mike was still gone.

Under her pillow, where she knew I'd look, I found a note: *Going to get the witch ball.*

Oh. Mike. Please, no. The sun would rise soon. If she didn't hurry, she'd be trapped. Like the crabs. Like Anassa.

If I went back, I could get trapped there too. But Mike was already there.

I didn't think any further than that. I crawled under my bed again and dove back into the river.

I fell through, then landed hard in deep water. The river knocked my breath right out of me. I felt the current start to pull at my clothes and spin me.

I struggled to stay on my back, trying to catch a stuttering lungful of air. Then I turned over and swam diagonally for the nearest shore, toward the bridge and the nightmares.

+++

Near the inlet, the sound of horses blowing mist and pawing at the sandbar grew louder.

I tried to keep my own splashing down, swimming low, using long breaststrokes until the sand ground against my clothes and my fingernails filled with grit.

When I stopped swimming, the river tried to pull me with it. I dug my fingers into the wet sand and the grasses along the riverside. My lungs ached, and my arms and legs felt like they were made of worn cloth.

One reed moved, dipping its beak close to my ear. I heard the *snick* of garden shears, saw a glint of beach glass and the glow of driftwood in moonlight.

The Heron.

Its red eye came closer. I sank lower in the water.

When I whispered, "What do you want?" it turned to look right at me.

"The same thing you do." The Heron clacked softly. It sounded like reeds brushing together. "To fix the river. To send you home."

"You wanted us to stay before." I shivered. The night breeze was cold, but the fact that the Heron hadn't said "you and your sister" was colder.

"You can protect the other side better, I decided. Anassa's too strong for you."

I broke things everywhere. Even when I tried to fix them. *Who would want you anyway.* I started to crawl away, toward the horses. "Anassa said you would throw me away. I'm going to get my sister. Go pick on the broken dreams."

"You misunderstand." The Heron followed me on stilt legs. "I want to help you. Your sister doesn't belong here either."

Without the lighthouse beam, everything was edged with moonlight on the river. I smelled the salt-edge of the water, the green of the reeds, and smoke. The nightmares. The cloud-veiled moon and stars weren't strong enough, especially this late, to let me see them. But when the horses started to run, I heard them. The Heron's head turned too.

The light broke through the clouds and I saw the dark forms of the herd more clearly, just as they turned toward my hiding spot. Mike rode the lead horse, her fingers curled through its mane, her eyes blank with fear or something worse.

If I'd stayed home, this wouldn't have happened. Mike would be safe. I'd be warm and dry, in bed. Pendra would never know about the river.

Probably.

. . . Probably not.

My shoulders shook with guilt. "How could you possibly help now?"

"I can help you make a new agreement."

"Why didn't you do that earlier?"

"I was trying to save myself. I was running out of glass." The bird showed its wings. Most of its feathers were missing.

"No." I didn't want the bird's help after everything that had happened. Anassa was right about the Heron. I crawled forward, up onto the shoreline, and the first of the horses swept past me.

I saw the crabs from the tunnels being pulled behind one of the nightmares in a net. The two of them clung beneath James's shell, trying to avoid the hooves.

But if I didn't take the Heron's help, how would I rescue Mike?

More guilt. I'd led Anassa and the nightmares to the tunnels where the crabs had been working. I'd made the cracks in this world worse. Just like the snake had said on the bridge. If I'd just followed the rules, let house magic work, there wouldn't be any cracks. Mike wouldn't be here. The old agreement would never have broken. Poppa wouldn't be so mad. And we'd be safe, me and Mike.

Well, safer.

A nightmare whinnied.

No one was safe now. Not here. Soon, not on the other side either. I imagined the dock and my house growing dark beneath storm clouds, then the rest of the neighborhood.

More hooves beat the ground and the low water. The Heron rose and flew away.

I felt it go, a missed chance.

The nightmares' breath tangled with mine, they were so close. I tried to stay as still as a reed. As quiet as a new dream. The 'mares' velvet sides brushed my shoulders.

I couldn't see the horse Mike rode any longer. The 'mares were circling me too fast.

It grew darker. I could hear their teeth chattering with excitement. Mirrored eyes reflected my face.

I saw my own face, grimacing. Angry. The part of me I always fought against. The part of me that yelled at my sister—that cried and stormed.

I saw scenes play out in the horses' eyes. The sound of my yelling rose up in their breath.

"That's not me," I murmured. "I'm not like that."

Mike heard me. Her eyes cleared for a moment. "You are. So am I."

And then teeth gripped my pajamas at the shoulder and lifted me. My wet pajamas dragged in the sand and then dried against the hot side of a 'mare's ribs. I was set astride the horse closest to Mike's. The teeth released my shirt. The smoky horseback felt solid against my tailbone, jarring me as the dark mare began to run.

The crabs bounced in a net behind Mike's 'mare. Their metal shells struck rocks on the beach and sparked in the brightening air. We ran up the beach and farther, passing the bridge pilings. I could hear Anassa laughing. Past the barge. Dishrag saw us and began to chase but wasn't fast enough.

The weather grew dark and wind tangled my hair. Mike bent close to her horse's neck and wound her fingers in its mane. We were riding toward the sunrise, toward the rocks. The broken profile of the jetty rose black against the sky.

I became motion. My heart began to pound out my fears. That I was bad, that I was broken, that I would disappear. That my sister would too.

As the 'mare ran faster, I lay on its flank and cried. The fears sank away from me, into the 'mare's skin. I couldn't remember anymore why I was crying. I felt the nightmare take my worries. But I didn't feel any lighter.

And then Mike began to speak. A ribbon of words spilled from her lips.

She fed the 'mare flickers of stories. Her horse grew larger and faster with them in its teeth. Every bad thing she'd ever done. All the rules she'd broken. The fights.

"No, Mike!" She was saying things that had happened to her, that she hadn't done on purpose. And the nightmare was turning them into strength. The words slipped from her lips, curls of white mist. Mike had stopped making any sound.

Once I saw what was happening to Mike, I pressed my lips tight together and refused to speak any more of my fears to my horse.

Mike's nightmare passed mine, and as it did, I pulled the net holding the crabs free of the horse's back. I watched James and then Sheila tumble back, rolling on the sand, avoiding the hooves behind us. They dragged themselves out of the nets and scrambled up the dunes.

My hair clung to my forehead. My 'mare and I were no longer keeping pace with Mike. I was going to lose her. I spoke to my horse, telling it about the time I'd gotten in the way of a fight, how I'd said nothing hurt until I believed it. The nightmare sped up, growing faster, even as I grew weaker.

But we once more matched, then exceeded, Mike's pace. And pulled alongside her.

When I could reach her, I grabbed her hand. "Listen!" I shouted. "Don't forget!"

Both 'mares slowed. One tried to bite away my hand, but I held fast. Then I pulled Mike off her horse and onto mine. In her pocket, I felt something sharp scrape my leg. Pulled the hilt of a paring knife from her pocket.

My sister's skin was cool. She leaned limp against my shoulder as we continued to move forward with the herd. I held her fast with my left hand and used my right to stick the paring knife into the nightmare's neck.

The horse bloomed into a puff of dark smoke and Mike and I fell through it, hard, all the way to the sandy ground.

The herd of nightmares, one fewer in number, began to circle us again. Eyes rolled back, teeth bared, they came at us.

Mike clung weakly to me, her eyes half open. "Eleanor? What are you doing here?"

"Keeping an eye on my sister," I said.

The horses circled us again, speeding up and pulling closer. Their hooves made no sound, their smoke bodies pressed tight together until it was hard to breathe. They swirled around us like gray glass, sealing us up. The sun peeked over the edge of the dunes, but it looked like a lighter gray smudge against the darkness of the horses. I pushed the knife into the air and cut an opening for the light to come through.

The herd split apart. Heads reared, holes tore in the smoke, and shards of smaller horses galloped away. I stood on the beach in the predawn light and hugged Mike tight. She was quiet, staring after the 'mares. She didn't follow when I started to walk toward the water, where Dishrag and the Heron were paddling closer.

"Mike, get up."

She didn't say anything.

"Mike, come on." I shook her.

"It's just a dream," she whispered.

The forgetting. It had her—or she had it.

"No, it's not. Remember the stories? Once upon a time, there were two girls . . ."

Mike stared at me. Then blinked slowly. Nothing.

"What about Someday?"

Nothing.

"Mike! Someday our real parents . . ." All my hope went into that one. That was her line. She always said it.

But there was silence. Then: "That's just a story."

"It is not just a story, this is not just a dream. Mike, remember! Someday our real parents will—"

"No one's coming for us." She sat down on the sand. I felt like sitting down too, but I forced myself to stand.

The barge ground against the beach and Dishrag stepped off. "I am. And your sister is."

"And we are," the Heron said, with its flock behind it. The birds landed on the beach, their small feet erasing the dips and drags where the nightmares' hooves had chopped the sand.

"We're trapped here," I whispered to Dishrag. "The lighthouse beam is broken; it's morning." I tried not to think about what was happening at home. Of the oncoming storm, of parents waking up and discovering us gone.

Then the Heron croaked, "Once upon a time." Exhaustion weighed each word. The bird's beak was rusted nearly through, its driftwood wings, cracked. Its feathers, mostly fallen away. Fighting the 'mares had cost it dearly. The bird's frame looked white as bone.

It began again. "Once upon a time, the nightmares won."

Then it stopped. Waves slapped the shore. Dishrag's barge ground on the sands.

"Tell the rest," I said. I pulled the glass feather from my pocket and held it out.

The bird slumped, shaking its head, refusing to take it. "This is the end of the story. You fell through the river and everything broke. I have nothing left to tell. The horses are crossing the river. Anassa has finished her bridge. They'll break through the lighthouse and head for reality soon."

We'd lost. I held my sister and watched the gray shapes move across the purple-lit bridge, toward the now-dark lighthouse.

Mike sighed and buried her face in my shoulder. "Tell me a story," she breathed.

Would it help fix Mike's forgetting? Would it make things worse?

Dishrag nudged me with his towel nose. "The Heron might be done," he said, "but you know more of the story. It's your turn to tell it."

I knelt at the edge of the shore, my feet and knees in the water. In the distance, the nightmares had reached the lighthouse and were swirling around it.

I didn't want any more stories. I didn't want to make things up any longer. Or to have to stick to the rules.

I thought of Pendra, who always wanted magic and truth, and of the Heron, who'd never given up until now. And I thought about Mike, about school and the science fair. If the weather let up, that might still happen tomorrow. I hoped it would. We'd worked so hard. But more than that, I didn't want to be stuck here.

I thought about the story the Heron had told, the first one. Where the young girl fought her way home and brought back her mother. And an agreement made of glass.

She'd made it here and brought it back by making the lighthouse too. *Out of fishbones and* . . . I thought for a moment . . . *glass*.

The crabs and their underwater tunnels. The glass shards that patched the cracks.

I would bring back my sister.

Don't tell anyone anything, or the magic will stop working.

That was the rule. The biggest rule of house magic.

But the river, and the Heron, and the pony weren't *anyone*. And Mike needed me to try.

I looked at my sister. She elbowed me back.

"Tell a story, Eleanor."

I would, but I would tell a true one this time. Maybe Mike would hear it and not forget as much.

Broken or not, it was who we were. And maybe we could use that to get back home.

I stared at the water. Began to think of the way things had happened for a long time. A story grew in my mind that had scary parts and sad parts. Enough loss to make it fragile. Enough hope to make it float. It wouldn't sound like a fairy tale, not after a while.

I put the glass feather into the water.

"Once upon a time, there were two girls who knew their real parents hadn't gone away."

I spoke and the river began to bubble. I gave Mike the last pieces of the ancient witch ball. She skipped them across the shallows and into the deep.

"No one knew their house was magicked. No one could know. Not even their best friends. Not even their gran. If they told, the magic would stop working. Until one day, it stopped working anyway, and the river broke through everywhere."

I let the river hear my anger. "It wasn't fair. It was hard to be scared. It was harder to lie."

I told the river about the broken pictures. About my missing books. About the paring knife I'd stolen. I described my friends' faces when I'd told them everything was all right, even when it wasn't, and how I felt when they'd smiled and believed me. I told it how much I loved school. And how much I hated home. "But I don't want to be sent away," I said. "Or forgotten."

The river kept bubbling, water spilling over a small, submerged sphere.

"I don't want my sister to disappear," I said. Mike squeezed my hand. "She is wild and brilliant and when she was born, Poppa was so angry, at both of us. Because we were in the way. Because we weren't worth anything." I heard again his silence on that topic. The anger that never quite ebbed. "We'd pretended we were worthy sometimes. Heroes. On a quest. We pretended to be birds too."

I told the river my dreams. Told it the properties of glass. I spoke about quiet and magic and lies and truth. "And then there was Momma," I said. "Who is maybe a good witch and maybe isn't." And then there was Poppa.

I gave everything to the river and let it make me something in return. The first small bubbles looked like a pot boiling, air trapped beneath the water. Then those joined others to make bigger spheres. I didn't stop talking. Blue and turquoise, threaded with light, the bubbles rose to the surface. The sun's beams brushed them and made them solid.

Things work differently here, the Heron had said.

Whorls of water and air, story and sunlight. Mike waded out and gathered a few. Her face lit with memories, sad and bad and good also. "I remember," she whispered.

I spoke and spoke until the surface of the river glittered with witch balls. More than we'd ever need.

Mike stood among them, holding four in her arms.

"Now you tell," I said.

She spoke about coffee mugs and ponies, about not wanting to fight. "There's no happily ever after," she whispered, "and there are monsters, and that's not fair. But once upon a time, there were two sisters who rescued each other."

"And we kept on doing that, until we didn't need to anymore," I added.

As we spoke, one perfect turquoise witch ball bobbed to the surface. The birds rose as one—a flock of ravens and gulls, led by the bone-white Heron—and dipped their claws in the water, lifting out the float, and then more.

They put these on the barge. Some were dark, some light.

"Scary ones in there," Dishrag said.

Mike reached into the pile of glass spheres and pushed several aside. The glass clinked as the raft swayed against the river's pull.

With both hands, my sister offered the pony the darkest witch ball.

One that swirled with charcoal and smoke.

Dishrag's lip twitched. Mike strung the float on a piece of netting the birds brought. She tied it around Dishrag's neck.

The pony's nostrils flared and his tail lifted high. He stepped carefully with his new weight.

"We have to stop the nightmares," the Heron whispered. The bird was a pile of bleached wood on the beach, its glass feathers nearly gone. "They'll darken the world if they run loose. Eleanor, I believe in your stories. In what you did here. You were honest. You are stronger than Anassa, stronger than the 'mares."

The Heron's words settled around me like a dawn breeze. I breathed them deep. We'd done things I never thought we could. Maybe we could do even more. "We will try," I promised. "For you. And for us."

"I believe in you both," the Heron creaked.

The ravens pushed the raft from the sandbar. Dishrag worked the treads hard and the wheel spun, throwing water everywhere.

The flock followed, but the Heron stayed on the beach, no longer able to fly.

When we reached the lighthouse, the last few nightmares were passing through a crack they'd broken in the thick, low wall of the lighthouse. They'd knocked down the stairs. The light was shattered.

My mouth felt dry as paste. There was a pale-green shape among the nightmares.

Anassa, moving through the crack with the last of the horses, turned back and laughed. "You've lost," she gloated. "We're going through. All thanks to you. You can try to follow, if you're fast enough, but we'll arrive long before you. You can't do anything right, Eleanor. Better than that? You won't remember a thing before long. You'll want to forget how you failed and the 'mares will help."

I slumped. We'd tried and it hadn't been enough. I'd missed my chance to stop Anassa at the bridge.

Across the river, the sky began to glow red. The sun pushed at the clouds. If the past was any guide, we might not remember any of this. Not the dream reeds, not the Heron—if we made it home; not the real world, if we stayed here.

Mike looked as if she was ready to throw one of the floats after the snake.

Breathe, Eleanor.

Suddenly, I had a better idea. I gathered up the glass balls into the garbage bags that had fallen off Anassa's dress. The birds helped me, and soon Mike did too.

"We're not giving up," I said, looking at the birds. "You can't give up either. You help us and we'll help you. Deal?"

One young raven stepped forward and nodded. Its glossy black feathers were made of curled, tarnished forks and plastic combs.

Its black beak, pieces of tires. "A deal. Which is an agreement," it said. "When you take the witch balls to the other side, you'll have several. They should last you a long time."

"If the nightmares can get through." I pointed at the crack in the lighthouse, so narrow, and getting smaller now. "So can we."

I ran my hand along Dishrag's mane. The pony nickered at me. "How?"

"Want to be a nightmare?" I winked at him.

Dishrag cocked his head and blew hard through his nose. Then he pawed at the barge. Once. Twice.

"I'll need you to run really fast. With us on your back. Can you do it?"

The crack in the lighthouse was growing darker. I could hear the wind whistling through it.

"Maybe," Dishrag said.

I turned to the birds. "I need you to carry the witch balls. And to follow us through."

The birds cackled at one another in distress.

"We've never been out of dream," the comb raven cawed. "We're not allowed."

"Come with us just for a moment, to do a job. For the Heron's sake," Dishrag said.

The raven's tire beak closed and opened. Then it picked up one of the trash bags, and the other birds followed. As they rose, glass shifted and clinked. The flock hovered in the air.

I helped Mike onto Dishrag's back. Then I climbed up, too, and held on to my sister.

The towels felt warm and soft. Mike leaned forward and hugged his mane and neck. "You are the best pony," she said.

"I'm trying to be a nightmare," Dishrag said. "Shhh."

Mike lifted the witch ball to Dishrag's mouth and the pony took a large bite, like an apple. The glass broke in his mouth, but he crunched it, then swallowed. He began to paw the beach and move forward on the sand. We clung to him, tendrils of smoke moving through the rolled towels.

The birds rose in the air as we began to move, their wings colored red and purple by the sun. "Will we make it?" And would we remember on the other side?

Dishrag shouted, "Yes!" as he threw himself at the hairline crack running up the tower. Darkness split the bone-white wall and the crack began to widen as we moved forward.

My panic rose and then turned to fear. I heard the nightmares whispering in the passage ahead. We slipped through the darkness. Then the light disappeared behind us as Dishrag's hooves beat the ground faster than before.

I couldn't breathe. I was so afraid. But Mike began to yell and I did, too, because we were riding through the dark on the fastest pony ever. We caught up with the herd, passing Anassa, passing everyone.

Still shouting, we rode with the nightmares out of the river and into the real.

CHAPTER

WATER AND WIND

SIXTEEN

Our yells were loud enough to make my ears ring. But the noise was nothing compared to the sound of the wind's howl on the other side.

No one heard us arrive.

Mike and I lay on a soaked pile of towels beneath the bed frame, disoriented and shivering. When I lifted the bed skirt, the bells jangled merrily. Jarringly. I watched shadows move on the walls all around us as the nightmares began to come through.

Downstairs, Poppa shouted, "We are not evacuating! Not now, not ever. This house is our anchor." That's how I knew we were home.

"Dishrag," Mike whispered. She grabbed a pale towel. I searched through the pile for the pony's mirrored eye but couldn't find it.

Mike began to cry.

"Shhhh," I said. I stroked her hair. I had my sister back. That's what mattered most.

Outside, a rattling sound grew louder.

I waited as long as I could before I said, "We have to hurry."

We scrambled from beneath the bed feeling at once too big and too small for the room. Rain and hail struck the windows. A strange sound rippled outside. The river had risen to lap at the neat stone walkway. The dock had disappeared.

And inside my room, a flock of dark birds beat against the windows, panicked.

Feathers swirled to the floor. The birds were going to hurt themselves.

I ran to the window that faced the front of the house. Flipped the latch and threw up the sash. The wind blew cold and tossed my homework from my desk. Mike opened another window.

Now the wind that had been outside was in.

And the dark birds, carrying most of the bags of witch balls, pushed out.

Up the road, I saw Pendra looking out her window, toward me. She stared as birds erupted from my house. Lifted her hand to point, to wave. In her driveway, Mrs. Sarti was packing their Subaru with suitcases. Other neighbors paced their garages and driveways, putting valuables in their cars and preparing to head for higher ground. I heard a weather radio squawk.

Our father would never leave. I knew that.

"The storm's coming fast," I whispered to Mike. "Come on." We had work to do.

The witch balls glowed in the stormlight. Green clouds outside—the same color as Anassa—built heavier and higher. My ears popped with the pressure.

This wasn't a normal storm.

Downstairs, the shouting grew louder. I heard the television screen crash once more to the floor. "Moira," Poppa shouted. Then: "Eleanor! Mary!"

Mike looked at me, eyes wide. "I'm not going down there."

"We have to finish this or Anassa will win. She'll bring all the nightmares here, the river will leak through to reality, the dream reeds will die, and the crabs and the birds too." It would look like an enormous storm, the clouds building to huge fists on the horizon. It would spread like darkness. The thought of nightmares running on the shores of our river scared me more than Poppa did.

Mike wiped her nose with her sleeve. "Okay."

I lifted the bag with the five witch balls the birds had left for us. It rustled and clanked in the wind. We tiptoed down the hall. The light in the house was strange. Bright and dark at the same time, the shadows nearly dark green. Stormlight. Like being trapped inside thick glass.

"We need to prepare to evacuate. The girls . . ." Momma began, standing in the foyer. I could see her, small and birdlike, sweatshirt and jeans, her hair a ragged mess. She held a bucket and a mop.

Poppa cut her off. "We're staying. It's just a storm. The news is making money off of scaring people."

"Simon, I don't think . . ."

The hard sound of hand striking cheek came again. I winced at the quiet that followed.

Then he spoke. "You *don't* think. Imagine what's going to happen to the house when everyone leaves. We'll get robbed, or flooded. Or both. We're showing your mother we know how to take care of things."

Mike and I were on the landing now. We stayed in the shadows. Outside, the wind rose and sounded like hooves on the roof, the windows.

I reached inside the bag and lifted out the turquoise ball. The one Mike and I had made together. Mike cupped her hands around it as I untied the yellow suncatcher.

"What are you doing?" Poppa's voice climbed the stairs before him, and his footsteps fell fast. He was on us in a second. "Leave that alone." His face folded around a deep-set scowl. "You didn't learn a thing yesterday."

I knew that look. It meant no matter what answer I chose, it would be wrong. He'd looked that way last night too.

Worse, his voice sounded like Anassa's. And mine. Angry.

There wasn't any good choice. Only bad ones.

So I chose to look him right in the eyes. I saw something dark looking back, trying to get out.

"No. We won't leave it." I reached up and knotted the cord so that it would hold the witch ball.

Poppa raised his hand, aiming for the glass sphere.

I stepped in front of the swing. He caught me hard on the cheek and I knocked into the witch ball. The ball swung, but it didn't break.

I stumbled but stood back up, daring him to do it again.

His face got redder and redder. "We have a situation here and you're wasting time. Worthless."

Mike stepped next to me but let me put an arm in front of her. We both stared back at Poppa, watching him swell with anger. We did not answer him.

His fists balled up. "What do you have to say for yourself, Eleanor?"

I said nothing. I waited. I wasn't going to cower. I knew that would make him mad too.

A rush of air and his hands were on my neck. His face close, eyes nearly black. I flailed and tried to back away, tried to put my hands up, poke at his eyes—something. Mike shouted for Momma, but it sounded squashed, like I was hearing her underwater. I heard Momma yell too. Quieter.

And then a wisp of dark smoke formed, nightmare black, about shoulder height, just at Poppa's side. If I'd had air to scream, I would have.

Poppa said something through gritted teeth. My name. Pressed harder on the "nor."

Dark smoke built at the sides of my eyes. Along the hallway.

Then the smoke nickered in my ear and rose to swirl around Poppa's head.

He pulled one hand away to swat at the smoke, and I jerked back, freeing myself.

He wobbled on his feet, teetering on the landing. "What is this?"

My skin pulsed where he'd pressed, an angry beat. I could feel where his fingers had been.

Now his hands danced in the air, trying to push away smoke. He turned and nearly fell down the stairs. "Something's burning. Everything is flooding and something in this house catches on fire." His voice rose in pitch, then curled into a sharp laugh.

No smoke alarms had gone off. The house remained quiet except for Poppa's laughter and the crackle of the storm radio. But Poppa chased the smoke downstairs anyway, leaving me and Mike standing at the top of the landing, the turquoise witch ball swinging in the breeze.

Mike let her breath out in a rush.

I watched the smoke recede from the foyer. "That's a really good nightmare." My voice sounded rough, like I'd swallowed sand, but my hands were steady as I tied a second set of knots around the glass sphere. *He'll have to work harder to cut it down next time.* My only goal.

The power flickered and the house grew stormdark. The new witch ball's blue-green surface caught a light shining in from the river. One that disappeared and reappeared. I looked out the guest room window. A small boat bobbed within the river's bend, a searchlight mounted on its bow. An amplified voice asked repeatedly for us to signal if we needed assistance before the worst of the storm hit.

I nearly flashed an upstairs light in reply, but the boat motored away before I could find the switch in the dark.

There is a quiet before a storm—like all sound is sucked into powering the wind.

There is a quiet during a storm when the power goes out, or the wind dips.

In those moments, you forget how loud it was a moment ago.

Downstairs, Momma carried buckets and mops. Brown water rippled on the clean foyer's floor. "Help, Eleanor," she said. "Get the spray foam from the basement." She bit her lip, but otherwise, her expression was calm. "We can make do."

Making do meant we weren't leaving. Momma was trying to clean things up instead. The house smelled like the river and was, for a moment, as quiet as water. Water lapping at the floor.

The rules of house magic didn't apply when everything outside was intent on coming in.

At Momma's urging, Mike reached for a mop. The wooden handle stood as tall as her.

I looked back up at the witch ball on the landing, at the closed office door. I could get the spray foam. I could help patch the house against leaks.

My neck throbbed, which helped me remember. But Mike seemed to already be forgetting again. "We just need to fix the hall," she said. "That's all. The rest will be fine." Everything was normal. Anassa had been right: Forgetting was easier. It made things simpler for everyone.

I went to help them mop the floor.

When Momma's cell phone rang, we all jumped. The sound snapped me out of my forgetting. I ran to the kitchen and grabbed it from the counter on the second ring, even though Poppa had said no phone. Pendra's phone number glowed on the display.

The line crackled with static, like damp wires in a flooded tunnel. I heard Pendra's voice. She sounded very far away.

"Mom says we have to go to the school, to evacuate. Are you going? Did you find Mike? What's happening? Did you get in trouble?"

Her words saved me. I found my voice. "We're shoring up the house. Mike's here."

"Come with us, Eleanor. We'll give you all a ride if you can't get your car out. Your parents too."

I stood in the dark kitchen, wanting to go. Now. Poppa had nailed boards over the kitchen windows.

"They said we're staying," I said.

"That's not safe! I'll tell my mom to come get you. Tell your mom you want to go to the evacuation point, at the school."

"We can't just leave without—anyway, we're grounded."

"You have to leave, Eleanor!" Pendra said. "Hey, weren't you grounded last night too? Think about that. You snuck out, right?"

She meant the sleepover. That seemed so long ago. Maybe Pendra had already forgotten the rest. Her voice reached through the phone, from all the way up the hill, from beyond the house that was almost magically sealing itself shut. It made me feel stronger. "I'll try."

I'd told Momma I'd help her; I told Pendra I'd try.

My voice was still scratchy and my cheek stung, and I just wanted to get through this storm. To go back to normal.

But.

Nothing was really normal, was it?

I peered through the cracks between two pieces of plywood. Outside, Poppa paced through the rain, his curses pounding against the thick glass and wood. Smoke played against the window and the wind kicked higher. Poppa dropped his hammer and picked it up again. I shivered and walked backward, away from the window, so I wouldn't have to turn my back on him or the storm. My feet splashed on the floor.

Water was coming up from the basement, under the doors, and the leaks were darkening too. I grabbed the spray foam from the shelf by the stairs, then turned to find Mike right behind me. So close that I jumped. She didn't say a word at first, just chewed on her hair.

She held the bag of witch balls tight to her chest with her other hand.

When Momma wasn't looking, we climbed up on the counter and hung a small witch ball from a light fixture near the leak. Like boarding up the windows and trying to mop up the river, we couldn't fix everything, couldn't hold everything back. But we could try something.

I climbed off the counter and took Mike's hand in mine. "We'll be all right," I said.

She didn't say anything. Her face was moon-pale. Even the freckles. On the way back to the foyer, we peeked through another boarded window at the bay. Over the river, dark horses ran with the clouds and stirred up the water. Mike pulled me away, tugging at my hand wordlessly.

We splashed into the landing and Momma took the can of spray foam from me and began to seal the front door.

Still, we followed Momma to the front door. The foyer floor was already damp again.

"Storm surge," she muttered. "Wind is driving everything up the bay."

"Momma," I said, thinking that if she sealed the front door we'd be stuck, "we can go with Pendra's family. We need to go."

"We can't," Momma said. "I can't . . ." She looked from me to Mike.

Poppa had stopped hammering.

While the wind began to slam things outside, the house became a container of silence. The dark smoke passed us once more, and through the cracks between the boards, I saw it wrap

Poppa once, twice. He waved his hands as if he could bat the nightmare away, then dropped his hammer and came inside, into his office with the radio, declaring, "We're staying. No arguments!"

I'd argued. It had hurt.

I'd do it again.

Momma began to mop the floor once more.

"Momma," I said. She'd forgotten so much, but this wasn't a fairy tale. She wasn't a good witch. She just wanted things to be all right really, really hard. Even when it was impossible.

She forgot things so that she could pretend everything would be all right. Normal, even. She was forgetting now. "Please? Let's go?"

Around the house, glass spheres caught the last of the light before the storm and held it fast. The last few witch balls in Mike's hands seemed to glow, too.

Momma glanced toward the study, where the radio crackled. She looked at us.

I pressed. "There are nightmares running in the clouds, Momma. There are monsters. Like on the river."

She blinked. "Nightmares?"

"You remember?" The storm pressed against the house. "Did you ever go?"

She looked up at the witch ball Mike and I had hung. "A long time ago, but I couldn't—there was a storm. The rowboat sank and I—" Then she shook her head and put the mop down.

"I lost. I was terrible at everything, including managing that dinghy. And then your father took over. And the dinghy sunk. And I thought no one was coming to help and I just forgot. And then . . ."

I waited for her to finish. But she shook her head again as if waving away a small bird. "It wasn't a really good dream," she finally said. "But we make the best of—" She stopped. Blinked again. "No."

She gripped the mop handle tighter. "You go. Eleanor, take Mike and go up the hill. Hurry." She opened the closet. "Get coats and boots."

The leak in the closet had darkened. The wallboard bubbled. Momma ignored it and grabbed our coats. I found our boots, damp on the floor.

"Momma," Mike whispered, "come with us."

Outside, the rain began to salt the glass with hard taps. Momma looked out the window.

"Moira!" Poppa shouted from the office. "Get in here. Bring the mop."

Momma hugged us both. She pushed our coats and boots into our arms. Bent close and kissed the top of my head.

"I'll come as soon as I can. Go to the Sartis'." Her voice shook but she pushed us out the door, into the cold electric air. "Run."

+++

Outside, I struggled to force my feet into the rubber boots. The last three witch balls swung heavy in the plastic bag on my shoulder. More glittered in the trees around the house, but I couldn't see the birds. I helped Mike, who was moving slower, get her boots on too. She grumbled at me. "I can do it."

"You can. Let me help anyway." The clouds spun overhead. Finally, she nodded.

We stayed in the shadows. We couldn't see into the house, and our parents couldn't see us.

The nightmares ran the waves, down the river, around the house. A few began to climb the trees, shaking and bending them. The trunks held until the horses reached branches where the birds had hung the witch balls. Then the branches began to bend.

Each time one of the smoke-shadows reached a float, the glass ball gleamed. The shadow disappeared. That might have been the storm, which was in full swing now, but the number of 'mares lessened. The magic was working.

But not fast enough.

There were nightmares pulling on the house shutters, trying to batter the sealed door. They looked like dark waves of wind and water.

One nightmare came running straight at us, galloping up the hill toward Pendra's. Anassa rode on its back.

"We didn't forget!" I shouted, not caring if anyone heard me inside the house.

I pulled on Mike's water-slick sleeve, yanking her out of the way. The 'mare skidded to a halt. Blew warm mist at us and stared.

"You go back where you came from," I said.

The 'mare snorted. Anassa did also. "You can't think you have any power here, child. Your stories won't work now. Your baubles are broken, and I am back in the world." She looked at her hands then, and blinked, disappointment welling in her eyes. Then her tongue flickered out and she curled her fingers in the nightmare's mane. "Still a monster. But I'm strong. Here, even more than on the river."

The nightmare's eyes reflected my face. Made me seem bigger.

I pulled a witch ball from the sack. "Mike and I made new agreements. And they're stronger than stories. Stronger than you." When I held it up, it reflected the horse and its rider and the wind and rain pouring over them both.

She rushed at me, her hand raised to strike me, to smash the ball. I held my ground.

I was so focused on the incoming hit, I ignored her other hand, which grabbed me by the jacket.

When she picked me up and shook me hard, I nearly dropped the witch ball. Mike grabbed my ankle and held on. I felt like I was being pulled apart.

But I wasn't afraid. I wasn't panicked. I knew what I had to do.

"I won't forget," I said. "I'm watching for you."

"Both of us are," Mike yelled. And I held the witch ball up to her scaled face, her dark eyes.

The threads inside the glass sphere dazzled her. She couldn't turn away.

"No one will want you, once they know what you're really like, lovely," she whispered, but only half as loudly as before.

I didn't let go of the ball. I didn't falter. Mike held my ankle. I took a deep breath and let it out.

"Yes," I said. "Yes, they will."

And at that moment, I believed it, because it was the truth. That mattered the most.

Anassa's shocked face drew closer to the ball, and then she was inside it. Suddenly tiny and trapped.

I could hear her fists pounding on the glass curve.

A flock of ravens and crows flew down and snatched the witch ball and flew away. The nightmare turned and sped after the flock, toward the river. Chasing its mistress.

I fell back to the ground and Mike helped me up.

We watched the birds go as the rain flattened our hair.

The sky lit up in layers of lightning and cloud.

"The storm's not easing!" I pulled my sister up the road.

Already, Riverland's empty driveways and dark houses—some with boarded windows like the blue house at the bottom of the cul-de-sac, the one that wasn't magicked after all—looked desolate. A few lights flickered, but the driveways had emptied. Four cars waited at the top of the subdivision, their headlights laced by rain, their brake lights glowing red. One by one, as we climbed the hill, our neighbors turned left out of the subdivision. Headed for the evacuation center.

From the cul-de-sac, I couldn't see Pendra's garage. Would they still be there?

Mike and I ran up the road, the wind pushing at us with all its might. We ran toward the bus stop and Pendra's house. Rain needled at us, coming in sideways. Pooling in our collars. Plastering our hair to our cheeks and lips.

Mike clung to my arm, jostling the remaining two witch balls in her bag. I wrapped my arm around her and pulled her through the storm. "We can make it." I said.

Her teeth chattered.

"Once upon a time," I shouted over the storm, "two brave girls finished their quest."

"And returned home and ran away again," Mike said sadly. "What will happen to Momma? And Poppa."

"We'll make it," I said. "We can tell someone to go back for them."

Hoofbeats. A single nightmare galloped behind us. Three ravens swooped down and plucked it away. I saw them flying back to the trees. We kept running.

At the top of the hill, in the Sartis' driveway, red lights glowed. The Sartis were still putting things in their car, preparing to leave. Up here, the wind was worse than the water. The big Subaru's doors were open. Mrs. Sarti struggled to get one of the dogs into the back of the truck.

"Wait!" I called. I thought about all the questions they were going to have. All the lies I might have once told. "Our mom asked if we could leave with you."

"Where are your parents?" Mrs. Sarti squinted down the road at our house, which sat in the middle of a grassy lake now. Then she looked at us and grabbed two towels. Handed them to us. "Never mind. Get in."

Inside the car, Pendra peered at us. Her brothers too. "Pendra said you had birds in your house this morning. A whole flock."

Pendra stared at me and I stared back. She was waiting on me to deny it. To say she'd been seeing things.

I didn't say a word.

She spoke instead. "It was a figure of speech, Mo. You take everything so literally." She unbuckled her seatbelt and helped us get in and out of the rain.

The car smelled like gym socks and damp. Pendra sat quietly. I'd pushed her away after she'd helped me. Now I didn't need her help, but I still wanted to fix things. On my terms, not hers.

"I can't always tell you everything," I whispered.

"I know."

"But I got you a birthday present." I held out the small witch ball. One with a happy story. "Good for keeping away nightmares." The blue-green sphere reflected our faces in the car.

"You said it was a dream," she whispered so her brothers didn't hear.

Mike stared at me as I nodded. "I wasn't telling the truth, but I wasn't lying either. Magic is like that sometimes. So is glass. Something in between. But you have to promise never to go back."

"I promise." Pendra's eyes went wide and she put her palms on the glass ball. Her brown fingers wrapped the blue and green whorls. She closed her eyes and gasped. Whispered, "I see . . . you and me."

She cradled the witch ball. Behind us, beyond the car's back window, the storm rolled around the bay. Floodwaters rose up against the perfect house at the bottom of the street. Mike and I, dripping but safe in the Sartis' SUV, looked back at the house lights as they flickered again. I saw my father's shadow in one last unboarded window. Then the lights went out.

Fear broke over me. *How could we leave?* Mrs. Sarti started the car. The dogs barked in the very back of the Subaru. Pendra's brothers played with their phones, taking pictures of the storm. We were leaving. Mike's fingers pressed white on the car seat as we watched the darkened house get smaller. Momma had told us to go. We were safe, and that was a different kind of magic.

My throat didn't hurt much anymore. And the bright spot on my cheek had faded. That was lucky. I didn't want to explain those things. Not yet. I had my sister, who I'd gone back for. I had more than one agreement with the river, and I was spreading those far and wide to keep them from all getting broken.

We would figure the rest out as we went, but we were done making the best of things.

Back down the hill, I saw two more dark horses pounding across the water toward the house. The witch balls hung in the trees caught the lightning and the horses turned, bewitched. Then the nightmares disappeared, one by one, transfixed into the witch balls. As I watched, a flock of gray gulls teetered in the wind, then descended to the trees. They lifted the floats away, taking them back to the river.

As we pulled away, all I could see were storm clouds. No more nightmares.

+++

When the Sartis' car reached the middle school, the parking lot and the bus line were already crowded.

Almost everyone who lived near the river had come to the evacuation point. Some were talking about the last storm that had blown up the bay, how they hadn't left then. Saying, "We've had too many close calls before." And: "The storm might have blown through already, but the surge will flood everything."

One side of the gym was filled with green cots covered with gray blankets. On the other side, a large television flickered news. On the screen, I saw the Coast Guard rescuing people from houses up and down the bay, and even from row houses in the city.

"They'll pick up your parents too," Mr. Sarti said. "If your father doesn't refuse to go."

"He might," Mike whispered.

"He probably will," I said.

Pendra elbowed me. "You did the right thing." She'd wrapped her jacket around the witch ball. Now she pulled something from the pocket. "You forgot this."

A plain brown box, stripped of paper. My birthday present. I took it from her again. "Thank you."

The box felt solid in my hands but complicated too. A memory of the night before, a promise maybe for the year ahead. "I'm going to open it when things are calmer, all right?" I asked.

Pendra nodded. "All right."

Mrs. Wunner and Mr. Divner walked the gym, passing through loose knots of families, sharing news and snacks. Mrs. Sarti touched my elbow reassuringly. Mrs. Wunner passed me a bottle of water. "You girls all right?"

I kept my eyes on the screen. The rumble in the room calmed as the rain on the roof and the thunder began to ease. We weren't all right, but we were better.

"We'll be able to go home soon," Pendra's brother Mo said. He turned to me. "I hope your house is still there."

"Shut up, Mo! El's house is magic. They'll be all right," Pendra said.

"You should call someone." Mrs. Sarti nudged me. She handed Mike a dry sweatshirt and me a blanket. We huddled in them like owls. "Who would you like to call?"

I took a breath. "My grandmother."

She nodded, peering at my face. "She's a good one to talk to now."

We walked from the gym to Mrs. Sarti's office. She gave me the phone and left Mike and me alone.

Mike bit a fingernail and looked at me. "What do we tell her?"

I thought about the silences between people. Between us. About glass paperweights and the witch balls. About how Gran had said sometimes reaching out is the hardest part.

"Everything. We tell her everything."

Mike stopped biting her nail. "Okay."

I hoped Gran was right and Poppa was wrong.

The phone rang twice before Gran answered. "I've been watching the news! Are you all right? Is Mike? Moira?"

I'd break the last rule of house magic for real if I told her.

I was ready to do it. But I wasn't sure how to begin.

I took the last witch ball from the bag and put it on my lap. Touched my fingers to the glass. It felt cool and hard, liquid and fluid. Mike rested her hand on it too. I looked at the surface of the sphere. At the space inside, the space outside.

Breathe, Eleanor.

"Eleanor?"

"Gran, I need to tell you a story," I said. "A true one."

CHAPTER

MEMORY

SEVENTEEN

After the storm, a lot of things happened. Gran didn't go to Venice. She found a bigger apartment in Baltimore instead. She took the light rail down to the museum.

We framed the map Mike had made when we visited Gran the first time and hung it in one bedroom. Strung the witch ball in the window of another.

The schools rescheduled the science fair for three weeks after the storm. The crowded gym looked different than it had the night of the evacuation. Instead of cots, there were tables, holding posters and screens. But it sounded the same. A lot of people talking all at once. Like a flock of birds.

Pendra and I had been busy.

When I finally opened the box she'd given me for my birthday, I found a gift certificate inside. Clipper Mill Glassblowers: a group class.

"I thought we could go together," Pendra said.

I couldn't answer at first and she'd stammered, "If you want to? I mean, you can go with whoever. I just thought I'd ask."

My smile had nearly cracked my cheeks. I wanted to go. I'd worried we wouldn't see each other if I was living somewhere other than Riverland. But we would. We did.

At the fair, two glass spheres and three paperweights sat on our table, next to a few long tendrils of glass Gran had made. All different shapes, all catching the light and reflecting our faces. There was a story behind each piece. The time Pendra had blown too hard and the molten glass slumped nearly to the floor, but we reheated it until it was fixed. The time I'd folded and pinched a paperweight until it was more bubble than glass.

We repeated our lampwork example for the fair. Talked to the people gathered by our table about how glass has memory but can change.

Momma came by to watch us, weaving her way among the different schools' displays until she found our group. She shook Mr. Divner's hand and admired our second-place ribbon. Smiled at Mrs. Sarti and Mike and Gran, who were standing together near the table.

"I'm proud of you," she whispered while Pendra was talking to a curious sixth grader. A small gold necklace was clasped at her throat.

"We miss you." I held her hand.

She blinked tears back. "We just need some time to sort things out, fix up the house again," she said. "You know your father. You're doing fine with Gran?"

I nodded. Smiled maybe a bit too much. "We're fine."

Gran nodded too. "Both of them are," she said. "They have their own rooms at my new apartment."

Momma drew back then, a little. She put a hand to her cheek. "Just for a while."

Then she hugged Mike and me and left to go back to Poppa. We watched her go. Her jeans and sweater, her dockside shoes let her easily blend with the crowd as she disappeared. She looked so normal.

Mike and I knew that sometimes magic worked this way.

"You okay?"

"Just a nightmare. Can I come in?"

"You don't need to ask. I'm finished with my homework. What kind of nightmare?"

"The kind that only makes you a little sad. Not really a nightmare at all. More like a friend that's moved away."

"Aw, Mike."

"Can you tell me a story?"

"Okay. But don't wake Gran."

"She won't be mad. She'll just tell me to go back to bed."

"How about we tell it together."

"Once upon a . . ."

"What about someday instead?"

"Someday, two sisters will have amazing adventures, and they'll travel a lot and . . ."

". . . they'll always remember to come back home."

"Wherever home is . . ."

"That's simple. Home is where we keep our stories."

"I like that."

"Should we say the spell?"

"Do you think we need to?"

"Yeah."

"You say it."

"YOU say it."

"Mike."

"Eleanor."

"Okay, fine. Together?"

. . .

"Someday our real parents will come for us."

"But it's okay if they don't."

"Yeah. It's okay."

Acknowledgments

Writing a book like this pushed me far beyond what I thought I could do, and no matter how hard it was, I kept pushing because I knew the story was important. It is my hope that when it's needed most, it will be right there on the bookshelf for whoever needs it.

If that's you, I see you. I believe you. You are important.

This is a tough story to tell. There was no way I could make it through writing *Riverland* without a cast of magical beings of my own:

To Susan, Chris, Tom, and Iris for everything, each step of the way. To Stacey Cunitz, Kat Howard, Aliette de Bodard, Sarah Mueller, Liz Argall, Shveta Thakrar, D. T. Friedman, Michelle Burke Kelly, Sarah Pinsker, Natalie Luhrs, Constance Callahan, A. C. Wise, A. T. Greenblatt, Siobhan Carroll, Stephanie Feldman, Kate Martin, Eric Smith, Will Alexander, Alexander London, Eugene Myers, Tiffany Schmidt, Kate Milford, Katherine Locke, Nanita Cranford, Nancy Caudill, Lauren Teffeau, and Raq Winchester for reading drafts and encouraging words. To my consulting teachers, especially Kathryn Gullo,

Harriette Bode, Dan Cunitz, and (again, and always) Stacey Cunitz. To my parents and families everywhere.

Many thanks to the Crefeld School and the Crefeld Glass Studio and especially Josh Cole and Kristy Modarelli.

To my amazing editor, Maggie Lehrman, at Abrams Books—you saw this book for what it was and helped it become what it needed to be. I loved working on this with you. To my agent, Barry Goldblatt, thank you for believing in this strange world, these girls, and this book. To the production and PR staff at Abrams, including copy editor Kylie Bird, cover artist Robert Frank Hunter, and Emily Daluga, thank you for your careful work.

Thank you forever and always to Camp Tockwogh in Worton, Maryland: the water knows why.

Read on for a sneak peak at Fran Wilde's new fantasy adventure

Winner of the Nebula Award

FRAN WILDE

THE SHIP OF STOLEN WORDS

Part One

Chapter One

Sam

On the last morning of fifth grade, Sam Culver lost his favorite word. Then, right after that, he lost two more words.

Sam didn't notice at first. But then his sometimes-best friend, Mason McGargee, and his teacher, Ms. Malloy, noticed. And after that *everyone* noticed. Which was embarrassing.

"Sam! Easy on the screen door!" His stepmother, Anita, had called as he ran from the house. Too late—the door hit the frame with a WHAM right between *screen* and *door*.

"Sorry!" He shouted over his shoulder, hoping that would smooth his exit. He heard Anita say something about Mason, but he was already late. He'd see Mason in a minute anyway, because they walked the three blocks to school together.

But today, she wasn't waiting for him.

Just in case Mason was running late, Sam strolled slowly toward Ursula K. Le Guin Elementary alone. He took his time stepping over cracks and dodging the ants making lean trails across the already-hot pavement. Mason and her mom had missed their families' latest Saturday movie night, and the first meeting of the Mount Cloud summer baseball league, which they'd been waiting for all year. He had a lot to tell her.

As Sam walked, he whistled. He wasn't very good at whistling, and the notes sounded flat. He tried to remember the bad guys' theme in the monster movie that he, his sister, Bella, and their parents had just watched. But he couldn't quite get it right. Mason would have known which notes he was getting wrong, because she never forgot things like that. But she hadn't caught up to Sam on the way to school yet, so he couldn't ask her.

Sam was also thinking about baseball—how could he not? The first practice of the summer was that afternoon. At the end of last season, he'd played second base instead of his usual right field position, and he and his dad had been working on his throws ever since. The Mount Cloud coaches, Mr. Lockheart and Mason's dad, Dr. McGargee, had hinted Sam might move to the infield for good.

He was so busy thinking about baseball and movies that Sam almost tripped over a miniature white pig rooting around the base of Mrs. Lockheart's Little Free Library, two doors up from his house.

The pig's snout was deep in the last of the tulips, upending the flowers and pushing dirt onto the sidewalk. *Boy, Mrs. Lockheart hated when her flowers got messed up*, Sam thought. Then he realized there was a bigger problem.

The pig's leash—a long, leather strap that matched the saddle it was wearing—had gotten tangled around Sam's ankles. He'd blundered right into it when he was looking at the wrecked tulips and wondering who was going to get in trouble and have to apologize to Mrs. Lockheart.

Mrs. Lockheart hated apologies. Sam knew this for a fact, having messed up her tulips before.

The surprise pig was very odd, and its leash and saddle even more so. But what most immediately concerned Sam was the small, silver-haired old woman poking a willow stick at his face while trying to untangle the pig's leash with her other hand.

Her skin—both on her hand, which was way too close, and her face—was wrinkled like a dried apple. When she shook the stick, the end almost scraped Sam's nose. And then she started scolding him.

"Watch where you're going, young man!" The old woman bellowed; her voice was much bigger than should be possible for someone so small. Even Bella—who was five, and taller than this woman—couldn't get so loud. The old woman waved the switch at Sam again. "Kids should be more careful, especially—"

"Sorry!" Sam said for at least the second time that morning.

He tried to back up and pull his foot free from the leash. The pig made a watery snuffling sound and gazed at Sam doubtfully, sideways, with one black-ink eye.

Sam couldn't free his foot fast enough. He ended up splat on the sidewalk, next to the tulips, where he couldn't avoid the old woman's stick. She tapped him on the cheek with it, which itched. "Hey!"

Something shimmered near Sam's cheek, like a spiderweb or a long piece of ribbon—the kind Bella sometimes tied to Sam's backpack. He pushed it and the stick away. Sam waved at his hair too, for good measure. Leaves and spiderwebs sometimes fell from the big oak onto the sidewalk near the Little Free Library.

For a moment, Sam felt the same way he did when he'd just pulled a tooth out—where that one raw spot was just *lacking*, before it became a point of pride to stick his tongue through. And then the feeling went away, and he grabbed for the ribbon. Mrs. Lockheart didn't tolerate littering any more than people messing with her tulips, and if she caught Sam on the way to school doing both, he was going to have a lot of explaining to do.

But the ribbon—or whatever it was—sparkled just out of reach. Then the white pig snorfled it up gleefully. Most of it disappeared before Sam could grab it. "Hey!"

"You shouldn't be so careless!" The old woman scolded him. She glowered and yanked at the leash. The pig snuffled, and Sam finally freed his foot. He was going to be so late for school.

"I really apologize for running into you! I have to go," Sam shouted over his shoulder as he sped off, a little embarrassed that he'd managed to get so tangled up with the pair of them. The strange woman waved at him with her stick. And Sam got the missing-tooth feeling again, but then it went away.

A pig! With a saddle—in Mount Cloud! Sam almost stopped and turned around again to make sure they were real. But that would make him even more late. And who would believe that he was late because of a wandering grandmother and her miniature pet pig? No one. Especially not Ms. Malloy, his fifth-grade teacher, who lived right next door to the Lockhearts and likely had never seen an old woman walking a tiny pig on a leash. Sam knew he hadn't.

But then he did look back. And when he didn't see the old woman or the pig—or anything other than the Little Free Library and a few uprooted tulips—he wondered if maybe he had imagined it all.

He quickened his pace and made it to the school's front steps just as the bell rang. He'd climbed two of the five big stone stairs that led up to the blue doors of Ursula K. Le Guin Elementary before Mason caught up with him.

"What is that you're whistling?" Mason asked. She wore her hair in curly pigtails and had one of last year's Mount Cloud baseball jackets wrapped around her waist so that it cinched her yellow sundress in a blue hug.

Sam hadn't realized he was still whistling the song.

"There you are! I can't remember the tune right—it's from Ghostbusters IV, which you'd know if you'd been able to come watch the movie last weekend," Sam teased. He and Mason had been teasing each other a lot lately. Sometimes not so nicely.

"This one?" Mason repeated the tune and did it perfectly. She so good at remembering. And at whistling.

Sam felt his face go red. He didn't really know why, but Mason barely having to try to remember made him want to turn invisible. She was better at everything than he was, really, except reading and baseball. And maybe fixing stuff, when Sam had Anita's help. He spoke without thinking. "It's hard to tell. You whistle kind of like a goldfish." He puffed his cheeks and pressed his lips into a fish face.

Mason's smile fell.

One thing Sam liked about Mason was that he rarely had to worry about hurting her feelings. She was tough and always said she could give as good as she got. But today felt different.

"It's not like you can whistle well, either, Sam. You should practice more instead of teasing people." Mason was blinking hard, and her face was scrunched. "Can we not fight today?"

Sam winced. Mason knew he was touchy about having to do extra work to get stuff right, like with math this year—but she still teased him about practicing. It wasn't fair. Even though he did wish he could unsay the bit about the goldfish.

He tried to smooth things over. "Sure. And I'll definitely practice. As long as it's practicing baseball!" He opened Ms. Malloy's classroom door. It was the first room down from the principal's office, just after the main entrance. A wave of air-conditioned coolness washed out, smelling a little like very cold tin cans. "Instead of spending all summer doing math problems, like a nerd!"

Mason elbowed him. "It's called Math Olympics and I like it." Now she grinned.

Sam smiled too. He started to describe what had happened on his walk. "You'll never believe . . ."

But with a few words, his mostly best friend made him forget all about pigs and grandmas. "Don't worry, you're getting a lot better at math too," she said with a wink.

Mason wasn't letting up! Even if she'd dropped the joking tone and was trying to sound nice. Sam focused on his shoes, betting he was turning bright red and that everyone in class could probably see it. Math *had* been hard this this year, and Mason knew it.

His parents had even talked with Ms. Malloy about extra summer work, but he'd managed to pull his grade up before the end of May. Unlike Mason, who ate math for breakfast, Sam wished he could disappear every time the subject came up. Why didn't she get that?

Mason took her seat and Sam slid into his desk right in front of hers. His embarrassment simmered then quieted. Why had they been fighting? He couldn't remember how it started. Now he felt a little sad. Mason would have loved hearing about the pig.

She'd have said the old woman was a witch or a fairy, probably.

Sam almost turned and tried again, but Mason was already talking to her neighbor, Gina. And Gina thought Sam was weird. So he decided to leave it alone, for once. His dad said that it was good to leave well enough alone sometimes.

Maybe when it's summer, I'll tell her about the pig, Sam thought as he stared at his desk. *Meantime, only a few more hours of school to get through and I'll be free.* He knew he'd earned it: the bell was going to sound like a winner's gong.

That final bell took a long time to chime.

School ground from math (games, thankfully) to history (a movie, with everyone dozing off, including Ms. Malloy) to English. The playground outside Ms. Malloy's classroom window shimmered with waves of heat. Sam couldn't take his eyes off it.

That shimmer meant freedom. Schools in Mount Cloud's district weren't built for this much summer. The air conditioner—an old window unit with colored strips of paper in the vents that let the students know it was still working—coughed and sputtered. It couldn't keep up with the heat.

Sam could almost taste the lemonade Anita would set on the porch after the last day of school. She'd done that every year since he was six. He could feel the sweaty surface of a baseball—Mount Cloud Community League (MCCL) Sharpied in fading black ink near the red stitching—as he caught it and tagged a runner out. Summer was less than an hour away.

On the playground, a tongue-red kickball someone had left out after recess seemed to deflate a little and stick to the pavement. As he stared, the curl of a pig's white tail appeared behind the ball.

He blinked to clear his eyes. Then he heard a snort.

The pig, not the ball.

When Sam looked again, after giving his head a good shake, the pig was gone.

"Sam! Pay attention!" Ms. Malloy waved a fan-folded worksheet in his direction. The less-warm air cooled the sweat on his cheek. "We have forty-five more minutes of your time, my friend. We're going to make it count. Let's take a look at your summer book projects."

"Yes, Ms. Malloy," he said, while his sixteen classmates, including Mason, snickered. Sam momentarily considered tacking a half-hearted apology onto the end of his sentence, then looked up at his teacher with wide eyes.

Sorry was the kind of word that had always rolled off Sam's tongue like a bright coin and made everyone relax. Before he said it, he'd think of something sad like chocolate melting uneaten, or Bodie Jacobs, the youngest player ever for the Mount Cloud farm team (who might get to play for the Mets someday) striking out with all the bases loaded. That was Sam's secret formula for getting out of trouble. It wasn't just the word that mattered. It was the delivery: Say *sorry* and look really sad or serious. Adults ate that stuff up.

But it was the last day of school, and when he said certain words around Ms. Malloy, he had to mean them. She was strict. Sam learned that from the first three-paragraph essay he wrote for her: wasted or excess words got him extra work like looking up things in her huge classroom dictionary. But Ms. Malloy said Sam was a great storyteller, so she'd wanted him to fix it.

No, she'd said she *expected* Sam to fix it. So he had.

When anyone did what Ms. Malloy expected, she never said thank you. She just nodded like they'd finally lived up to her standards and moved on. That made her a little scary, for a teacher, but also as a neighbor.

Ms. Malloy, when she left Ursula K. Le Guin Elementary, would walk the five blocks to her house, which was catty-corner to Sam's, and sit on the porch fanning herself all summer, except when she disappeared inside.

She wastes summer, Sam had told Bella once. She didn't come to baseball games or go to cookouts; she didn't go to the neighborhood parties either, his parents said. She sometimes chatted with people on her porch, but that was it.

Sam couldn't imagine anything worse, and neither he nor Bella could figure out what Ms. Malloy did at her house for three whole months. They'd spent some time the previous summer imagining Ms. Malloy's house had hidden tunnels and secret portals to the other side of the world. Like in the stories that Sam's sister loved.

But Ms. Malloy didn't seem like the kind of adult who would have secret tunnels. She was the kind of adult who could sit on her porch all summer long without the perfect bun on top of her head getting the least bit out of place.

In the classroom, the heat-damp curls of Sam's own too-long hair already stuck to his neck.

"Sam!"

He stopped staring at the small holes in the ceiling tiles and smiled at Ms. Malloy.

She shook her head then returned to discussing their summer book projects. "You'll be partnering with someone in your neighborhood to take care of the nearest Little Free Library and make sure it's stocked with books for the community. Ones you've read. I want you to write recommendations too. And if there isn't a Little Free Library near your home, I can help you find a way to build one."

Sam grinned. This would be easy. Ms. Malloy's neighbor, Mr. Lockheart, had built his block's Little Free Library—with Sam's help—and it was always well stocked. The recommendations? Those depended on who Sam was teamed with. He liked sharing sports and comic books. He hoped he got someone who liked a lot of different things.

"Sam, your partner is Mason."

His smile faded. This wouldn't be so easy after all. While Mason liked science fiction and graphic novels, she also liked to read math and science books. Maybe, Sam decided, we can add in some of Bella's favorite recommendations too, and it would work out.

The whole summer might still have gone great if Mason hadn't decided right then to whisper something about Sam and math to Gina Dulaney that sounded like more teasing.

And if Sam hadn't decided to fire back.

"I hope you won't have to spend the whole summer with your grandmother again, Mason," Sam whispered, trying to get her to be quiet. At least about him. "I don't want to have to do the whole project myself."

Mason's face folded shut like a book. She looked hard at her desk.

And *WHAM*, Ms. Malloy's hand came down loud on *Sam's* desk. "Apologize, Sam. Immediately."

His stomach cinched up. He'd gone too far, probably. Somehow. He had no idea how. But it was definitely too far.

As the window unit air conditioner hummed loudly, stirring the chalk dust and sweaty-feet air of the classroom around without actually cooling anything off, someone pig-snorted near the window, and Mason glared at Sam.

He thought of Bodie Jacobs striking out with three people on base. Then he reached for his trusty word.

"_____ . . ."

Sam gaped, tasting the empty space where the word should have been. He couldn't for all the summer baseball games in the neighborhood make the sounds that formed his magic get-out-of-trouble word.

The adventure continues in

Fran Wilde's novels include the 2019 Nebula Award-winning middle grade *Riverland*, which was also a Lodestar finalist and an NPR Favorite Book of 2019. She's also the author of the 2015 Nebula Award-winning *Updraft* (part of the Bone Universe trilogy). She writes for publications, including *The Washington Post, NPR*, *The New York Times*, and Tor. com. Fran lives in Philadelphia with her family and a rescue pup named Luna.